Constellation Eden

Maria L. L. DeWillow

Psy Fantasy Crusades

DEDICATION

For the kiddos, my parental units, and all the kindred souls I've loved in this crazy life.

PLAYLIST

"Whore" - In This Moment

"In the Year 2525" - Zager and Evans

"You Can Do Magic" - America

"Wicked Game" - Chris Isaak

"She Blinded Me With Science" - Thomas Dolby

"Just Tonight" - The Pretty Reckless

"Handlebars" - Flobots

"Dies Irae" - Giuseppe Verdi

"Fire and Rain" - James Taylor

"Shout to the Lord" - Darlene Zschech

"Only You" - Yaz

"Mary Jane's Last Dance" - Tom Petty and the Heartbreakers

"In the End" - Black Veil Brides

"Welcome to the Black Parade" - My Chemical Romance

"Science Fiction" - Richard O'Brien

AUTHOR'S NOTE

My writing may contain triggers. This book is for mature readers. Read responsibly.

CONTENTS

ACKNOWLEDGMENTS

I appreciate my proofreaders, alpha readers, and beta readers. Amy Loggins, Dale Barnes, Christine Reed, and Nicholas Salcido, thanks for encouraging my creativity, laughing at my quirks, catching inconsistencies in my stories, and copy editing my oopsies.

I've drawn lifelong inspiration for all aspects of my life, to include writing, from Anne Rice. May her gorgeous spirit live forever to inspire many more generations of gothic beauties.

Christopher Moore deserves a shout-out. His perfectly absurd stories made me realize my own silly ideas would be fun to shape into novels.

I tip my pointed hat to all fellow witches from the late, great Granger Enchanted fan-fiction archive, thanks for many magical nights of creative prompts and spirited writing contests back in the early 2000's when I first started to love writing fiction as much as I love reading it.

Daddy, I know your spirit is somewhere out there watching, so thank you for loving me and passing your strength and audacity to me.

Momma, thanks for always making your house my home when I need a place to breathe. I love you.

PROLOGUE

2282 A.D.

Iridescent air cradled her as if her body was in a pool of water. She appeared submerged in liquid even though that unexplained phenomenon did not affect the rest of the room and its contents. Characteristic of a mermaid, her crimson hair moved and flowed around her, reflecting the harsh florescent light that lined the ceiling above her petite prostrate form. There existed a lulling low frequency that sent slight ripples, or waves, through the air around her, making her slumber seem peaceful.

She opened her eyes for the first time in over a hundred years. The green one was immediately more sensitive to the florescent light directly above, so she winked it shut tightly, forcing a tear to escape her eyelid. The mahogany-colored one searched her surroundings carefully.

She was acutely aware of the force around her, though she could not control it. She concentrated on the gentle waves that flowed around her. She thought the strong unseen prison must have been the work of her lover, but what exactly was the place? She became angry at the thought of languishing there and being forgotten, so she continued to focus her strength. With a cry that felt like it would rip out her throat, she released all the power she could muster from within herself. It accomplished little. Glass broke somewhere in the room. The door swung open. Her prison expanded and contracted again, but she was still trapped inside.

જી જી જી

Joe's disdain for his part-time job was equal to that of any college kid who thinks they'll be doing something much more glamorous the very moment they graduate school with a wealth of technical knowledge and little to no practical experience. It wasn't that he thought being a nighttime security guard was a bad job for someone else, but he knew it wasn't for him.

It was certainly easy enough; the facility guarded itself. All he needed to do most nights was sit in a control room, listening to the building's artificial intelligence ramble off a list of security checks every hour on the hour. Far too infrequently he'd glance at the myriads of screens set up to monitor all the security camera feeds. That night, after a particularly long game of Tetris with his girlfriend on his phone, he scanned the kaleidoscope of images on the wall and leaned forward in his chair as something unusual captured his attention.

"Lisa, what is the status of level zero, section five?"

"Status normal," a feminine voice said confidently with a sigh.

"When did you learn to sigh?" Joe spat in no direction.

The artificial intelligence deadpanned a response. "I didn't know I could until just now. You asked a stupid question, and I reacted as programmed, I assume."

"In that case," he returned an over-the-top sigh, "maybe you can tell me why the door is wide open, and lights look like they're on in that area?"

Lisa argued, "My scan of the building shows no anomalies in any section of the building."

Joe took control of the corridor camera in section five and zoomed in on the door. He noticed a few things missing.

"What the . . . there's no room number . . . and where the fuck is the doorknob? Are you seeing this, Lisa? It looks like the wall just coughed up a new door."

"I see it, sir. I'm already searching the entirety of the company's files for an explanation—I've found something. I'm looking at the building's blueprints, and also accessing cameras in the rooms on both sides of this . . . anomaly. The blueprints say both rooms should be larger. The most probable explanation is a secret room, but you'll need to do a physical security check. Additionally, this is creepy," Lisa stated.

"Yeah, you're lucky you don't have to walk down there. If I sound distressed at all, don't wait for the direct verbal order to call in an emergency. You just do it," Joe said as he grabbed a flashlight and a pistol.

"If you enter that room, it is possible I will not be able to receive your verbal commands, so . . . be loud?"

"Great."

᠄᠄᠄

A young man appeared in the doorway, and she smiled. She tried to speak, but a raspy whisper broke the silence before she dissolved into a brief bout of coughing.

Joe couldn't make sense of what he was seeing, and he wished Lisa's system included a body cam, so she could validate the impossible dreamscape he had interrupted. There was a woman—

no, there was a goddess. She was absolutely gorgeous, making the least sexy noises he'd ever heard, and almost definitely floating in the very air around them.

Beneath her was only the floor. The room was otherwise empty. A single window at the rear of the room glowed from the moon's light, sitting high on the wall as they were in the basement level. Its glass was shattered all over the concrete floor.

As he sidestepped around the edge of the room, keeping his eyes on her and trying not to freak out, he noticed thin, shiny threads that seemed to originate from her body and web out in all directions. They grew faint and became less visible until he couldn't tell if they were still there or where they were going. He cautiously reached one hand out and tried to touch one, but his hand passed right through it.

Her smile faltered as she watched the boy grasp at the air, and she managed to whisper, "You can see them?"

When he didn't answer, she took a deep breath and managed another word.

"Witch."

"Indeed," said a new voice as another man stepped into the room.

The woman growled his name. "Adam."

Joe found himself face to face with the boss. Not his boss, no. Adam was the big boss. He was the famous boss. Adam ran the company, which was more of an empire. Joe's complete astonishment gave way to naked fear. He was suddenly aware of being the only person standing between a powerful man and an obvious secret.

Adam took in the young security guard's appearance and said, "You see what others cannot."

Joe wasn't sure if he understood Adam's meaning or not, but it sounded to him like a threat.

"I don't see shit! And I don't want any trouble, Mr. Godwine. I'm here to do a job. That's it. I don't know what she is—but, um she doesn't look hurt to me. Hell, she doesn't even look human. Even if I thought she needed saving, who would believe me?" Joe asked.

Adam said, "One way or another, I'm afraid the course of your life has just been altered tremendously, son. You will wait for me to put her to sleep, and then you will follow me upstairs. We have much to discuss."

As the boy walked past her on his way back to the door, she noticed the writing on his shirt and laughed mirthlessly as she read it.

"Dust."

She waited until he exited the room, and uttered, "Amusing, Adam. I've always enjoyed your wit . . . your style. It's too bad I'll have to kill you one day, my love."

She fixed her eyes on his, her voice and expression becoming sultry and alluring.

Adam placed his hand on her forehead. "Hush. Sleep now, lest you lead us into sin and ruin."

NEW YEARS EVE, BLUE EARTH, 2319 A.D.

"Ruby!" Jeremy Cohen stalked around a vast library. It was part of the ancient castle that the venerable Mr. Adam Godwine called home. "Ruby!"

At twenty years old, Jeremy was the youngest of two children by four years. Just like his sister, his bright red hair was his most distinguishing physical trait, although his height of six foot, four inches made him a favorite with the females at school. He was incredibly athletic and excelled at several sports, but his favorites were gymnastics and soccer, neither of which he pursued collegiately even though he could have easily done so.

He felt like he could do all the things he loved anytime he'd like as soon as he focused on his education and finished college, which he was on track to do early. He would soon be joining his father to work for Adam, which suited him just fine. After all, his family had quite a successful legacy due to all the benefits Adam afforded them. It was that brand of apathy born of affluence in Jeremy that aggravated his sister.

Jeremy's older sister, Ruby Cohen, called out from above him. She waved her hand in the air to signal him, expecting him to climb the staircase and come to her as she lounged on a chaise. The antique sofa wasn't made for a woman of her proportions. Although she wasn't as tall as Jeremy, Ruby was five foot, ten inches. Half of her calf and her bare feet dangled from the edge of the plush seat. Her shoes were tucked under the furniture, and she had a blanket wrapped around her body.

When Ruby wasn't breathing interest into every party, media event, and news story from Manhattan to East Hampton, she was alone for days on end. In a quiet, dark room wrapped in blankets was where one could find her when she was switched off for a few days. Her life could seem unbalanced at times. Her father disapproved of her tendency to always color outside the lines so to speak, but that dichotomy allowed her to enthusiastically reach out to the public for her work in journalism, and then use the solitude to reflect, write, and produce.

Simply put, it suited her career at The Times, which was the country's biggest multimedia news and entertainment organization. In the last century the company had bought and absorbed multiple print and visual entertainment and news sources, including, The Daily Earth, The Washington Globe, Discover Warner, and Disney Brothers.

The library had a skinny mezzanine that was high above the main level and wrapped completely around the room. The only access to it was a small spiral staircase situated in the front corner of the library, which was quite a walk back in the opposite direction.

Jeremy had no intention of walking all the way back to the entrance. The rolling ladder would get him there faster. He climbed it to the top of the empty shelves, but the ledge was still about ten feet above him. Balancing himself on the top rung, he jumped up and grabbed the ledge. He climbed his way up and over the railing. With the sound of his feet hitting the hard wood, he saw the top of his sister's head pop up above the back of the furniture.

"I got you," he said with enthusiasm.

"No, you didn't. You called out to me when you came in, loser. I was obviously expecting you," Ruby snapped.

"You're a damned liar, nerd. You were expecting me in about five minutes from now when I would have made it here by the stairs and walked all the way back here again. Just admit that I surprised you." He shoved her legs over as he sat next to her. "I climbed up here as quiet as a mouse in less than thirty seconds."

"You stomped up here like an elephant. Now, what do you want?" Ruby kept her nose in the book she was reading.

Jeremy snatched the book from her hands, but she wouldn't give him the pleasure of a response. She remained reclined, with her eyes fixed on him, waiting for him to state his business.

Jeremy closed the book and read the cover, "*The Great Gatsby* by F. Scott Fitzgerald."

"Congratulations. That's the most you've ever read from a book," Ruby replied.

"Dear, sweet, abnormal sister. I read tons of things. I read the normal way just like everyone else . . . except for you. I'm as I should be. You're the mutant."

Despite the wishes of their father to the contrary, both Jeremy and Ruby had accepted Adam's invitation to spend the holidays in the massive house along with many of their friends, colleagues, and relatives. Basically, everyone who was anyone was vacationing on the estate for at least part of the winter. The night would see the biggest New Year's Eve party of the decade, which even though Adam was technically the host, Ruby's best friend had planned every detail.

Ruby sighed. "You're mad because I've discovered something better than those tablets lined up on the cart by the door. I found this place first, and you wish it could have been your hideaway. But as your older and much more mature sister, I don't mind sharing the space with you. Just get over yourself and grab a book. There's plenty up here."

She kicked him off the sofa's edge, but he caught himself and sat on her legs. Since she knew he wanted a reaction, she didn't give him one.

With a plethora of gyms, lounges, bars, studies, conservatories, game rooms, theaters, and any other posh room one could think would be included in such a home, the upper level of the library was a paradigm of peace, quiet, and seclusion. Even when someone entered the library, they typically grabbed a glass tablet from the front and sat in a chair by the fireplace, never venturing far enough back to be a nuisance.

"You think I care this library actually has paper books, like in all the old stories—and in boring History classes?" Jeremy asked. "When all those empty shelves down there were full of books, it was a waste of space and paper. I'm much more practical than you."

"You mean you're much more ordinary," Ruby sneered. "I can't believe you went into cyber tech after you completed your core curriculum last year just like everyone else. You'll never find work that way. You need to explore some options."

"Not everyone can understand languages and grammar like you. Not everyone can write. Don't be a jerk about it." Jeremy was letting her get to him.

Ruby could tell Jeremy was upset, which wasn't her intention. All the same, she couldn't stop herself from offering unwanted opinions.

"Why not? You can read, can't you? It's just as easy to learn how to write those words down. Forming them on the screen is as easy as saying or typing them and making sure they're arranged so that most people can make sense of them or enjoy them. A hundred years ago, people did it all the time," Ruby argued.

Jeremy redirected the conversation. "Where do you think he got all these books anyway? I haven't seen one since Mother left, and she only had a few."

"Well, let me think . . . A castle that's been around since physical money. Empty bookshelves still everywhere . . . Adam obviously had them since before The Conversion." She took the book back from Jeremy and placed her hand gently on top of it. "And now they're priceless."

"Be serious, Ruby. Adam isn't old enough to have had this place before The Conversion."

"If you actually take a look around up here and read some of the stuff I have, you'd not be so sure about that," Ruby whispered.

"What the hell? He's Father's age, isn't he?" Jeremy asked.

Jeremy didn't like when Ruby tried to trick him. It made him feel stupid, and even though he liked to call her a nerd, he also liked to be smart, too.

Ruby abruptly changed the subject.

She knew she'd sounded crazy before, so she said, "I need to go dress for the party tonight. I must ring in The Roaring Twenties properly. This book was getting me into the right mindset, and now I'm ready for jazz and hooch."

Jeremy spread out across the whole sofa as Ruby left. "I'm more excited about the tommy guns that are sure to appear from the 400-year worm hole, right?" He smirked and watched his sister walk away.

Jeremy then started looking around. She'd caught his attention with that last comment about their gracious host. She'd be going back to work in New York in a few days anyway. That gave him the rest of winter break to peruse the place.

❧ ❧ ❧

The décor in the ballroom and the attached outdoor terrace was bordering on obscene due to the fact Camilla Giselle Rosemont did nothing by half-measures. The champagne fountains were flowing, holograms of legendary musicians sang and played their music on two stages, and everything was sparkling gold. Even Giselle's ivory flapper dress shone with golden beads, sequins, and fringe.

Giselle's life and work revolved around making her family look good. Whether she was involved in philanthropy, campaigning, or simply running the household, her jobs and her goals were always centered around her brother, Hayden, and her father, Jameson. Therefore, she had no independent career, but she did boast a rather eclectic and impressive resume, nonetheless.

Giselle loved big, and there was nothing she loved bigger than her family, except for Ruby. The drawback to her having an exceptionally big heart was that every yin has a yang, and Giselle hated as big as she loved. The woman was an emotional firecracker, who had been notorious for making dramatic scenes back in her partying days with Ruby. Her best friend's calm and calculating manner eventually influenced her a bit.

She spied Ruby talking to Hayden and waited for their eyes to meet before making an exaggerated face of disgust.

Ruby mouthed, "What?" and then excused herself from Hayden's company to link up with Giselle.

Entwining her arm with Giselle's and launching them both into a turn around the room, Ruby said, "Is it your brother, or is it my dress that's got your pearls in a knot?"

"Both are making me sick! But that dress clashes with everything in here; its vile. I told you the palette was going to be warm and gold . . . you look like a gothic ice princess, Ru!"

Ruby giggled and twisted around in her black and silver dress, making the beads sound like a thousand pin drops. "And just how is your beloved brother making you sick?"

Giselle said, "You know what I mean. I love him, and I love you, but I don't love you together. I don't care if our families say you two should partner up. You'd be a ridiculous couple, and you know it."

"Don't be silly. Don't you think I have enough personality to cover Hayden's severe deficit?" Ruby asked through laughter.

Giselle's eyes went wide. "See? This is my point! You know he'll bore you, and you'll agitate him. I don't understand why you flirt, or why you encourage our parents' notions about you two."

Ruby smirked. "It's fun to enjoy the moment and test the waters. I don't have a real partner in mind yet. There's no reason to get worked up over it. I don't make him promises or lead him to believe that there's anything between us other than the relationship we actually have."

"Which is?" Giselle asked timidly. She wasn't sure she wanted to know, but she also did want to know.

Next it was Ruby's face that dissolved into a disgusted expression. "I'm absolutely disinclined to share details about me and your brother with you."

Giselle sighed. "So there are details. That's both gross and what I wanted to know."

Ruby rolled her eyes. "Anyway, I don't get why you wouldn't approve of two people you love finding happiness together. I'd be ecstatic if you and Jeremy—"

"Shut your mouth, Ruby Cohen! He's in high school," Giselle squealed.

"He's about to finish college, hello? It's going to be 2320 in a few hours. With you still stuck back in our party years, I daresay he's grown more that you have," Ruby said.

"Well, that wasn't necessary." Giselle pouted.

"And I've seen him looking at you in a certain way." Ruby sighed dramatically.

Giselle held a look of disdain in place until she and Ruby linked arms again and walked together, then let the slightest trace of a smile break through her expression as soon as Ruby glanced away.

Carolus Hayden Rosemont worked in finance and had a good family. That was all the public knew about him. Even those close to him found little about him interesting to the point where that seemed to be his schtick; his dullness made him shine. Extreme to the point of being equally amusing and impressive, it was his most defining quality even above his considerable intelligence.

Since people on the outside saw him as the epitome of boring, and he seemed to take little interest in life's material pleasures, he had far more business acquaintances than actual friends.

He knew Ruby wouldn't end up being his partner, but she and her brother were among his few true friends outside of his family. He'd let her define their current relationship however she wanted as long as she remained in his life, and he took it for granted that she would always be his closest friend. There was no doubt in his mind that the Rosemonts and the Cohens were bonded for life.

Jeremy walked up to Hayden and handed him a glass of beer. Neither of them spoke. Although they appeared idle, both men were actively engaged in watching attractive women arrive to the party. Giselle and Ruby appeared within the fashionable crowd, walking in the men's general direction, so both brothers abruptly paid more attention to their drinks than to the surroundings. Jeremy especially wanted to avoid whatever polite conversation was headed their way. Every time he tried to speak in front of Giselle, Ruby teased him about it at home.

꧁ ꧁ ꧁

Adam watched Hayden, Giselle, Ruby, and Jeremy entertaining each other as they had always done since they were children. They were still his children just as the entire room was peppered with his descendants although unknown to them, but someone was missing.

One dangerous woman wandered the world beyond his reach, while the other slumbered in a makeshift bedchamber below the castle. Faustina, Joe's partner and the mother of Ruby and Jeremy, needed to be found. She knew too much and was too armed with connections and intelligence in the world at large to be in the wind. Watching Ruby laugh at Hayden, Adam came to a drastic decision.

Joe approached Adam, noticing where the older man's interest was focused and asking, "You're not going to respect my wishes for you to leave my family be, are you?"

"No." Adam's tone was cold.

Joe Cohen owed his life and success to Adam, but as the years went by, he felt more and more like Adam was manipulating him rather than mentoring him. He alone was privy to Adam's extraordinary secrets in New York.

Over the last two decades he had not only become the CEO of Adam's company, but he had also been assuming ownership of a large portion of Adam's assets. Although Joe didn't even know how vast Adam's unseen empire really was because he had parts of it hidden under different names all over the world, so it was impossible for him to know the percentage for sure.

"I've already lost my children's mother. Have you no decency at all? Or at least some shred of loyalty to those of us who've devoted our lives to you?" Joe wasn't hiding his desperation.

"I do what I must," Adam said to Joe, but his tone turned true and regretful.

Joe's anger brewed deep inside like a quiet storm. He whispered, "And you still pretend to care. You stand here, plotting schemes that will likely cost everyone dearly. Everyone, but you that is. And yet you pretend to care as if they're not your decisions to make—as if you couldn't decide not to fuck with us."

Adam had an abundant supply of patience. It kept him sane over the years. His long game was legendary.

"My curse is that I do care," Adam replied. "You can't know the responsibility I've taken here, but my decisions are all necessary." He turned from the crowd and looked Joe in the eyes. "I'm sorry, son . . . and this is the last time you'll hear me say that. You will not question me again. I've given you too much leeway as it is, which is why Faustina is lost. Had I not shown you favor from the very beginning, you'd still have your partner and be much better off. Now I must fix it."

Joe knew there was no use arguing. "I'm not your son," he replied as he promptly turned to leave.

"I'm not finished with you," Adam called. "We need to discuss a release date for the Companion."

The Companion was the biggest innovation in consumer technology since autonomous cars all thanks to Adam's elite lackies.

Just as the automobile industry of the centuries prior had kept vehicles with the internal combustion engine essentially the same to the consumer for over a hundred years, so his company and its competitors kept devices such as tablets, bracelet phones, and other wearables reliable and popular with consumers.

Despite advancements that had taken place in the last hundred years in both the government and private sectors with various implants and artificial intelligence, neither had initially appealed to the average consumer. There had been too much spiritual, medical, or ethical backlash for his team to remain involved in much technology they had initially backed. Then in the years to follow, the Defense Advanced Research Projects Agency had surpassed them with similar projects, and Adam knew it was once again time for a change.

The Companion was born of his ability to corrupt an organization, take their technology, and mold it into something he could sell to the masses exactly as he had manipulated the printing press, the telegraph, the computer, and so many other groundbreaking advancements into existence.

The Companion was an artificial intelligence so advanced that it upgraded its own chassis, appearing to grow like an organic being. It could function as the sole computing, communications, and entertainment device for an entire household or for one user. Its initial availability was limited to five models: dog, cat, horse, sloth, or human.

Joe wasn't in the mood to talk business. "We'll talk about it tomorrow. Maybe bring in Ty for his insight . . . Right now, I need a drink and a room without you in it."

❧ ❧ ❧

Chloe Phoebe Rosemont Astor wasn't born into privilege. She had no friends at the party other than her family. She barely tolerated the Cohens and felt endlessly obligated to Adam. Her passion was social work, but she also annoyed her family by adopting too many animals. It made her sad to think that her own daughter had organized such a wasteful event as the party sprawling around her. In the morning, she'd take the leftovers into the city and make sure they'd be distributed to the needy.

Phoebe hadn't known her mother, and her father had operated a bodega in The Bronx, New York. He'd died when she was fifteen, and she had been forced out of their apartment above the store when the property owner came calling a week later. Her only known relative left was her great-aunt in Astoria, who was still running a brothel known to half of the men on the party's guest list.

The greedy woman had taken in Phoebe as a teen only to turn her out to a handful of unlucky wealthy clientele. By the time the fifth man had gone missing, Adam had appeared at Phoebe's door. She thought back to her first encounter with Adam and shivered.

⋘ ⋘ ⋘

2290, Queens, NYC

There was a determined knock at Phoebe's bedroom door, but she was scared to open it. Every time one of those men touched her, they died right there in her bed. The only thing that disgusted her more than those perverted animals was the death on her hands. She couldn't stomach another.

She saw the lock turning on its own and cried out, "Stop! Go away! Please . . . please."

The metallic click of the doorknob turning prompted Phoebe to flee to the window and try to pry it open. It didn't budge, and she was surely out of time. She thought he must be right behind her by then. She turned, expecting the monster to be bearing down on her, but he wasn't. She slammed her back against the window and waited for the worst.

Patiently closing the door behind him, Adam remained standing in front of it. He didn't want to crowd or threaten the girl further.

"Hello, Miss Astor. My name is Mr. Godwine. I'm not here to touch you, or to hurt you . . . I want to talk to you. Is that okay?"

"Yes." Her tiny breath of a voice betrayed the terror she felt.

Adam asked bluntly, "I think you killed five very bad men, is that right?"

"Please, I'm nobody. I don't have anything. And I know they did; all the men she brings home are so rich. And Aunty said I'd be in trouble if I didn't stop, but I couldn't. I don't know where she took them." Phoebe began crying.

"Everyone is somebody, Phoebe Astor." Adam explained gently. "I'm not here to punish you, but I am here to take you away from this place if you agree to come with me. I can make sure you have a better life, but first you need to tell me what you did."

Phoebe couldn't see how her situation could get any worse, so she said, "They died when they touched me. I didn't want them near me, and when I felt them on me . . . I screamed out, and, um. And—and it was like I was electrocuting them." She paused and thought for a moment. "I'm not crazy, I don't think. It was real."

Adam smiled at the scared teenager. He wanted to reassure her and keep her safe.

"You're not crazy, no. You've got a power in you that most people don't understand. For your own sake, you must learn not to use it. I can help you, if you'll let me. Would you like that?" he asked.

❧ ❧ ❧

Phoebe sighed as Adam approached her. "Good evening, Mr. Godwine. It's rather disconcerting, and slightly annoying, that you're looking as young as ever. It's possible I've finally caught up with you."

"Behave, girl. I've already abided enough rebellion for one night . . . Where is your partner? Wasn't he able to get away from work?" Adam asked gently and scanned the room.

Phoebe laughed. "You know nothing can keep him away from Sands Point and these snobs when your invitations come . . . I left him playing billiards about an hour ago. What do you want?"

"It doesn't concern you, but I want to speak with him before you both leave tomorrow," Adam said without emotion.

"He's the only man I've ever loved, and he believes in you. Do right by him," Phoebe reluctantly pleaded.

"Don't be dramatic," Adam replied. "You love just as many men as he loves women. Between the two of you, you've loved half of New York. Don't pretend he's all you have. You're not a poor young woman anymore."

Adam knew he was being too harsh, but he was tired of his flock of whiny youths.

"Maybe you're right, but only Jameson loves me for who I am and who I was, and I him," she said.

Phoebe snatched a flute of champagne from a passing waiter and downed it, rolling her eyes to confront Adam's gaze, offering him a coy grin.

"The rest are just distractions for me, and lucrative connections for him. Besides, I wouldn't call the four—maybe fourteen—people between us in the last twenty years 'half of New York,' but nice try." She dared to push him a bit. "Say, you think you could help me tap back into those powers you had me bury deep down when I was a 'poor young woman' as you put it?"

"You think I should have Hayden fired from his job?" Adam snapped back.

Phoebe clicked her tongue. "And now it's weird. You took the conversation too far, and it's weird."

She saw Jameson was back in the ballroom and dancing with Ruby Cohen. She rolled her eyes at seeing her partner whispering in the younger woman's ear.

Nodding in their direction, she said, "There's the man you're looking for. Why don't you go make sure he's not seducing Ruby along with 'half of New York'?" She walked away without another glance at Adam.

⁓ ⁓ ⁓

Aside from being a zealous member of Adam's entourage, Casey Jameson Rosemont was New York's governor. And despite being a politician, he was well-known as a genuine person. His charm and wit were what drew people to him, but even though he always strived to be straightforward, he found it difficult to let people down with tough decisions. Adam helped him with that. Jameson was guileless, which worked out fine with Adam in the background pulling strings that Jameson either couldn't reach or didn't know about.

With both people he wanted to talk to in one place, Adam had to decide which situation to tackle first. He made his way to the dancing couple and said, "May I cut in? I'd like a moment to dance with a lovely lady before midnight."

Ruby smiled, signaling that she didn't mind, and Jameson took her hand and gave it to Adam.

Before Jameson could excuse himself, Adam added, "You and I need to set-up a meeting before you leave. Does a morning run work for you?"

Jameson nodded. "Sounds good . . . I should find my partner before the countdown."

"I just saw her on the other side of the bar." Adam looked in Phoebe's direction.

"Thanks." Jameson took his leave of them to join his partner.

Ruby always enjoyed Adam's parties, but she knew little about him. They'd never spoken alone before. Joe had always been present for their earlier encounters. Recent events and discoveries on her part only made him more of an enigma to her. There was something slightly dangerous about him, but she wasn't ready to accept that.

Adam held firm to her and asked, "Would you give me the pleasure of your New Year's kiss?"

Pretending not to be utterly shaken, Ruby replied, "I'm flattered, but I've already promised it to Hayden."

"Well then I'm fortunate to have stolen a dance before he comes looking for you." He smiled at her. "What if I came to Manhattan next week and took you out to lunch instead?"

Ruby blushed, but quickly recovered her signature charm; she was willing to flirt if he was. "As long as I get to pick where we go?"

Adam smirked and agreed. "Lady's choice it is."

As they continued to move together, Ruby couldn't banish the thought of asking Adam his age. She'd seen his name referenced in several old periodicals in her hiding spot in the library. Her father had pictures of them together from at least thirty years ago in which her father looked like a teenager, but Adam looked exactly the same. His linguistic patterns were sometimes unlike anyone's.

She also had a gut feeling that their lives weren't normal, and that Adam was the reason for it. The man had been reclusive for her whole life. Her parents said that he used to run the company, and she knew that he had been a public figure, but now the average person didn't seem to remember him even though she could look around the room and see corporate icons, celebrities, and even world leaders.

Her father's attitude towards Adam had changed after her mother's disappearance. He tried to hide it, but she could tell. She didn't want to upset her father, she didn't want to sound unreasonable, and she also didn't want to find out she was the only one who felt odd about their lifestyle. She'd keep her peace for as long as it seemed practical to do so.

There was a couple standing along a wall across the room watching Adam and Ruby dance, and the third time Ruby met their eyes as Adam spun her around the dancefloor, she realized they were purposefully staring at her. She stiffened at the realization. Those two pairs of eyes were deeply disconcerting for a reason she couldn't grasp. Taking a breath, she tried to relax again. She was embarrassed that Adam might notice she got spooked.

Adam felt Ruby's body quake.

"What's wrong?"

Ruby hesitated.

She said, "It's silly . . . There's a couple behind you; they both have bright white hair and very fine clothes."

Adam didn't have to turn to look as he said, "That's Duncan and Sylvia Cavendish. They're my oldest associates here."

"Funny, they don't look as old as some of the others. It's only their hair that's completely white," Ruby said, trying to make small talk and downplay her nerves.

"They've been managing certain interests for me in Europe since—" Adam started to argue but realized something important about them he'd overlooked, so he redirected his comment. "But I'd rather not bore you."

Adam had been living for so long that sometimes years slipped by like minutes in an average human's life. People came and went many times over, but the important thing he'd overlooked was the fact that Duncan and Sylvia should have gone to dust and ash a very long time ago.

Ruby was right; they didn't look as old as some of the others. They could easily pass for around sixty-five to seventy years old. Even though life expectancy for most people was around 105, most modern witches lived a bit longer, reaching 120 years of age, but they usually looked elderly by that point and died no more than three decades after becoming centenarians.

Taking a moment to think back over the years to recall specific events with those two, Adam formed a rough timeline. He estimated they were about 250 years old.

With Faustina missing and security being paramount more than ever, he would immediately have them investigated and followed. If they had used some type of unauthorized magic, he'd need to take severe action.

Adam and Ruby's dance ended, and Hayden was there on cue to spend the rest of the night with her. It was then that Adam did the oddest thing; he kissed her hand before wishing them a good night. She'd never seen anyone kiss a hand before. Hayden was in her ear commenting on how bizarre he thought the gesture was as he'd obviously never even heard of the practice, but she had read about the custom from several older sources. The question she didn't ask continued to burn in her mind.

Giselle and Jeremy joined her and Hayden to ring in the new year, and she put everything else out of her mind except for kissing Hayden and laughing at Jeremy's surprised expression when Giselle grabbed his face and put a sloppy lipstick kiss on his forehead.

In the nauseatingly bright light of New Year's Day when most partygoers from the night before were either sluggishly departing or nursing severe hangovers, Jeremy commandeered his sister's place in the library. Hours passed quickly while he immersed himself in a rich history he barely knew existed before.

He then understood why his sister loved her obscure reading nook. A book on a bottom shelf caught his eye because it was dusty on top, and he thought it would be interesting to open it for the first time in many years. He took it and then went to a bench by the nearest window to get a good look at the lettering in the natural light. When he dropped it down on the seat beside him, the sound it made gave him pause.

He knocked on the seat with his knuckles. The thud his hand made against the wood sounded like he was sitting on something hollow and empty, so he leaned down for a better look, raising the throw blanket up a bit as well. He then realized he was sitting on an old trunk.

The metal clasps looked brittle, so he took his time and care in opening each one before gradually lifting the lid. Inside were only five items. They were all portraits. Two of them were on strange silver glass, and the others were paintings. He took them all out and placed them side by side in front of the windowsill. Immortalized in oils were a man who looked like Adam and a woman with thick, flowing red hair. One of her eyes was green, and the other one a bright brown. Jeremy looked at her for a long time. There was something almost inhuman about her although she was beautiful. The subject of the oil paintings alone wouldn't have been disturbing to him since likenesses were often altered in paint at least a bit, but he knew that early photographs were a different story. What he didn't know was whether that type of photo predated historic photo editing software.

The resolution and speed of his personal tablet was far inferior to the clear glass ones belonging to the library, so he ran downstairs and grabbed one to search different types of early photography. After a few dead ends, he found it—the daguerreotype.

"Ruby is going to shit when I show her this," Jeremy whispered to Adam's likeness, which stared back at him in shades of silvery gray.

ONE OF US

Ruby thought about the historical fiction she loved so much and how different her New York seemed compared to numerous stories of old.

Any given street of New York City at noon on a weekday had once been like a parking lot—a stagnant river of pink taxis salted with delivery trucks and privately-owned transportation. The pristine avenue laid out before Ruby, as she exited the metro station and briskly started walking the quarter mile to her building, was far removed from any sites that could have been seen in the New York where her grandparents had lived.

As was typical of any street in the city, it was lined on both sides with healthy trees. The sidewalks were wide and the pavement unblemished. With full autopilot standard on all vehicles over the last several decades, the machines drove in a precisely woven stop and go rhythm, guaranteeing speed, efficiency, and safety for all passengers to all locations. Ruby's peace wasn't shattered with honking horns and loud motors as she enjoyed her walk home.

Indeed, the nation's biggest city, the birthplace of the National Metro System, no longer had streets festering with traffic and pollution. The metro was more popular than ever before and included a mixed network of cable cars, cargo trains, bullet trains, and trams that spanned the United States from coast to coast. Every major city was connected, with more smaller towns and rural areas across the country joining the transportation network every year.

Increasing availability and efficiency of public transportation also meant fewer vehicles on the streets, and many cities were able to easily incorporate extra bicycle lanes for both families and athletes. That's why Ruby loved New York. She loved to ride when she had free time, which wasn't often enough.

Ruby stopped a few doors down from her building to pet a familiar dog that was sitting in the basket of a bike. A neighborhood kid appeared and hopped on the bike, so she waved goodbye to them both. Smiling, she glanced ahead to her stoop and noticed her brother sitting there. Her grin intensified and she shouted, "Hey! What are you doing here?"

Jeremy stood as his sister walked up. "I have something to show you."

"That's it? No 'hello, loser,' or anything?" When he didn't answer, she added, "But I just left you three days ago. You couldn't show me back at Sands Point?" Ruby walked up the steps to the door.

Jeremy picked up a large satchel he had with him and followed her. "I didn't have it then."

He kept up with her as they walked down a corridor and up a flight of stairs.

"You couldn't send a picture?" Ruby asked.

"No! I couldn't, okay? And this . . . this is serious. Um, I really need to talk to you, so can we hurry up and get inside your door? It took you long enough to get home, by the way. I know you got off work three hours ago." Jeremy fidgeted and waited for Ruby to let him into her building.

Ruby shrugged and opened her door. "I met Adam for an early dinner first."

"Seriously?" Jeremy's flustered voice echoed down the hallway before the door shut behind them.

❦ ❦ ❦

Phoebe knocked on the thin metal door of an old Airstream travel trailer parked at a campsite outside of Foley, Alabama. She hated the gulf coast, but at least it was warmer than Albany that time of year. She heard someone thumping around inside before the door opened the tiniest bit, and a brown eyeball peeked out at her.

The eyeball spoke. "What's happened?"

Phoebe checked her surroundings then pushed on the door. "I'm here by myself, and there's not anyone watching us. Open the damn door and let me in," she said while continuing to push the door open. "You're the one who's supposed to be from a classy family, yet here you are not welcoming a guest. Rude is what it is!"

Once she was inside, Phoebe silenced her rant, looked around the interior, and then turned to face the trailer's inhabitant.

"You look well, Faustina."

Faustina Cohen Rothschild stared back at Phoebe, waiting for an explanation. She stood in front of a blanket-laden sofa that was obviously also her bed, wearing sweatpants and a thin tank top. She kicked fuzzy slippers from her feet and sat down.

"You seem to have adapted to your new environment," Phoebe joked.

Faustina repeated, "What's happened?"

"Adam has set a trap for you." Phoebe sighed and continued carefully, "He's been spending time with Ruby . . . alone. There's talk he's interested in partnering with her."

Faustina screamed incoherently and then grabbed a tote bag and started throwing stuff into it. "I have to go to her . . . ugh, disgusting!"

"You can't go! That's what he wants!" Phoebe grabbed at the bag.

Faustina grabbed it back. "Yet, I can't not go, right? What kind of mother would stay?" She looked through the window. "Is that your car outside?"

"Obviously. I hired it to drive me here from the airport." Phoebe sat down to think. "Look, I know you only told me where you were going because you needed someone to watch your family—"

Faustina interrupted, "We can get back faster if we hire the car to drive us all night and leave right now."

Phoebe ignored her and continued, "And I'm the last person Adam would suspect you to tell . . . But you can trust me. Whatever he did to you, I'll believe it. I've known him a long time . . . I know he's not innocent. Let me help set this right."

Faustina stopped fussing with her bag and stared at Phoebe. "You owe Adam your life, and I know it. I haven't been in his circle as long as some of you have, but I've been around long enough to know he took you off the streets, and now you're first lady of New York . . . Why would I tell you a secret so big that I—a Rothschild—am hiding from it?"

Phoebe stared at the floor for a long time while Faustina grabbed a bottle of water from the fridge and added it to her bag.

"Faustina, please stop and listen to me. I think I've proven myself. I mean, nobody else came knocking on your door, did they? But if I told you why I don't trust Adam, you'd think I'm delusional."

Faustina did stop, shaken by Phoebe's words. "Delusional?"

"Um, yes." Phoebe was recognizing that whatever had taken place between Faustina and Adam, it had to do with his unexplained powers. "You're not insane either, you know? Adam collects people and things that are . . . supernatural."

"How do you know I'm not one of them?" Faustina asked carefully.

"Because I'm one of them. Joe is one of them . . . You either need financial, social, or supernatural power to be in Adam's network, and people like me—we recognize our own kind." Phoebe paused to observe Faustina and gauge her reactions. "Besides, you have brown eyes and blonde hair."

Faustina hesitated, reflecting on a detail that had seemed insignificant until that moment. "All of you have red hair . . . or bright eyes?" She realized for the first time that her crowd had certain characteristics in common. Her partner had red hair as did her children. Her son's eyes, however, were also bright green. So many of them had bright green eyes, including the woman standing in front of her. Even Adam's eyes were green, which was a feature in contrast to his dark brown skin. It was a striking signature characteristic of his.

"I feel . . . stupid. And we still should leave now. Your car?"

"Yes, but I need you to tell me what happened first . . . I don't think he's going to suddenly kidnap Ruby. According to Hayden, she's at work today. We have time to plan. You need to focus." Phoebe sat down on the sofa and encouraged Faustina to do the same. "Spill."

"Right . . . okay. I'll tell you . . . about Eve."

❦ ❦ ❦

November 2318

Faustina was accompanying Joe on an important job he had to finish. The company's headquarters was moving from California to New York, and there was some valuable cargo that Joe had to personally load onto Adam's private jet and fly with to Hamilton Airport, and then hire a chinook to take it to Sands Point where Adam would receive it at his residence. It was not clear to Faustina why the container was going to Adam's residence instead of the new headquarters building in Hell's Kitchen.

It was Faustina's birthday, so Joe wanted to spend as much time with her as possible even if it was supposed to be a working weekend. Adam's home and its amenities would guarantee them a relaxing weekend as soon as he finished that last important job for the headquarters' move across the country.

Their day had started well before dawn, and as they climbed the formidable stone steps to greet Adam at his door, she admired the view of Autumn twilight's subtle hues that colored the sky all around them. She was exhausted and ached for the comfort of the spa and then a long night resting in Joe's arms.

She was grateful for Joe. Although he was dedicated to his work and wildly successful, he made room for her wherever possible. He was an honest and loyal partner. Above all she believed Joe was honest, which had always been an attribute paramount to any relationships Faustina maintained throughout her life.

Intimacy was, to her, not only laying herself bare physically before a lover, but also allowing them to strip her naked mentally and emotionally. If she was willing and ready to trust someone enough to show them every inch of her imperfect body, then she was equally ready to trust them with her thoughts and secrets. What made her partnership with Joe last was that she believed he wholeheartedly shared her philosophy.

She went to their guestroom, changed into a swimsuit, and covered up with a robe before walking down to the gym and spa to have a quick swim before soaking in a mineral bath. At the end of a long corridor, she saw Joe turn a corner and felt compelled to follow him. She wanted to ask him how much longer he'd be and if he'd be hungry later.

When she approached the end of the corridor and turned the same corner, she encountered a dark stairwell. Since there was a glow coming from below, but no light at all coming from above, she took the stairs leading down below ground level. On the first landing, there was but one door, which was locked, and the area still wasn't fully illuminated. Thinking the source of the light had to be on the next level below, she kept going. When she reached the next landing, there was indeed a light overhead, and a door opened to another corridor. She called Joe's name as she crossed the threshold and continued walking.

Just outside of the next door she approached was the crate they'd brought with them. It had been opened and was empty. Beside it was an object roughly half the size of the crate.

Faustina went from carefree to guarded in an instant. Whereas seconds before, she'd felt so welcomed in Adam's home that it hadn't crossed her mind not to wander into the bowels of the castle, that feeling changed with the site of a silver casket vault sitting opened before her. The casket was right behind it and Faustina shivered at the thought of what might be inside. Wanting to quickly find Joe and not get any closer to the casket, she approached the door. She was relieved to find it unlocked, and she slipped onto the room.

Panic initially kept her still when she saw a person floating in the center of the room, but worry for the poor soul soon overrode her paralysis. Faustina stumbled skittishly to the body. It was a young woman in an impossible position, but Faustina needed to make sure the woman was okay. She laid her hands on her and felt for her pulse at her neck.

"Can you hear me?" she asked. "My name is Faustina. I want to help you."

Almost directly after her skin contacted the other woman's skin, she felt an energy she'd never felt before. It was like a warmth entering her body through her palms, and then she didn't feel jet lagged from the day's journey anymore. She felt more refreshed than she'd felt in a long time.

A voice in her mind spoke a single word to her—a name.

"Eve."

Entranced and completely in awe of the woman, Faustina repeated, "Eve."

She didn't hear the door open and close behind her, but she did hear Joe's voice speak to her in fear. "Tina, take your hands off of her and come here."

"What's happening?" she asked. "I think she needs our help."

"She's fine. Just come here, please. I'll explain everything once we're back on in our room," Joe pleaded.

Faustina reluctantly let go. She turned to Joe, and as the realization hit her that he had been hiding kidnapping from her, or whatever crime it was, she ran past him.

❧ ❧ ❧

Faustina paused her story to organize her thoughts.

Phoebe popped up from the sofa and started searching through the kitchenette cabinets. "Eve. Adam and Eve. Please tell me you have whiskey . . . and also please tell me you're not referring to Abrahamic mythology."

"I don't know. I don't know where they came from exactly," Faustina answered. "All I know is that Eve is Adam's prisoner, and they've been alive for . . . I don't know—centuries."

"Whiskey?" Phoebe asked again.

"There's scotch in the one above the sink." Faustina pointed.

Phoebe busied herself pouring her drink. "This bottle is worth more than this trailer. Fuck, my life is weird . . . Why don't you know? I thought Joe tells you everything."

"He obviously didn't tell me about her until I found her . . . and he never mentioned to me he's apparently some kind of witch—thank you very much for that massive reveal—or that I've birthed two children just like him . . . He swore to me he didn't know any details about her—just that Adam said she was sick. He did explain that some people weren't regular people, and what he described to me was essentially witchcraft . . . He said Adam was keeping Eve safe and that he had been keeping me safe by not getting me involved. I was devastated, of course. But because of the extreme nature of the situation, I believed him and forgave him." She held out her hand, silently asking for a sip from Phoebe's glass.

Phoebe gave her the glass and asked, "So then what happened? How and what did Adam find out?"

Faustina drained the glass and gave it back. "Eve sent me visions. Joe said it was likely because I touched her. I'm not a witch, or whatever. I wasn't prepared . . . I went back and tried to free her. Witchcraft or not, the whole situation is a gross case of abuse."

Phoebe said, "I want to know what she showed you and how Adam stopped you. Then we can leave."

❧ ❧ ❧

December 2318

Faustina knew she was dreaming. There were images of dead witches—men and women slaughtered all around Eve, who was crying and covered in blood. Adam stood above her in a fit of rage, lashing out at her both verbally and physically as she crumbled at his feet.

The massacre dreamscape was followed by a montage. It was the same every night. Eve told her story in a barrage of images of her life with Adam. Adam leading the world away from belief in magic. Adam replacing magic with technology. Adam convincing people to believe science instead of earth magic. Adam telling witches to suppress their power. Adam squashing all other avenues to which the power flows, concentrating it and redirecting it back to Eve and himself to keep them alive and bound to the earth.

Then she awoke.

Faustina didn't remember calling for the car to take her from Brooklyn to Adam's house. She didn't remember how she got past the armed guards or back into the basement. She had a faint memory of Eve guiding her dream, but it was fading from her mind as she stood awake, alert, and scared in front of Eve. She'd been having visions about Eve since the night they'd touched, but never before had she sleepwalked.

She whispered, "I don't know why you've brought me here. I don't have powers; I can't do tricks or miracles or anything. I wish I could help, but I can't even see what's keeping you here. You look like you're floating—like I could just . . .pick you up?" She hesitated and stepped forward, putting her arms under Eve.

"What is in the air that's keeping you here, but not affecting me?" Faustina asked the unconscious Eve as she lifted and held her.

Faustina was the reason Ruby and Jeremy were tall; they'd gotten their size from their mother. Even though she was slender, she was five foot, ten inches and fit.

Eve's form was delicate and petite. As they moved through the corridor as quickly as possible, Eve gained consciousness and held onto Faustina's neck. They slipped back up the stairs and rounded the corner. Upon reentering the main part of the house, they slowed down, listened, and kept to the shadows as much as possible. When they finally made it outside, Faustina made sure to creep around the side of the house and into a little secluded garden space before placing Eve on a bench and catching her breath.

"I can call us a car to pick us up on the main street. It isn't far from here, but it would be faster if you could walk. Can you?" Faustina asked, almost breathless.

Eve looked down at her bare feet and placed them on the cool grass. She stood, looked up, and said, "I can command my feet. Thank you, child."

The lingering silence between the women was broken when the sound of crunching gravel rang through the night. There were people coming towards them from out on the driveway and only one way out of the alcove. They had no choice but to run and possibly confront the danger.

"Eve!" Adam's strong voice boomed in the distance.

Faustina looked back at Eve, and said, "His security. How did I get past it in the first place?

"There was a big problem with it today. I can sense, and I am aware of, many events that happen around my person when Adam has me sleeping. I knew when the machines and the guards wouldn't *see you . . . but unfortunately something still betrayed us,"* Eve *explained and sat back down.*

"Eve!" Adam's voice called again.

"Get up. We have to go!" Faustina pleaded.

Eve glared at her as if offended or annoyed with her tone. "Not today. The odds are against us now that he's on the hunt, and all the others I sense . . . He doesn't seem to know you're here yet. He's only calling my name . . . You need to run. I shall distract him and his men. Hide as well, for he will discover you were here. Come back for me when the time is right," Eve explained.

Faustina hesitated, looking at the diminutive woman as if enthralled. "Will you be okay?"

"Away, anon!" Eve commanded.

❦ ❦ ❦

Phoebe sighed. "All this time! I knew I should have been using the power inside of me." She grabbed the bottle of scotch, commandeered a cheap pair of wayfarers off the counter, and added, "Well, Adam won't be stealing any more years from me, that's for sure . . . Come on, heiress. Let's jam!"

"You get the car ready. I've got to take care of one last thing." Faustina disappeared into the bathroom.

Phoebe threw open the door and walked straight to the car, leaving Faustina to her privacy. While she was giving the car an address and approving the payment amount for the trip, Faustina sprinted to the running vehicle's open door, slid into the seat, and urgently shut the door.

Faustina said urgently, "Go now—go."

An explosion shook the car as it sped away, and Phoebe looked back at the incendiary carnage left in their wake. "Really?"

"Is there a problem? I can't come back or leave anything for Adam to find," Faustina explained.

"But a random explosion in a small town in Ala-fucking-bama isn't exactly incon-fucking-spicuous, is it?" Phoebe yelled.

In contrast to Phoebe's natural rawness, Faustina maintained her focus and said, "Here's the address of the next place I'll hide if it comes to it. Put it in your private memory and destroy the paper."

Phoebe stared at the paper, which contained an address in Texas—another town she didn't know existed called Magnolia. "How do you find these bypass places?"

She didn't want to admit it, but she was impressed that Faustina had thought to use paper instead of sending it to her the usual way. As rare, expensive, and inconvenient as paper was, it was also much safer than saving the information anywhere else when Adam had so much access to everything.

"It's a shame I'll have to burn such beautiful paper. And your penmanship—exquisite," Phoebe said, admiring the ornate stationary.

"Yes, well. Some of us were raised well." Faustina straightened her posture.

Phoebe replied, "Yes, well. Since you're an ordinary woman among extraordinary people, it's good you have something to be proud of."

They both smiled, amused—drunk. Then Phoebe poured more scotch for them both.

Phoebe finally asked, "How have you not made a plan to go back for Eve yet? You've been hiding this whole time for what?"

Faustina said, "She said to come when the time was right. I thought there'd be a sign?"

"Yeah, okay. A sign. And instead, you got a messenger who's drinking all your good liquor." Phoebe turned up her glass.

Faustina snorted and then made a dainty gesture to cover her mouth before stating, "You're right. Even better. Whatever plan we come up with under the influence is definitely going to work."

Adam followed Sylvia Cavendish from her hotel room in Bucharest to a castle perched atop a rocky mountain north of the city. According to his investigators, she and her partner traveled to Romania often, taking detours along the way. The erratic travel patterns had worked to obscure their movements many times, but eventually they'd caught Adam's full attention.

He thought about how to deal with her and Duncan. He'd confront them at the hotel later that night and get answers.

"Hello," a voice said from directly behind him.

Shocked, Adam spun around and expelled a surge of magical energy. Nobody had been able to approach him undetected in hundreds of years, so he assumed he was facing a foe and aimed to disarm it.

The powerful being blocked his attack without moving. It was a woman clad in a midnight blue leather catsuit. Her black hair was in a high and tight bun. She wore black combat boots laced up to the middle of her shins. Her eyes were gray, but they glinted in the sunlight like specs of silver.

He stood still and willed his energy to shield him, wondering if she was as fast as she was quiet.

"Yes, I am faster than you, Adam Godwine," she answered his thoughts with words.

Mindreading like that, as if hearing every thought, was not a witch's gift, and Adam had the double disadvantage of not knowing who she was, but also not knowing for sure what she was. He had an idea, but he'd believed they were extinct.

"My name is Sorina. Like you, my coven came from Eden. Long after your time, we were created and brought to the Blue Earth . . . The Cavendishes were under my protection as children, and I watch over them still, even from a distance while they serve in your court."

They weren't extinct, then, he thought.

"In my court? I don't hold court . . . I've built a global empire from technology and innovation. What has your kind done apart from falling into obscurity?"

"I know what you've done. You've fought against your mortality, slowing your decay by replacing magic with technology and controlling those still capable of wielding magic . . . While my kind— my kind possesses a peace you cannot."

"How do you know these things? Is my mind so open to you now?"

"Yes," Sorina plainly announced.

"The Cavendishes are not like you; they are my descendants," Adam boldly stated. "Why were they under your protection?"

"Centuries ago, we hunted witches in this region, but we embraced peace and a better way of life. Two of my brothers refused and fled the continent, slaughtering a small witch commune in England. Everyone died, including my brothers when the rest of our coven finally tracked them there. Only Sylvia and Duncan survived. On behalf of my brothers, I owed a great debt."

Adam nodded with a thoughtful look evident in his eyes. "I remember that time, though I was sequestered in the New World then and never had the pleasure of meeting any of you."

"It's against your nature to retain as much magic as you have. You'll end up as lost as your partner one day," Sorina uttered a warning.

"I know there is a way for me to acquire envito," Adam whispered.

"You put too much stock in legend," she answered. "My high priest is no friend of Eve."

"All the more reason to help me. It will ensure the peace you care so much for endures . . . I can pay him anything," Adam said.

Sorina replied, "You can start with allowing the Cavendishes to retire and leave your court unharmed and with their powers. I will speak to my coven about the rest."

꙳ ꙳ ꙳

"Did you earnestly just suggest time travel?" Ruby scoffed.

Ruby was locked in her office with Jeremy. They had the portraits of Adam and the mystery woman scattered about her desk while they grasped for any meaning that made some iota of sense.

Jeremy threw up his hands and asked in an exaggerated tone, "Did you earnestly just use the word 'earnestly?' Who the fuck are you? Our mother? . . . Why couldn't it be time travel?"

"Why *would it be*, dear brother?" she asked.

"Because it's Adam. What technology doesn't he have access to?" he persisted.

"Wha—I—Ah. Hmm." The dumbfounded expression on Ruby's face that morphed to one of sobriety, told Jeremy that she agreed even though she seemed to have trouble voicing it right away. "You believed in bigfoot until you were fifteen, so—"

"Oh, right!" Jeremy interrupted. "Because someone living for a thousand years or more makes so much more sense!"

His voice echoed off the walls and attenuated into nothing, leaving a stark silence between them. Neither knew what to say or what to suggest.

Then the muffled shuffling of metal and scratching of canvas pierced the air between them, providing a bit of comfort to both. Ruby was doing something—she was accomplishing something, and the sound lulled Jeremy away from the anxiety that had been building in the nothingness. She locked the portraits in her safe and walked to the window to draw warmth from her city's happenings below. Clearing her mind, she exhaled and turned to Jeremy.

He spoke before she could, "I don't want you alone with him anymore. Something is weird about him, and I can't have anything happen to you after losing Mother."

"Oh, really? Because five seconds ago your life goal was to work for him with Father!" Ruby snapped.

"You're suggesting I shouldn't reasonably change my mind about someone when presented with substantial red flags? Brilliant argument." Jeremy thew up his hands.

Ruby couldn't hold back her thoughts any longer; she needed to vent. "But Mother is exactly the reason we have to pretend everything's copacetic . . . I've been noticing things that are . . . out of the ordinary for a while now. Adam's accent. His age. His lifestyle—

our lifestyle even! We're not like anyone else. And then Father—he started treating Adam differently after Mother left. Remember? He didn't even want us going to Sands Point. Not to mention the fact that Mother is gone in the first place, and then you find these portraits."

Jeremy was quiet and pensive during Ruby's rant, but then he asked, "How is that even connected though, Ruby?"

"I'm not sure, but all these things are too bizarre, don't you see? They must be connected! And I'm going to stay close to Adam to find out how . . . so are you." Ruby went to Jeremy and took his hands in hers. "I need your support. We can be careful—we won't lose each other, but we might find Mother."

"You want us to be like spies?" he asked.

"Exactly."

"I'm in."

A CLANDESTINE HOMECOMING

During Jameson's initial term as governor, the Rosemonts had been the first family to live in the New York State Executive Mansion in several decades. His predecessor, hoping to leave a legacy of culture and graciousness, had successfully orchestrated an effort to turn it into a public museum instead of an official residence. Although the tourist attraction had been both charming and popular, the added expense of maintaining a museum with free year-round admission ended up being enough for the legislature to entertain another change to the mansion's status by the time Jameson took office.

The fact that the former governor fought hard to keep it operating as a state-funded cultural landmark had been the main catalyst for Adam's subversive move to purchase it from the state at a price so ridiculously gargantuan that no legislator felt that they could reasonably argue—especially since the mansion would always remain protected as a historic site.

Adam's feud with the former governor had run deep ever since Adam had discovered the man's involvement in the perpetual escalation of the amount of red tape and expenses involved in the company's move to Hell's Kitchen. Turning his museum into a private residence had seemed to Adam like an effective warning, or a peaceful way to assert dominance.

The coup de grâce had finally taken place when Adam found out how much Giselle loved the house growing up, so he had ensured the historical plaque was redone, renaming the property after the winning opponent's daughter before giving the property to her as a birthday gift.

As much as Phoebe avoided material possessions, she loved living in the Camilla Rosemont House, but it wasn't the house she loved; it was the living she loved. Her family was happy there. Having a space for her family to congregate and enjoy their time together was all she needed from a house.

She could have, in fact, made any house into a home, and that was the extent of money's import to her—to enable her basic needs as well as memorable experiences. If she had the means to see every country in the world or go on every adventure that interested her with her family, she needn't buy luxuries or stay at the best hotels. As long as her family had the food, clothing, shelter, companionship, and personal fulfillment they needed, she didn't care where they lived.

The only problem was convincing her daughter of the importance of experience and time over money and things.

Hayden was already of the proper mindset. The only reason he worked so hard to make so much money was because that's what he was good at doing. He enjoyed his work, even though he didn't enjoy excessive spending or luxuries any more than his mother did.

Giselle, on the other hand, loathed the fact that her mother never splurged on designer clothing or high jewelry, and it embarrassed her when Phoebe hired practical vehicles to transport them to special events especially when she let the animals ride along like some sort of mobile zoo.

As Phoebe poured a cup of coffee, Hayden entered the room and said, "Giselle is causing a ruckus upstairs, and it's too early for me to deal with it."

Phoebe noted that there was a tired tremor in his voice and his complexion was a bit wan. She was doubtless the end of his romantic fling with Ruby was to blame even though he'd said it was inevitable.

She prepared a cup of coffee for him as well and said, "Here. A warm cup of coffee will help you feel better this morning. What's wrong with your sister?"

Hayden followed his mother as she exited the house through French doors that opened into a veranda. The air was brisk, but not too cold that the fireplace in the outdoor seating area couldn't make the temperature comfortable.

He answered, "She's rather upset with you actually. Snoopie ate one of her shoes."

Phoebe patiently listened and tended to the fire she had started prior to making coffee. Then she sat next to her son and breathed in the air, which was fresh with a bit of smoky scent and just the way she preferred it.

"Not that I care, but she could easily replace the shoes," she eventually replied.

The conversation was quiet and sparse. Neither wanted to say much as they enjoyed the fire, the coffee, and simply sitting together.

Then came the mingled sound of Giselle shouting and Snoopie barking from somewhere close, but still inside of the house. Phoebe lazily glanced towards the doors in anticipation of the inevitable interruption of her quiet morning, while Hayden leaned back and massaged his temples.

Phoebe frowned when Giselle came into sight, dragging the chocolate labrador by his hind legs. He was on his back but trying to roll over and escape.

"Oh no you don't! I'm getting you out! This! Door!" she screamed at him, while sliding the door handle down with her elbow and using her backside to push open the door.

Snoopie hit the floor of the veranda while Giselle made sure the door shut behind them so that he couldn't get back inside.

Phoebe called to the dog, "Come here, sweet boy!"

She held her arms out as she spoke, and Snoopie flipped himself upright and ran happily to her.

"Don't reward him, Mother!" Giselle ordered. "He chewed up a pair of shoes worth thousands."

"Fix your tone," Phoebe snapped back. "You might be grown, but I'm still the parent . . . You kicked Snoopie out of the house. Surely that's a severe enough punishment."

"My house! It's not just *the* house. It's mine! And there's too many of your animals in it!" Giselle continued shouting.

"Shut up, Giselle!" Hayden interrupted. "Nobody cares that it's technically yours. You have a bedroom and stuff at our other residences even though they belong to Mother and Father, right? Because we all agreed they're for the family, remember? Especially this one since we've been here most of the year every year since we were still in middle school, and—"

"I don't care! I'm sick of this shit!" Giselle interrupted.

Phoebe hugged Snoopie in silence as the conversation deteriorated into shouting between her children.

"You're so damned selfish!" Hayden declared.

Giselle's face turned red. "Everything I do is for you and Father! Don't call me selfish, asshole!"

"Fine! You're a fucking conceded snob, then!"

"Well at least I'm not lame and boring like you!"

As the bickering continued, it took a moment for Phoebe to realize her cheek was getting warmer because of the fire and not just because she was agitated. In fact, the side of her face closest to the fire was getting downright hot. She turned and looked at it. What had been a few small flames licking at smoldering embers moments before had become a raging inferno . . . and it was blue.

It was very blue and too hot.

As Phoebe slowly got up and moved all the furniture farther away, Giselle and Hayden kept arguing. They didn't even notice when the dog whined and hid underneath a chair. Phoebe knew someone's magic was out of control and causing the fire, and she knew it wasn't hers. But which one of her children was it? She wished that she could wait and figure it out, but the fire was getting too dangerous.

"Both of you look at me!" she shouted.

Hayden and Giselle both looked toward Phoebe, who was standing in the direction of the fireplace. Seeing her and realizing that she, and much of the veranda, was bathed in blue light, both children experienced a sudden departure of anger from their minds. Humbling fear overwhelmed them both, and the fire imploded into ash.

Hayden spoke first. "Mother? How did you do that?"

"I didn't. One of you did." They stared at her dumbfounded, so she continued, "Have either of you seen anything like this, or anything otherwise unusual happening around you—"

"What?" Giselle interrupted. "You—you're talking like what we just saw is normal. In what world is that normal?"

"No. Not normal. But . . . expected," Phoebe explained.

Hayden said, "Well . . . we both have a thing—"

"No, we do not," Giselle interrupted her brother.

Hayden continued, "When we were little kids, Giselle talked to animals and I—"

"Hayden! That wasn't real. You sound crazy."

"What could you do?" Phoebe asked.

"Giselle would try to . . . burn me with matches or candles or whatever. But I was never hurt," Hayden said.

"Giselle?" Phoebe asked.

"What?" Giselle replied defensively. "We were kids! I remember trying to play chicken with him—make him admit he was hurt. But I must not have kept the flame on him as long as I thought . . . I just thought the flame needed longer to make him blister. That I never held it there long enough. It was the only thing that—that made sense . . . And then he used to tell me he could light candles with his mind, but then he could never do it in front—"

"Because you made me nervous . . . I could do it when I was alone . . . I distinctly remember," Hayden explained. "And you used to tell the animals what to do, and they told you things too. I know it, and—"

"Stop." Giselle whispered.

She was sort of pleading, and her eyes were vacant like she was trying not to be there, whether out of embarrassment or fear, Phoebe couldn't tell.

Hayden continued, "Then one day you decided you were too old to believe it anymore—that you were too old to play with the animals or with me anymore even."

Giselle kept arguing. "We were pretending. We were—"

"No, we weren't," Hayden said.

"You don't sound sane right now, Hayden." Giselle had tears in her eyes.

Hayden continued, "Sane or not, I could see that even though you chose not to understand them anymore, they could still understand you. The animals have always reacted based on your moods . . . And now that you're always so bitchy to them . . . Why did Snoopie ruin your shoes? What did you say to him this morning?"

With tears running down her face, Giselle pleaded, "Mother? This isn't real—it isn't true. I'm not a freak. We're not weird. We're—we're normal."

Phoebe hugged her daughter close and kissed her wet cheek. She reached for Hayden's hand and held it tight too.

"No, Giselle. We're not normal . . . But listen. You can't tell your father, and you can't tell anyone else. Not yet. Not for a while. And what I'm about to tell you won't make sense, but it's crucial—it's so, so important not to volunteer the information to Adam."

Hayden said, "I think the sensible thing to do is to get Giselle's face washed off, and all of us calmed down. Then we need to sit inside at the table and discuss this as thoroughly as possible before Father gets back tonight."

Phoebe smiled and said, "There's my logical, darling son . . . I think you're right."

❦ ❦ ❦

Ruby was sure her heart would explode from her chest at any second. The sound of it pulsing rapidly was permeating her skull and was the only thing she could hear given that the scream she desperately wanted to release was stuck in her throat. She was silently choking on it while clenching her eyes shut.

There was no ground beneath her. Pointing and flexing her feet a few times told her that she really did levitate or fly or otherwise climb rapidly into the air somehow. Looking down was a terrifying option, but also the only option. Surely Adam was down there somewhere and could help. She started controlling her breathing, taking several minutes to calm herself enough and finally working up the courage to open her eyes.

Whatever she expected to see, she certainly didn't anticipate Adam being eye to eye with her in the air as soon as her eyelids lifted. The added shock jarred her loose from whatever was holding her suspended in the air, and as her body plummeted downward, that's when the air's force against her falling chest pushed a scream from her mouth.

Within seconds she was in Adam's arms, but still screaming into the brisk night air.

He dug his fingers into her shoulders a bit too roughly and said, "Stop screaming now."

He commanded her to stop twice more before she stopped cold and stared at him.

"What happened?" she asked.

Looking around, she realized that she was back on his private rooftop lounge and sitting on a bench in front of the bar exactly where she was prior to . . . whatever happened.

Adam let her go, and said, "I think you should tell me what happened. How long have you been able to fly?"

"Wait, what? What did you put in my drink?" She knew it was an outrageous question, but the last thing she remembered before being stuck high in the sky was Adam kissing her. "Did we . . .?"

"No, we didn't. Not yet. And I also did not drug you, Ruby. And furthermore, I'm going to pretend you never asked that," Adam said in a low, growling tone.

"But the last real thing I remember is us kissing . . . Flying? You've got to be toying with me." She put her head in her hands.

"And then? What next?" He was coaxing her to elaborate.

She looked away in an effort to withdraw herself slightly. "I opened my eyes, and you were there. It scared me. I felt as if the shock jarred me loose from whatever energy was holding me there."

"But where did the energy come from to begin with?" Adam asked impatiently.

Ruby was so confused that she'd been panicking, but Adam's attitude was sobering her wits. His bullying inquisitiveness in the wake of her apparent trauma was starting to anger her as well. She concentrated on the memories leading up to that moment.

She gathered up her strength and finally returned his gaze, saying, "It came from you . . . You did this to me. I felt your . . ." Ruby searched for the right word and continued, "I felt your energy flow into me, and then I ascended."

Adam smiled.

Ruby wondered why.

Then Adam said, "It felt good, didn't it?"

"It scared me." Her response was too immediate, and she mentally kicked herself for not thinking before speaking. The whole moment was just too weird and complex for her to fully comprehend on the spot.

"Yes, but before that if felt good. Euphoric, perhaps. Isn't that right?"

"Yes." She didn't see the harm of a simple answer, and the thought of how good his energy had felt put a dent in her resolve. She wanted to be defiant, but the feeling had been like an orgasm.

Adam tried to seem less ruthless with his questioning. He really needed her to be open to him.

"Have you ever experienced something similar before? And I'm not referring to the flying. That's only a byproduct per se . . . because I can fly. What I mean is, have you ever physically felt like you absorbed energy from someone else and then displayed a strange . . . talent?"

"What? No!" She was afraid her wince had been visible that time. She needed to gather her wits and play his game. She had verbal skills but needed to stop allowing them to abandon her. "I apologize . . . this doesn't seem possible."

Adam nodded but continued promptly, saying, "Nevertheless, you're going to be careful with whom you have physical contact until I can teach you how to control yourself. Now this has happened to you once, it will happen again, and we can't have that—you must suppress it. Some powers can harm you if you take them without knowing how to use them, so it's crucial not to do it at all unless it's with me."

"I am not feeling well. I'm leaving."

Ruby needed to find her brother and discuss what was happening. Adam was some kind of super-villain or something, and she could barely play their game anymore.

It was another afterthought—the thought of spoiling her rapport with the object of their investigation—that had her saying, "Thank you for a lovely evening, but . . ."

Adam reached out his hand and touched hers, but rather than an accidental transfer, he sent some of his energy to her on purpose—just a taste.

"Are you sure?" he asked. "I can make you feel this way all night. And now that I know what you are, I can control it for you . . . You'll be safe with me."

Ruby trembled in ecstasy and instantly knew she was going to stay. It was already terribly late, and she could talk to Jeremy when morning came. She rationalized her situation by thinking she'd learn much more about Adam much faster if she stayed, but she knew that was an excuse to tell her brother if need be. She hadn't spent the night with someone since college. The night could be something for her, too.

The Cohens' primary residence was Faustina's ancestral home in Greenwich, Connecticut, which was a Greek Revival mansion built in the mid twentieth century by her great-great-great-grandparents. Joe and Ruby rarely spent time there; Ruby because she'd been in love with New York City since becoming old enough to strike out on her own, and Joe because he was always working. Faustina and Jeremy, however, were often at home, that is, until Faustina had to go into hiding.

Faustina had been checking in on Ruby in the city for a couple of days without contacting her or the rest of the family. She wanted to be close in case she saw any signs that Ruby was in distress, but she also needed to bide her time until she found a completely safe opportunity to reveal herself to her children.

The weekend seemed the best time to catch Jeremy at home without the household help afoot to blow Faustina's cover, so she had Phoebe go home to Albany, going through the normal motions of life and checking in with the family, before coming back down to Greenwich to help Faustina break into her own home.

Fresh out of Faustina's cheap hotel just across the state line, Phoebe's car drove up to the wrought iron and cut stone gate in front of the Cohen-Rothschild home and requested entrance to the property. Knowing that lights would come on, revealing the car and its contents to security monitors, Faustina had slid into the trunk through the back seat.

As the car crept up the driveway and around a sizable roundabout, Phoebe asked the car to park. She looked up at the gray stone and columns, the entire façade bathed in too much light for her liking.

She spoke loud enough for the woman in the trunk to hear. "I'm going in alone to speak with Jeremy. He needs to turn off the exterior lights before you get out of the car."

Faustina's muffled voice screeched, "Just drive around back!"

"I know you're getting impatient, but just wait here. It doesn't make sense for me to go around back since I've never been here before, right? He also might not be alone. I'll check it out and come right back, okay?" Phoebe waited for an acknowledgment.

"Fine."

Jeremy could see Phoebe approaching the front door from the monitor in the foyer and wondered what Ms. Astor could possibly want from his house at midnight. He didn't even think she liked his parents. Mr. Rosemont was the friendly one, not her.

He went to the door and opened it upon her approach. "Please come in, Ms. Astor. It's late. Are you well, or is there something you need?"

Phoebe glanced around briefly. "Yes, I need you to turn off your lights outside . . . Are you alone?"

"Excuse me? What?" Jeremy wasn't exactly alarmed, but he was uncomfortable.

Phoebe explained, "Jeremy, I need to know if you're alone because I have a message for you that nobody else needs to hear. Now is anyone else here?"

"No . . . I should call my father," Jeremy threatened.

"How about your mother?" Phoebe whispered back. "She's outside hiding in my car until you turn off those lights—actually, you better just kill all of the power just in case, and your mother would prefer it if you didn't call anyone until you've seen her."

Within a second, the home went entirely dark.

"Well, that was fast. Good." Phoebe exhaled into the darkness and waited for her eyes to adjust before taking a step back, searching for the door handle.

"She's here?" Jeremy asked. His voice trembled slightly.

Phoebe's silhouette nodded and said, "That's what I said, isn't it? Go help her out of the car."

Jeremy walked past Phoebe and opened the front door as a shadow ran towards him from outside.

Faustina was almost to the door when it opened. She was about to run through it when her son screamed, and the door slammed in her face.

Now standing by the window and gazing out of it with her hand slightly parting the curtain, Phoebe said, "I think it's just Faustina. You slammed the door on your mother . . . and yelped like a puppy."

"I know. But I wasn't expecting someone to be coming at me so fast," he said with agitation as he opened the door again, letting Faustina slip through before he closed and locked it right behind her.

He turned and embraced his mother, her arms already open to receive him. He felt them envelop him and squeeze tightly. He didn't want to cry, but it was too late by the time he noticed that he already was. He couldn't remember the last time he'd felt so happy— and so relieved.

Faustina pulled away from her son slightly and cupped his face in her hands.

With a tremor of amusement in her tone, she said, "I didn't mean to scare you, I could see the lights extinguish from a window in the back of the car, and just crawled out and ran for the door while I knew I could."

Jeremy sighed. "I don't care. I love you. It's perfect . . . Where have you been? Are you okay? What are we going to do now? Did you tell Ruby you were coming?"

He walked them into an interior sitting room and turned on a single lamp to light their darkness.

Phoebe parked herself in an overstuffed armchair while Jeremy and Faustina shared a sofa as the many questions lingered on the edge of the moment.

The women took some easy breaths for the first time in many hours, knowing they'd be safe from discovery for one more night, or until the time was right to make another move. Then Faustina placed her hand on her son's, preparing herself for the necessity of breaking the silence from which she was drawing temporary comfort.

"I know you want answers, and I have so many things to tell you about where I've been and why, but you need to get your sister here. What we are going to discuss is for both of you," Faustina explained.

Jeremy started, "Ruby—"

"And do not mention me or Phoebe. Tell her something mundane, but still urgent enough that she'll likely come see you," Faustina said.

Phoebe added, "Tell her you adopted a, um . . . what kind of animal do you want?"

Jeremy shrugged. "A bald guinea pig?"

"No," Both women simply stated.

Faustina added, "Just tell her you're fostering a dog, and you want a bit of help. She'll love that. Simple."

"What kind of dog?" Jeremy asked.

Ruby knew she wasn't awake. She'd always had a gift for controlling her lucid dreams, but the one she was experiencing felt different. The place was strange to her; she'd never been there. That was new since she usually dreamt of familiar places and people with familiar sounds, sights, and even smells. She'd often dream of a place she knew she'd be visiting the next day, and in the dream, events would play out as they did in reality, or she'd dream of people she hadn't seen in years, and then unexpectedly see them within the next week.

However, the place was dreaming wasn't somewhere she was going, at least not that she knew of. There were also no sounds. She was experiencing a complete absence of sound from the world around her. She stood in the cool shade of a giant tree, but no animals called out to each other, no sounds of civilization or machinery murmured in the distance, and no leaves rustled in the wind either. In fact, the air was dead still, but despite that detail, the tree looked more alive than any plant she'd ever seen.

The leaves seemed to pulse with the green glow that was their color. The bark of the trunk was so vivid that it was like rich velvet that seemed to glisten, or if she looked closely, it was like the bark was crawling with its own lifeforce. The entire tree was visibly alive and an entity unto itself in a field of golden barley and then secluded within a fence of mountains.

Ruby had a sense that she was at a rather high altitude. She took her first step and froze, startled at the sound of her foot disturbing the grass underfoot. Then she became aware of her breathing and heartbeat. So, she then knew she could hear in the dream, but her surroundings were naturally mute. She didn't belong there, and her mere presence was like amplified noise.

It was the most beautiful place she'd ever imagined—the most beautiful Earthly place she'd ever imagined anyway. She turned to look at the entire scene and to soak in every drop of beauty the dream had to offer, knowing it would have to end soon.

As she turned back toward the tree, there was something standing between her and the tree that wasn't there before. It wasn't *human, but it was humanoid in appearance. It wasn't even organic like the rest of the scenery, yet it made no sound as if belonging to the place. Ruby was face to face with what could only be described as a robot.*

Ruby's whisper rolled like thunder through the air between them. "Can you speak to me?" she asked.

"Yes, Ruby Cohen. My purpose in bringing you here is to speak to you," it said in a voice that wasn't a whisper, yet seemingly in tune with the quiet tranquility of the place.

Ruby wondered at the sound for a moment before asking, "Who are you?"

"You're not ready for that knowledge," it stated.

She then asked, "Where am I?"

"You're under the Gaia Tree."

"Where is the Gaia Tree—what is the Gaia Tree?"

"We're under the Blue Earth. If you were to travel here in your waking hours, you'd have to enter through a hidden, enchanted tunnel in Mesopotamia. And the Gaia Tree, is the Tree of Life."

Ruby stared at the robot's copper face with green glass eyes in confusion, and then looked up. Although she was standing beneath the tree's colossal canopy, natural light bled through. She looked out onto the field, and light pooled over the barley. She'd assumed the sun was somewhere above, but after she looked around, she didn't tangibly see it. Maybe the source was directly over the tree at that moment, but she couldn't be sure without walking very far away from the fascinating being that was patiently answering all her questions.

She continued, "How is it possible we're underground? How did the light come to be here? I can't see the source. Is this 'Blue Earth' different from my home?"

"This is your Earth. I made the light. You cannot understand the source."

"Well, that's fair, I guess," Ruby said and then hesitated before asking, "Why did you have to bring me here to speak?"

"Gaia keeps the door open and nourishes this place with her primal power."

"I don't understand your meaning, but I feel as if we haven't the time . . ."

"No, Ruby Cohen, we do not."

"Then, what do you need to tell me?"

"You cannot help Eve . . ."

❧ ❧ ❧

Ruby was awake too early. Something pulled her out of sleep.

Like most people, her communication device of choice for everyday needs was her bracelet. As consciousness crept into her body, the feeling of it pulsing around her wrist caused her to stir. Her brother was messaging her in the middle of the night about a puppy. She wondered if it was code for something, or if he was under the influence of either of his two favorite vices, narcotic candy or hard liquor.

She sighed at the possible antics of her baby brother and rolled onto her back in Adam's bed. She'd kill her brother when she got to their house for ruining the best dream she'd ever had, and then she'd certainly start researching dream interpretations for that one too.

Yawning and stretching, she glanced at the space beside her. Adam wasn't there. It was going to be a clean getaway.

AUTOMATON TRACES

"Ms. Astor, why are you here? And isn't it a bit late for dinner?" Ruby asked as she walked into her family home from the back entrance and into the kitchen where Phoebe was making a sandwich.

Phoebe looked Ruby up and down, noting her formal attire, smudged mascara, and messy hair.

"Ms. Cohen," she said sarcastically, and then looked her up and down again. "Yeah, and a bit late for excessive questioning . . . A bit early in the morning for a walk of shame, too, I suppose."

Ruby had always liked Phoebe's style. It had been Phoebe who'd got Ruby interested in journalism.

Likewise, Phoebe liked to have Ruby around as a positive influence on Giselle, but she really couldn't stand her inquisitive nature.

Ruby diverted the conversation. "Know where I can find my brother?"

"He's in the . . . well, whatever you all call that room with the piano and indoor hammocks. He's in there—with your mother." Phoebe looked up from her sandwich-making and smirked, then she went right back to her task.

"Mother?" Ruby asked breathlessly as she dropped her bag and ran from the kitchen.

Halfway down the corridor, the heel of her shoe got caught on the edge of a Persian rug. Stumbling, she kicked off both shoes and rounded the next corner. The double doors were already open, so she slid to a stop in the middle of the room the family called their "hobby room." Her brother had a guitar in his lap, but he wasn't playing. He and her mother were already staring at her as she stomped into the room.

Faustina and Ruby eagerly closed the distance between each other and embraced tearfully.

Faustina continued to hold her daughter close, rocking her side to side. "We could hear stomping and bumping around out there, and I knew you were home!"

"Mother." Ruby exhaled in relief and melted inside her mother's embrace.

By the time Phoebe entered the room, the Cohen children and their mother were already in an intense discussion about the events surrounding Faustina's disappearance and trying to reach an agreement on what to do next. She stood just inside the doorway listening as their debate intensified.

Ruby was pacing and visibly uncomfortable. "I don't think we should get involved with this Eve woman. I don't have a good feeling about it."

Faustina said, "What I saw was real, Ruby. You need to believe me and take this seriously. We need to do what we can to help Eve and to protect our family. Adam isn't what he seems. Phoebe says these powers are real, and that maybe you'll even get them one day."

Faustina's patience was failing. Her words were meant to be a parental command rather than a suggestion, but there was an underlying struggle to gain control of the situation.

Phoebe could sense that Faustina was failing to convince Ruby. There was some key element of understanding missing.

"Adam is dangerous. We need you to listen," Phoebe added as she advanced into the room, interrupting the unfolding argument.

"Then call the police," Ruby argued.

"More dangerous than that," Phoebe snapped back.

Faustina reiterated her fears. "Not only did my dreams feel real, but she's real. I was there, and she's been abducted. Adam isn't who he says he is."

"I believe you, but that's not why I don't agree . . ." Ruby struggled to explain.

Phoebe said, "You shouldn't be intimate with Adam. He's influencing—"

"That's not—I'm not—let me tell you something!" Ruby's frustrations climbed even more as she watched her mother's disgust at Phoebe's comment about her and Adam. "I have powers! I saw Adam's powers!" She exhaled deeply, gathering her thoughts.

"Gross," Jeremy interjected, but immediately realized his poor comedic timing as all three women in the room looked at him judgingly. "Fine. Sorry. You were saying?" he asked Ruby.

"Whatever." Ruby shrugged and continued, "My dreams have always meant something. They've always helped me. And maybe that's my inherited power—from Father . . . But maybe also because of you, Mother. Maybe my power manifests as dreams—or visions— or similar ways—because you tend to have vivid dreams, and a unique imagination. He gave me the power, but you gave me the form it takes in me. I think especially your creativity and the way you're always learning so quickly how to do things from others, which is usually a completely normal human talent—but for me, I think I can learn the powers of others . . . I flew with Adam last night."

"Adam flies?" Phoebe asked indignantly. "What a prick!" Then she stepped farther away from Ruby and added, "You're right. It's possible to inherit your powers in that way, and you should probably be careful around me until you learn to control how you take power from others. Mine can hurt people . . . if I even still have it." She grimaced. "Adam forces everyone to stop using powers when he 'collects' us. I think it makes his stronger. I'm sure you can understand that's not what a good person would do to his friends."

Ruby was skeptical. "But aren't you all more like his employees—or maybe, in your case, like his ward? I don't always understand decisions my parents make either."

Phoebe became defensive. "Seriously? This is not the time to give him the benefit of maturity . . . or responsibility. Parent?" she scoffed, looking to the ceiling with her eyes tightly shut. "Hardly. You'll understand too late. He's already manipulating you."

Faustina could see Ruby was readying an argument, so she stepped in first. "The fact remains that you don't know how dangerous Adam is. Unless you can tell me right now a good reason why he's been seemingly crippling his followers while in effect stockpiling their powers, and keeping a human being prisoner, we need you to help us."

Ruby knew everything her mother and Ms. Astor said made sense, and Jeremy had already decided that Adam was a super-villain with nefarious designs on his sister. Still, a voice in her head telling her to stay away from Eve lingered at the edge of yesterday's fading dreams. She was the only one questioning, and she wondered what Giselle thought about it all. She really needed her best friend's council.

Phoebe's voice pulled Ruby from her thoughts. "Now that a new part of you has started to grow, it will feel like that part of you is missing when he takes your special abilities. You won't feel whole if you let him have his way."

"For my own safety, I choose not to use my syphoning power," Ruby said and then asked, "But if he's so dangerous, why risk ourselves and our families? I was willing do to anything to get my mother back, but she's here now. We're all safe. Is the loss of our powers worth losing everything else too?"

Jeremy said, "You're wrong. We're wrong if we look the other way. And I don't think you should assume we're safe. If he's kidnapped one person, he's probably kidnapped more."

"I get your conclusions," Ruby said. "So, how much help can we get?"

※ ※ ※

Adam exited the stage after introducing the Companion to an auditorium filled with elite Dust partners, press, developers, and other distinguished guests to find Joe waiting for him in a private chamber in the basement below backstage.

Joe was holding an ornate metal box about the size of a shoebox. It looked more industrial than decorative even though it was copper with silver and gold tubing.

"Why go all in and expend our resources on the Companion now after years of keeping the fully developed tech on a back shelf?" Joe asked.

Adam answered, "I think you know I don't trust artificial intelligence of this caliber. I needed to do more research and slow the cycle of repeated history. Creation is flawed; I have a responsibility."

"You say that so often, as if you enjoy some great burden that you've imagined your lowly engineer cares about." Joe unbottled his rant. "I lie to my family for you. I use my magical gift only in service to you. I suppress it when you command me to. Technically I'm an accessory to kidnapping because you think you're a god—"

"No, I am not a god," Adam whispered with the attitude of a defeated man, "but a god made me . . . a god of metal, silicon, circuitry—all the things used in creating these robots we're marketing and more."

Adam paused. Joe said nothing, his eyes open as if seeing too much, or perhaps nothing at all.

"I don't believe the universe would benefit from our creations one day evolving into creators, do you? What would they create? Would they destroy?" Adam asked.

"You're saying—but what are you saying? God—*the God*—of creation, the one you never talk about, the one you lead me to fear, and the one who gave you the power you also make me fear, is an artificial intelligence?"

"I had no basis for comparison thousands of years ago when He left me and Eve on this planet, but that is my best guess," Adam said flippantly. "He is quite famously mysterious after all."

"No, not as much of a mystery if you've seen him—if you know with your own eyes that you were created. Most people must have faith," Joe almost shouted. "You have proof."

"You think I don't have faith?" Adam asked. "If I didn't have faith, I wouldn't play this game. He left us here to rot, but I still have faith."

Weary from oversharing, Adam pointed to the box Joe still held. He wanted to change the subject. More than anything, he wanted that box. It could change everything for the world's future.

"I'll take that now. I need to start using it tonight." Adam reached for the box.

"You paid dearly for it, and she still didn't want to hand it over." Joe handed the technological artifact to Adam. "She kept asking me how long you'd keep it."

"Her partner will retrieve it from me when the time is right," said Adam. "Have you used your sight on it?"

Joe's magical gift, which some of the witches referred to as "their power," was a physical sight beyond what others could see. He wasn't clairvoyant like some others. His sight was like he was seeing wider spectrums and sometimes across spacetime to look at tangible things in front of his face that were solid and real to him, but that others could not see.

It was a particularly tricky gift to wield during social interactions, especially since it hadn't manifested until he was an adult on the day he'd met Eve. The next day, he'd noticed a coworker's pregnancy and congratulated her, creating an incredibly awkward moment since her condition hadn't been visible to anyone else yet, and she hadn't told anyone.

"I can see multiple functions within it," Joe explained. "I see danger more than anything . . . Adam, the woman who gave it to me— I could also see she wasn't a normal person, but her aura wasn't like a witch, and it wasn't like yours. How can you trust this machine?"

"Sorina came from Eden just the same as Eve and I did, but she and her people came later." Adam put the box into his satchel and secured the strap across his body. "And I need this machine for Eve."

With that, Adam left in a hurry as Joe stood baffled.

Joe shouted after him, "We're going to unpack those last statements at some point, boss!" Then he whispered to himself, "Fuck all the way off with that shit. Fuck. Me."

Jeremy and Ruby lounged in the hobby room at their Connecticut home. They were swinging in an oversized hammock together while Jeremy replayed the recording of a private conversation between their father and Adam.

Being close to Adam while also a member of the press, Ruby had been invited to the Dust event for the Companion, and she'd known her father had been expected to arrive with some sort of vital information for Adam. Getting Jeremy into the auditorium with her and past the security measures backstage hadn't been difficult either, considering most employees knew they were Joe's children. While she'd worked and kept key people distracted and away from backstage, Jeremy had planted the bug.

"I feel guilty, don't you?" Ruby asked. "Part of me just wants to talk to Father about all this."

"No way. He's messed up in some pretty bad stuff and lying to us about all of it," Jeremy argued in frustration.

Jeremy switched off the recording and started absently eating from a large bowl of popcorn. Ruby held the bowl but snatched it away after he'd grabbed two handfuls of her favorite snack.

While chewing, he said, "Besides, I've already told Mother and Ms. Astor about that machine. We all agree. From what Father and Adam said, it's got to be a weapon. Hopefully we can get to Eve before Adam hurts her with it. I think Mother agreed to let Ms. Astor tell the rest of her family, or maybe just Hayden and Giselle. I'm not sure yet."

Ruby knew Jeremy was enjoying the research and the spy craft. Puzzles and mysteries always kept him enthralled, but she wasn't sure he fully realized the gravity of their reality yet.

"Father's magical power seems badass from what he said about the machine and those people," said Jeremy. "I wonder if he would have seen the bug if he had looked up?"

"We're lucky he didn't," Ruby stated.

Jeremy asked, "Do you think Adam was really made by a robot?"

Ruby didn't respond for quite a while, but Jeremy held his peace.

Ruby closed her eyes and took deep, calming breaths. "I think God's physical appearance is irrelevant. I think Adam's faith is shaken; he doubts who or what his creator is, and that's why he overthinks his decisions."

WITCH CABAL

"Tina . . ."

Joe stood in his Connecticut bedroom for the first time in months. He hadn't wanted to sleep in the bed without Faustina there. He'd either been staying in New York or traveling, but his son had asked him to come home for the week.

He realized his son, who was nowhere to be found in the dark and quiet house, must have called him home for that reason—for his partner, sitting at the foot of their bed and wearing what he knew to be her favorite pair of jeans with a simple linen shirt. Her hair was loose, and it framed her makeup-free face. In that moment, Joe thought about how perfect she was.

He inhaled the clean, sweet scent of her presence, his heartbeat steadily elevating as his brain registered her wellbeing. Relief washed over him; arousal followed. Sleeping alone for months while thinking only of her resulted in his desire pooling stagnant just below the surface of his psyche, only needing a slight spark to erupt.

"Mr. Cohen . . ."

He went for her. Dropping to his knees between her feet on the hard floor, he wrapped his arms around her waist and rested his head against her abdomen. His hands caressed the curve of her back. He took a deep breath against her shirt then lifted the material. Kissing her from her navel up to her chest, he slid his thumbs into her beltloops and pulled her completely against his body as his lips reached the valley between her breasts.

Faustina moaned and dug her fingers into his thick red hair. She missed intimacy with her partner so badly and needed to feel him again even if she ended up having to run and hide when the morning's small hours arrived.

She needed the moment. She craved it and fully lived in it. When he grabbed her jeans and pulled her flush against his body, she wrapped her legs around him and locked her ankles together behind him. As her back fell against the mattress, his body rolled on top of her while he licked a trail up her neck and teased her earlobe with his mouth. She could feel his manhood grinding between her legs through their clothes, and she wanted to taste it.

Joe knew what she was trying to do, but he needed to taste her first. He slid down her body and jerked her jeans down to her thighs and watched her wiggle them down to her ankles and kick them off. His eyes met hers and seeing each other's hunger, he finished shedding his pants too.

Twenty-five years as lovers, and they knew how to read each other and move together. They wouldn't waste any time; they'd taste sex together. Mutual desire mounted as they praised each other with their mouths and tongues, prompting their limbs to become laced together in a knot of sensual movements against each other's skin.

She felt it against her tongue. He was close to completion. She had to stop. Her desire to ride him was overpowering her, so she broke contact to quickly adjust their position. His small groan of protest died in his throat, replaced with a primal moan of pleasure when she sheathed him inside of her in one warm, wet stroke.

⊗◦ ⊗◦ ⊗◦

Hours after Joe and Faustina were sated and cooling off from their passionate reunion, neither wanted to break the silence between them. They were enjoying the condition of simply being there.

Summoning her courage, Faustina sat upright.

Joe felt the mood shift. He knew it was time for a fight, but he sat up and tried to hold her anyway.

"What do you see?" she asked such a terse, deliberate manner that he knew what she meant as she pushed him an arm's length away and reinforced her noble posture.

"I don't . . . I don't use it on you," Joe said.

His answer was pure, and he explained, "I see the best person to ever be part of my life. So gorgeous, confident. A woman who could have had any man, but looked down at me and chose to lift me up . . . Your generosity to me has been a blessing. The family, the trust, the time, and everything you've given me is more than I deserve."

"I physically and figuratively looked down on you that first night at the solstice gathering." Faustina giggled breathlessly with very little mirth, dreading the conversation they needed to have before the night was through.

Faustina stood an inch taller than Joe, which was a barely perceptible difference . . . unless she was wearing heels.

"I love your killer stilettos though," said Joe. "They might even be the reason I stay with you."

She genuinely belly laughed then.

"You're not going to make tonight easy for me . . . How well do you remember the night we met?" she asked.

Summer of 2292

Adam hosted a gathering on his private island in the Caribbean during every solstice, but it was Joe's first year to receive an invitation to pass a social evening among Adam's elite circle. He'd spent the last few years bringing innovation after innovation to the table while also accepting Adam's mentorship to control and contain his powers. His hard work and focus were finally getting him into the right rooms and seated at tables with the right people.

Joe spotted Jameson by a balcony with a tall, fit blonde. Jameson had a scotch in one hand, and his other hand was resting gently on the woman's shoulder. They exchanged a quiet conversation peppered with laughter.

Jameson was on the city council back in New York and had an expensive loft in Dumbo purchased with family money. There were always parties. It seemed to Joe like his friend knew everyone.

Like a professional social butterfly, Jameson took a pause from his conversation to glance around the room as he took a long sip from his glass. He met Joe's eyes and waved him over.

Jameson embraced Joe. "Joe Cohen, the smartest man at Dust, how are you, my friend?" he asked. "It's my pleasure to introduce you to Miss Faustina Rothschild, the most beautiful lady on the island with us."

Joe and Faustina shook hands. He noted the contrast of her firm grip and soft hands as he tilted his head up to see her face.

Jameson kissed Faustina's cheek and said, "I'll be back soon. You can get to know Joe while I'm gone."

Jameson nodded to Joe with a wink and left.

"So, I've heard you're going to be the next world-famous genius," said Faustina. "How does that feel?"

"For a guy who grew up in a free housing district, you mean?" Joe asked the straightforward question.

"If that's where your mind goes for an answer, then yes, because I want a genuine conversation," she said. "Especially now that I understand your perception of me, which is fine. Elitist heiress is one of my favorite games to play . . . Another question—Is 'poor boy' your favorite mask to wear, or have you brought it out just for the party?"

Joe smirked and changed the subject. "Were you and Jameson college friends? He talks like he knows you well."

"No, our extended families have been well acquainted our whole lives, and he was college friends with my sister, but I've only

recently become personally acquainted with him," she explained. "I went to Rice University."

"You went to Texas for college? I thought you all favored New England schools these days, or, at least, something prestigious within the tri-state area," Joe said.

Faustina replied, "I wanted to be far away from all that for a few years. Besides, there's better food down there."

"What did you study?"

"Terraformation."

Joe's surprise was evident from his expression, which Faustina found pleasant. She relaxed, leaning against the balcony railing and preparing to stay for a longer conversation.

"Intriguing . . . But don't you miss home when you're gone?" Joe asked.

Her smile broadened as if he had said the wrong thing. He understood he was an amusement to her.

"You've really never heard of me, have you?" she asked, nearly laughing. "My role is more of a . . . financier."

Joe's mind was reeling over how beguiling she was. He wished he could land a woman like that. He thought he'd work even harder to elevate Dust beyond what Adam expected if that would get her attention.

Faustina was instantly infatuated with how refreshing Joe's personality was. His handsome face certainly attracted her too. Short men were her usual type anyway, but their conversation was the best entertainment she'd had in months. He made her feel awake after she'd felt asleep in a dark place for a long time. The way he looked at her made her feel like she was the only person in the world, and she silently thanked the stars for sending him to her.

❧ ❧ ❧

"I met my soulmate that night; I'll never forget it," Joe whispered.

"What if you suffer from dementia?"

"Not even then."

"Or you get amnesia from head trauma?"

"I'd forget myself long before I could forget you."

Faustina said, "You say that, but you keep your most intimate secrets from me while I place my whole world at your feet year after year."

"How did you learn about my sight?" asked Joe, ignoring Faustina's statement.

Faustina raised her voice in anger. "Even now, you care more about your secrets than you care about your family!"

"Life isn't black and white, Tina. I know secrets that protect you. I know secrets that protect others. Most of the secrets I know are not even mine to tell," Joe said.

"Do any of those secrets have to do with kidnapping or false imprisonment?" she asked.

Faustina was standing, putting on her jeans and shirt.

Joe could see the moment going wrong and getting worse by the second, but he felt powerless to stop it.

"Eve is sick," Joe started to explain, but he struggled. He needed to be careful with his words.

"How dare you lie to me, Joe Cohen!"

"She's in Adam's care," Joe continued to tell her. "Again, this isn't my place to speak about. You shouldn't have run. Now Adam is suspicious and looking for you. You need to contact him yourself and smooth this over."

"Shut up! Just stop . . . and I suppose you don't even give a damn that Ruby has spent the night with Adam!" Faustina shouted.

Joe sat on the edge of the bed naked while Faustina yelled at him as she packed a duffel bag. He noticed her glance towards his muscular chest and then quickly avert her eyes. He knew that she loved his black tattoos in sharp contrast to his pale skin.

She threw his clothes at him, so he dutifully pulled his shirt over his head to hide his body from his conflicted partner and then started straightening out his pants.

"Ruby is an adult," he said, breathing a heavy sigh. "I don't like it, but—for fuck's sake, Tina. We're not talking about regular wealth and power here. This isn't like me standing up to your father. We're talking about dangerous, supernatural forces at work. Let me protect you."

Faustina didn't acknowledge him.

"Stay, please," he begged.

"I can't, yet, but I'll come back when I can," she uttered.

"Where are you going?" he asked. "What are you going to do?"

"You're keeping your secrets, Mr. Cohen, so I will have to keep mine. Just remember that you chose this status quo."

"No, that's not—" Joe didn't finish his sentence, but sighed as his partner turned her back on him.

Faustina left then. She didn't look back. She didn't see Joe follow her into the corridor and watch her walk all the way through the house and leave.

"I love you," he said as she slammed the door.

❦ ❦ ❦

Camilla Rosemont House was the site of an impromptu meeting to decide what the next steps to free Eve would be. With the knowledge of an unknown weapon in play, time was running short for the unlikely vigilantes, especially since they always had to find ways to communicate in advance of plans.

None of them underestimated Adam's ability to intercept electronic communications. With their eminent ringleader actively searching for Faustina, and Joe fully indoctrinated to his cause, they assumed all risks were high. The meeting had been arranged using two sets of couriers, each hired to relay half of the information via word-of-mouth to a hotel room in Poughkeepsie.

Jeremy lurked in the doorway of a stately sitting room. Within it he saw Phoebe and Hayden seated in chairs in front of opposite windows. They were quiet and still, observing Giselle.

Giselle was sitting in the middle of the room; she was in a lotus position on the floor. One of the family dogs, Snoopie, stood across from her with his tail wagging. Giselle and Snoopie appeared to be staring at each other endlessly.

Ruby walked up and leaned on the door frame across from Jeremy. She rested her head against the cool, hard stone and massaged her temples.

She'd been in a guest bedroom with the lights off and shades down, sitting in the middle of the bed and attempting to meditate. Phoebe had shared some of what she'd learned about the witches she'd encountered during her years with Adam. She'd said witches with clairvoyant dreams had the ability to receive premonitions anytime, even while awake, but the power had to be honed through meditation.

Ruby felt confident in her ability to hone her skills in clairvoyancy. She was afraid to develop syphoning skills without a powerful teacher, so instead she tried to suppress that gift during her meditation sessions as well.

"When did you get here, simp?" she whispered.

Jeremy whispered, "Why are we whispering, nerd?"

"Obviously, we don't want to break Giselle's concentration. Read the room." Ruby waved her hand around and rolled her eyes.

"What's she doing though?" Jeremy squinted and tilted his head.

"Can't you see? She's staring deep into the eyes of a perfect boy and sharing secrets . . . Jealous?" Ruby asked, referring to Giselle's eye contact with her dog, Snoopie.

"No!" Jeremy whispered, but it was a whispered shout. "I'm not jealous of other boys. I'm a man . . . And who said I care about Giselle?"

The volume of the conversation escalated. Hayden was looking at them.

"So, you don't?" Ruby asked, challenging her brother.

"What?" Jeremy asked, confused.

"Care about Giselle?"

"Well, I didn't say that—"

"You two realize I can hear you, right?" Giselle asked, not breaking eye contact with Snoopie.

"Can Snoopie hear us, too?" Jeremy asked.

"Look at the size of Snoopie's ears. Of course he can hear us, simp," Ruby said.

Jeremy replied, "I wasn't talking to you, nerd, and you know what I meant." Then to Giselle he asked, "Can Snoopie understand us?"

"No . . . He's a dog, Jeremy," Giselle replied, breaking eye contact with Snoopie and turning to face Jeremy with a mischievous smile.

Seeing the embarrassed expression on Jeremy's face, Giselle laughed, which prompted Ruby to break into a belly laugh. Even Phoebe and Hayden started giggling.

When Giselle went to Jeremy and embraced him, still laughing, he also joined the others in laughter. The levity was good medicine for the group after enduring so much stress.

Giselle explained her gift to Jeremy, telling him animals can't understand much English, but they understand basic feelings from most people due to voice tone and body language, but most people can't reciprocate. However, understanding between Giselle and animals was much more specific. She could reciprocate feelings through voice tone and body language, and she also felt like there was a special language between her and them that nobody else could decipher.

"I wish I had powers, too," said Jeremy.

"You've already done more for our cause without them, with organizing all of our communication plans, than the rest of us have done with powers," Giselle said. "Besides, Mother said you have a gift of your own."

Phoebe said, "Yes, powers don't always appear when you want them to, but now that people around you are exercising theirs, it will awaken what sleeps within you soon."

"What's the plan so far?" Jeremy asked.

"Adam still doesn't know Mother's back, and he's invited me out to Sands Point tomorrow," Ruby said. "I'll try to access the room where Mother last saw Eve and call for your help to disable security if needed. I'm still thinking about how to slip away from him unnoticed."

"And Faustina took a security token from Joe's wristwatch, fingerprints, and voice samples last night," said Phoebe, "so, she and I will go after dark tomorrow night. We have one of the janitorial staff uniforms. The night crew doesn't know Adam is looking for Tina, so they shouldn't be on alert or recognize her with the hat on, but if we get caught somewhere, we can try to get out of it by saying we're looking for the kitchen or breakroom, but got lost, or something, but none of that should be necessary since the Lisa monitors will be bypassed."

"Right, the night guy mostly keeps to himself, but he can call in armed assistance if he feels threatened, so be as passive as possible," Jeremy said, agreeing with Phoebe's assessment.

"Are there any others with powers we can trust?" Faustina asked as she joined the group.

She'd been the second to arrive after Phoebe, but she'd gone to change out of the wig and men's suit she'd worn to move through public transit and past the state security at the house's gate that morning. Sitting on a chaise to kick off her shoes, she'd leaned back and fallen asleep for over two hours. Her night with Joe had taken so much energy from her.

"There's only around twenty witches with power left in the inner circle," Phoebe said. "A lot of the older generation died off without children. The rest of Adam's set is made up of people like you. None of the inner circle should be trusted outside of the six of us and Jameson."

"What's Father doing for us?" Hayden asked.

"He won't be actively involved. I don't want to risk his position or have both of us in a bad situation if this goes sideways," said Phoebe. "We have his silence and our shared resources though."

⬡ ⬡ ⬡

Hayden almost ran into Ruby as he stepped into the corridor from his home office. She stopped, smiled, and opened her mouth to greet him. He scowled and pivoted away from her before she could voice the words she wanted to say. Determined to speak to him alone, she followed him.

"Hayden! Slow down. Please, I need to talk to you."

Hayden spun around and snapped at her. "What?"

Ruby wasn't deterred and quickly said, "I'm sorry. I should have told you I was moving on. We've always been friends, and I didn't respect that, or you."

Hayden crossed his arms and looked down at the floor while Ruby spoke, then he said, "When you were intimate with me on New Year's Eve, but then never showed up to the dinner I planned for us the next week, yes, I was upset. You didn't cancel. You never even contacted me again, so I was definitely upset—"

"I didn't mean—" she said, starting to interrupt him with an excuse.

"Let me finish . . . I was upset that you were ignoring me because, as you said, our friendship meant something long before we were dating . . . However, I got over it, Ruby. My ego was hurt that you'd ditched me for someone who is essentially an elderly billionaire, but it's not like we were in love. Your leaving didn't bother me for long, but your attitude now disgusts me." Hayden scowled.

"My attitude?" Ruby asked.

"Our mothers are trying to do something good for all of us. Freedom for our powers. Freedom for Eve," Hayden answered. "I think you question them too much. I think your allegiance is shifting to Adam . . . If you get any of us hurt, we'll be enemies."

Ruby stated, "You're wrong. I think you're still upset about us and letting that cloud your judgement, but I'm still sorry about before."

"I hope it's worth it," he uttered with a sneer.

"You say that as if I had a real choice," she cried.

She stepped closer to him and was close enough to smell the pomade on his perfectly combed hair while noticing his meticulously ironed and creased shirt. His nervousness showed through his tidy façade, and his voice faltered.

"From free housing district nine to Sands Point is the only real choice for your family, you mean?" Hayden asked just as Jeremy appeared from around the corridor's corner.

Jeremy stepped up to support his sister, but also stand up for his family's history.

"And who was your mother before your father and Adam met her?" Jeremy asked. "Don't pretend to be better than us just because Ruby doesn't want you."

"That's not necessary," Ruby said to Jeremy. To Hayden, she said, "I'm still sorry; I care about you."

She reached her hand out to Hayden, meaning to give his arm an assuring squeeze, but he jerked his arm away and stomped past them. No matter what Hayden said, Ruby knew he was hurt. His cool, rational speech was merely an upside of his square personality.

"Where is Father?" Ruby asked. "Did you see him at the house?"

Jeremy nodded. "He'll be out of the way. I overheard him saying he's hosting a conference on Adam's yacht. I think they're meeting with a new Caribbean team and taking them down there while they train or something."

"Perfect timing for us. One less obstacle," she said.

Giselle's house featured a central grand staircase made of marble that rose majestic from the first-floor entry hall to the second floor. From the landing, another open hall radiated in each direction, connecting foyers and rooms. All bedrooms were on the second floor. Through the north foyer, there were five guest rooms. The south foyer led to the family bedrooms. A spiral stairwell to the third floor was hidden behind a door on the west side.

Giselle waited on a sofa in the second-floor hall, lounging conspicuously in an emerald-green nightgown of thin silk. She was waiting for Jeremy to walk through on his way to bed, knowing he was alone in the library finishing some research for his college capstone. She'd made sure the mothers had already retired for the evening,

Ruby had left the house, and Hayden was in the pool house with a couple of his colleagues, playing chess and drinking scotch.

Footsteps pierced through silence in the muted, dark household.

As Jeremy approached the landing, he noticed a glint of color in the dimness of the hall. He looked closer as he neared a sofa, realizing Giselle was lounging on it. Moonlight through the high windows fell across her red hair and green gown.

He subtly smiled when she switched on a table lamp next to her and met his green eyes with her hungry blue ones. He had little experience but made up for it with a confidence common to young men, especially one of his height and athletic prowess.

His gaze swept from her eyes downward as he shamelessly admired her body. The outline of her breasts against silk hastened the tightening hardness in his jeans. As he looked down past her hips, she leaned back. Her spine arched while she spread her legs, letting one foot dangle off the furniture.

Jeremy gained control of his breathing and asked, "Do you—um—" He cleared his throat. "Want to come to my room?"

Giselle didn't say anything.

She stood and turned away from him, walking towards a door at the back of the hall. When she glanced back over her shoulder, she noticed he hadn't moved, but he was watching her.

Turning her body to face him again, she extended her right arm straight in front of her with the palm facing up and hand relaxed. The movement was bold and graceful. Her manicured index finger beckoned him forward, the repetitive curling gesture promising him secret pleasures.

Once they were through the door, she closed and locked it. Then she took his hand and guided him up the narrow staircase. When they emerged from the dark stairwell, they were in a pool of gentle moonlight shimmering down from above.

Jeremy looked up. The skylight was massive. It was as big as the hall below them and the center of a gallery that spanned the entire third floor. There was art hanging on the walls. Antique furniture was placed sporadically throughout the space.

"How have I never seen this?" Jeremy asked. "This is amazing."

Giselle placed her finger against his lips, wordlessly telling him to remain silent. His response was to pull her against his body and kiss her deeply. She entertained his embrace for a while, kissing and licking his lips, mouth, and neck. Then she pulled away slightly.

Her hands slid down the front of his body, as she dropped to her knees. She unfastened his jeans with patience. The excitement of what he knew was about to happen made a shiver roll through him, and he dug his fingers into her soft hair.

When she wrapped her hand around his manhood and cupped her other hand beneath, she enjoyed feeling his warmth and how hard he already was. Bringing him to her mouth and using the end of her tongue, she licked a single salty pearl of fluid from the tip before looking up at him and taking all his length into her mouth.

A tumble of fellation and massage was mixed with moaning and caressing as she teased him and brought him to the edge of orgasm.

She was ready, her gown sticking to the moisture on her inner thighs. Knowing he was younger than her and might not last, and knowing she wanted to feel him inside her, she stood. Raising her gown above her waist, she bent herself forward over the back of a chair and clawed her nails into the plush fabric, bracing, anticipating the fuck he was certain to deliver.

He couldn't think; his mind and body were consumed with the release he could barely hold back. There would be no more kissing or caressing. He took one look at her supple ass, her toned thighs, and the perfection budding between them, and he went straight for it.

Pleasure rocked her core. The sublime feeling of his strong hands gripping her waist as he began wildly thrusting into her compelled her to thrust back, grinding her backside against him and driving him deeper into her as she found her release. In only a few moments, he was spent and smoothing down her gown before pulling up his jeans.

Giselle stretched out on the floor, looking up at the sky. Jeremy laid down beside her.

"Are we allowed to speak now?" he asked.

She laughed, and he joined her in the kind of pure, easy laughter that two people can only share in the afterglow of sex.

"I'm sorry for whatever boneheaded thing my brother said to keep you from socializing with him tonight," she said, "but I'm also glad you stayed in the house."

Jeremy started to reply, but stopped short as he thought about the tiff he and Ruby had with Hayden. Ruby was thoughtful when it came to her friends, and she was also uninterested in drama. In fact, Giselle was more likely to gossip than any of them. He didn't think Ruby would have mentioned to Giselle what he had insinuated about her mother, but somehow, she knew what had happened. Embarrassment crept into his thoughts.

"Ruby actually told you about that?" Jeremy asked. "I'm sorry for my part in it—for what I said."

"No, Snoopie told me."

"But you said he doesn't understand words," he said as he realized he'd admitted too much. "So, you don't know what I said."

"I sort of know what everyone said," she answered as she laughed, then sighed at the imposition of having to explain. "I've been working on my gift—my connection to Snoopie's mind, specifically. He doesn't understand much English, but he hears it. Sometimes he remembers the sounds, and I can hear them through our connection, or sometimes it's just his feelings I can feel . . . Today he was upset with you and Ruby and came straight to me. What I know is from his point of view, which was skewed not only because he's a dog, but also because Hayden is his family."

"It wasn't Ruby's fault. Hayden was being cruel to her," Jeremy explained. "I'm sorry about my part in it."

"I gleaned from Snoopie that Hayden and Ruby were upset. Hayden spoke to her harshly. Then, you showed up, and I know Hayden said something about your father, and then you said something about my mother, but I don't know exactly what." Giselle asked, "Am I close?"

He nodded. "Magic is truly unbelievable sometimes. What we said was--"

"No! I don't want it repeated right now, and there's no need to apologize to me for something you said to my brother while defending my best friend," she said, and rolled to her side, facing him and resting her chin on his shoulder. "I'm mostly excited that my interpretation of what happened was accurate."

Jeremy said, "It's a badass power . . . I have an idea how you can use it to help us."

"How?" Giselle breathed.

He explained, "Send Snoopie with Ruby to Sands Point. I mean, she won't have to get away from Adam, and he can wander around practically everywhere without us having to worry about raising suspicion."

≪∘ ≪∘ ≪∘

Ruby opened her eyes, yet she knew her corporeal eyes remained closed. The dreamscape was familiar; it was comforting. Under the exquisite Gaia Tree, she again stood facing that automaton being with the copper face and green eyes.

"I know who you are now," she whispered into the quiet place. "You're Adam's creator."

With a voice exuding humanity, he replied, "Yes, Ruby Cohen. You have disobeyed me."

"You told me not to help Eve, but I haven't. I've helped my family, but I haven't even seen Eve."

"We are not fae folk. You cannot avoid taking sides through a loophole. You are lying to all by omission," he declared.

"I—" she said but couldn't find words. "I wasn't even sure you were real before."

"Do you believe I'm real now?"

"Y—yes, I do."

"Trust Adam," he commanded.

She wanted to stay in her dream longer and enjoy time under the tree's tranquil canopy. She wondered why she wasn't in control there like she was with her other lucid dreaming.

She felt a tug of reality piercing her mind and soul as she was ripped from the divine presence.

Sitting upright in the feel of heavier air and gasping loudly into dark reality, Ruby found herself back in bed.

❧ ❧ ❧

"Are we sure this is the best idea?" Ruby asked, biting her nails.

Giselle snapped at her. "Stop biting your nails!"

Hayden interjected, "Both of you shut up! Between my sister's dramatic temper and Ruby's lack of loyalty, this meeting is going nowhere."

"Nail biting is gross, just like your face," Giselle mumbled to Hayden.

In the early morning, Jeremy, Giselle, Ruby, Hayden, Faustina, and Phoebe met over a pot of coffee. The family never used the formal dining room. Their kitchen was more comfortable. On the opposite side of the room from the major appliances and food preparation area, there was a breakfast table, island seating, a coffee hutch, an old sofa, and a small corner dry bar.

Hayden managed to get off the sofa and join the others at the table. He nursed a hangover with medicinal powders and a rehydration drink while Jeremy and Giselle poured more coffee into their cups and tried not to acknowledge each other too much.

It was almost time for everyone to leave and carry out their plans for the evening, and tensions were running high over the new plan for Ruby to take Snoopie with her to Sands Point.

Ruby suspected Hayden wanted the dog to spy on her in addition to sniffing around the estate for traces of Eve. She didn't want her privacy violated. It would be embarrassing for her interactions with

Adam to have a witness. The thought of her best friend possibly being able to see her intimate moments with a man made her feel rotten. She already felt rotten, being the only person in the room unsure of her role in their benevolent collusion.

Phoebe said, "Ruby, this is a good idea. If nothing else, you have extra security. He'll protect you from—"

"I really don't believe I need protection from Adam. Besides, how am I going to explain having your dog?" Ruby interrupted and looked around the room for an ally, but she found none.

Giselle answered, "I think it's a perfectly reasonable excuse to say you're watching your best friend's dog. I mean, it's doubtful he'd even ask about details in a house that size. He'll probably forget there's a dog there, right? Why is this turning into such a huge discussion?"

Phoebe added, "You don't think you need protection from Adam, but you do. Just this year, two of his oldest associates have gone missing. Nobody has seen them since the New Year's Eve party."

"And you automatically assume he hurt them?" Ruby asked.

"It's happened before," Phoebe answered. "You—all of you here, to include your mother, don't know what it's like to live with nothing, and—"

Faustina started to interrupt, but Phoebe held up her hand to silence her, and continued, "You lived in hiding for a few months, Faustina. That's not the same, and your family resources made that comfortable for you more than you realize."

Faustina looked down at her coffee, seemingly embarrassed. Hayden and Giselle looked uncomfortable as if they'd heard their mother speak that way before, and Jeremy glanced sideways at Ruby to gauge her reactions. Ruby was focusing directly on Phoebe, who continued speaking.

"You all take the comforts of Adam's empire for granted. He could snap his fingers, and you'd all be suffering. Maybe you'd be dead. Maybe your loved ones would be gone. Maybe you'd be wondering where you'll find the next meager meal while your stomachs ache from hunger. Instead, you have succulent chef-prepared meals that you don't know how to truly enjoy, and you don't have to worry where the food comes from . . . And you can't even understand what that means—the blessing of how wonderful it is to have . . . just to have. If you did, not only would you fight to keep it, but you'd understand what it means to lose it."

"Then why defy him and risk losing it? If I'm going to suffer outside of his empire, then why would I do anything to get exiled from it? All for freedom of choice? What good is that if my choices without his wealth and influence are all shittier ones?" Ruby asked in an exasperated tone.

"Because, even if you're ignorant of this fact, we live with the constant threat of him taking things anyway," Phoebe answered.

"I don't want to end up like Eve, or worse," Faustina said. "If we did nothing, I'd always fear for all of us. I might not know what it's like to suffer poverty, but I know about taking risks. Sometimes it's necessary . . . You're a risk-taker, Ruby."

"Try thinking about more than your own comfort, and then you might understand our mothers' point of view," Hayden said to Ruby.

"Why don't you stop giving her a hard time?" Jeremy asked.

"He's right!" Giselle snapped at Jeremy.

Silence followed. Then Ruby stood up slowly, drained the last bit of coffee from her cup and walked across the kitchen to the sink. Nobody said a word as she washed the cup, dried it, and carefully walked back across the room and placed it in a cabinet above the coffee hutch.

She turned to face the table, confronted all the faces watching her, and said, "I'm going upstairs to get my bag. Get Snoopie ready to leave. You'll hear from us tomorrow."

As she was leaving the room, she turned at the doorway and simply said, "I love you all."

REBELLION

Jeremy arrived at Dust headquarters in the early afternoon, still wishing he knew what his power was. He wanted to help more than being the tech and communications expert among them. He imagined himself flying through the city, stopping evil deeds with power radiating from his palms. Then he'd be able to protect his mother and family.

His original plan had been to go to a late lunch with his father and slip into the security server room on the way up to meet him. After hacking in and setting up remote access for himself, he would have then bypassed the security monitors during the night while his mother could slip past the back entrance in disguise while Phoebe kept watch to distract the night guard if he left his office.

That plan went to shit.

On his way into Manhattan, he'd received a message from his father that he was leaving the office even earlier than previously planned. They could still go in without control of the monitors, but if Lisa's facial recognition tagged them, they'd be busted within seconds.

He walked past the headquarters building and towards the Hudson Riverfront, thinking about the best way to move forward with searching the building. Seeing Adam's yacht docked a short distance from him on his side of river, he groaned and turned to walk the other way.

❧ ❧ ❧

Giselle and Hayden waited in a Brooklyn Heights loft and practiced their powers. Since they needed an anonymous place to hide out until Jeremy sent a message, Hayden called in a favor from a fraternity brother who worked in real estate. The loft was a fully furnished rental that had recently been vacated, so it wasn't back on the market yet since it was awaiting some plumbing and lighting updates.

Giselle filled various styles of drinking glasses with water, using every glass from the kitchen. She placed them in a circle around the floor, staggering them between candles she'd placed earlier.

"Okay," she said. "Do your worst . . . or best."

Hayden moved to the center of the floor. Getting relaxed was the best way for him to concentrate on his powers, so he worked on controlling his breathing while adjusting his attire. He untucked his t-shirt from his hand-stitched tailored trousers. Rather than kicking off his shoes like Giselle would have done, he carefully unlaced the antique leather and Harris Tweed wingtip shoes on his feet.

Giselle coughed out a loud and graceless laugh.

"Brother, only you could make relaxation look so tedious," she said teasingly.

Hayden ignored her and sat down on the floor, resting his forehead gently on his knees while loosely hugging his legs that were bent toward his chest. His breathing became steady and calm. As he lifted his head and opened his eyes, small flames sparked to life at the tip of every candle's wick.

Giselle became entranced with the elemental show Hayden created as he practiced discipline and control over his powers. The flames grew to five inches high, casting reflections across the glass and the water around the circle. The room was brightly lit from below. It looked like an inverted chandelier. Then the water froze from within each of the glasses. Misty ice replaced water, causing an effect like a light dimmer, which continued as Hayden brought the flames back down to a smolder.

Then the flames were extinguished, and candle smoke twisted and snaked up into the still air. The fire alarm began to sound and flash. The sound ripped Giselle out of her peaceful headspace.

"No fire! There is no fire! Home is safe!" Giselle shouted into the room, deactivating the alarm. "I can't believe we forgot to turn that off. Hopefully we didn't attract too much attention."

Hayden replied, "These lofts have individual home management systems, so we should be fine."

A chime from the front doorbell echoed past them. She glared at him.

She sighed. "We should be fine?"

He shrugged, walked to a screen mounted by the door, activated the intercom, and said, "We're fine, thank you. Please have a good evening."

Hayden started walking away from the door, and Giselle was gathering up glasses from the floor and taking them to the kitchen. There were three loud knocks on the door, and Giselle lost her grip just as she reached the sink. Glass shattered against granite. Suddenly frustrated, Giselle dropped the rest of the cups and stalked directly to the door.

"Tell them to go away!" she snapped at Hayden.

He activated the video feed, and they both studied the screen. A well-dressed couple looked directly into the camera. They were maybe two generations older than Giselle and Hayden's parents, or perhaps younger. Their stark white hair in contrast to their slightly weathered skin made it difficult to tell. They were smiling, and then the woman waved as if she knew Giselle and Hayden were looking at the feed right at that moment.

"Wha—there's no way . . . How are they . . . here?" Giselle asked.

"You know these people?" Hayden pointed at the screen; his face was confused as if pleading with his sister to explain.

"Duncan and Sylvia Cavendish," Giselle stated in barely more than a whisper.

Giselle had personally sent out invitations to every member of Adam's circle for the New Year's Eve shindig at Sands Point. She had then greeted every guest. As a self-proclaimed social butterfly, she knew the elite set on sight, but it took her some time to accept seeing those two at her door because rumor had it, they were dead.

"But—wait. Didn't they disappear right after the new year?" Hayden asked. "All the parents were talking about it for weeks. Mother thought Adam did something to them, yeah?"

Giselle and Hayden simply looked at each other. Neither of them knew what to do next. Another knock on the door accompanied by a chime from the doorbell jolted them from shocked indecision. Giselle held up her hand, indicating that she'd deal with them.

"I'm very sick at present. If you need something, please come back tomorrow," she said into the microphone and activated the outdoor microphone to solicit their response and get the awkward moment over with.

"Miss Rosemont, let us in. The longer you keep us outside, the bigger chance you take of being discovered here," said Sylvia.

Giselle looked to Hayden for an answer, and they frantically whispered to each other.

"She's right; we need to get them inside before they cause a scene," he said.

Giselle argued, "But can't we just stop talking to them? Nobody knows we're in here. If anyone walks by, it'll look like they're talking to themselves if we shut off the doorbell, turn off the lights, and keep quiet."

"Giselle—" Hayden hesitated, searching for words to explain reason to his sister. "What's the harm in talking to them—carefully? If Adam really did try to kill them, then maybe they're allies."

"Or maybe he sent them!"

"If he sent them, we're fucked anyway."

She studied his face for a moment, activated the microphone, and said, "We're going to open the door. Come inside quickly and stand still once you're inside. We need your hands where we can see them, okay?"

"Yes, ma'am," said Duncan.

Jeremy had hatched a new idea. He was aware that after the Companion launch, Dust technicians had stored demo models in the storeroom adjacent to the back entrance where he could get in undetected and activate them to search the building. The monitors wouldn't alert security for Dust's own tech.

"Are you sure they won't be noticed roaming around?" Phoebe asked.

Jeremy explained, "Nobody pays attention at night unless the system kicks out an alert, which it won't. Not this time anyway. I'm sure they'll add provisions to prevent this sort of thing eventually, when the vulnerability is discovered." He laughed and added, "You and mother can stay out here."

Faustina nodded and said, "We'll stay in the dark inside the car."

Jeremy left, closing the car door gently. Even though their temporary meeting room was a hired car stowed in an alley the next block down, they needed to do everything possible not to attract attention.

It was a public alley, so it only had minimal crime surveillance. Jeremy double checked that fact, noting two city cameras at each end. They were the type that only sent alerts and recorded if violence or destructive crimes were detected.

Faustina watched her son walk to the back of the alley and slip behind a corner towards the back entrance of Dust.

When he was out of sight, she turned to Phoebe and said, "I don't think Eve is in there. I felt her at Sands Point, but not now."

"But the power is not yours," Phoebe explained. "She was using her power to communicate before. She could be incapacitated, or maybe she's simply not searching her surroundings right now."

"With her mental powers, why didn't she communicate with the household staff, or any number of people around?" Faustina asked.

"You're sort of like a perfect conductor—a conduit for magic . . . You grew magical babies in your womb. It makes you susceptible to a witch's communications, or so the old folks say," Phoebe said. "It could also be part of Eve's natural powers. You did touch her."

"I'm trying to keep my mind open and tranquil even though the visions came naturally like dreams before. I'm worried she needs to communicate," Faustina whispered.

Faustina closed her eyes and concentrated on breathing. She leaned back as if to nap with the seat slightly reclined, while Phoebe faced her, looking past her at a man walking up the alley.

Trent Pinkerton, the 31-year-old Dust nighttime security guard, made his way toward their vehicle. His hair was black as coal and shaggy, but it wasn't necessarily long other than covering his ears and neck. It fell three inches above his shoulders and was combed to fall over his left eye a bit. He wore a company shirt and a jacket with a security patch, but instead of slacks he had on fitted faded jeans with black and navy wingtip boots.

"He's too sexy to work nights," Phoebe said.

Faustina opened her eyes, turned to follow Phoebe's gaze and asked, "Who?" When she saw Trent, she slouched low in the seat and urgently whispered, "Fuck! It's Trent."

Phoebe smiled. "Yes, fuck indeed."

"Shhh," Faustina whispered.

"Relax," Phoebe whispered back. "The windows are tinted, and it's so dark outside. Just let him walk by. He's probably out for a walk to take a break."

"I suppose you're right . . . At least we know he's not bothering Jeremy—also he's not noticing anything else in the building."

The two women watched as Trent approached them, but when he stopped beside the vehicle instead of passing by, Faustina reached through the darkness and gripped Phoebe's forearm. They both tried to remain still and breathe quietly.

Trent surveyed his surroundings and leaned against the side of the car. Then he took a silver case from his jacket's inside pocket and opened it. Inside there were two rolled cigarettes and a book of matches. He rested one of the cigarettes between his lips, struck a match on the sole of his boot, and lit the cigarette.

"How—is he smoking something?" Phoebe asked in a low mumble.

Faustina poked her in the side and whispered, "Shhh."

Trent was seemingly in no rush and began to absently tap his knuckles against the car door as he continued smoking. He hummed a lively tune between puffs, taking his time to enjoy the moment.

Phoebe knew they'd be discovered if he touched the door handle. A hired car's alarm only sounded to protect passengers from immediate threats. Otherwise, vehicles could simply be tracked if stolen or abandoned. She slowly moved to the front of the vehicle to locate the security menu on the console screen, trying for an excruciatingly long sixty-four seconds to change the setting from the default setting to the off position. A barely audible sigh of relief pierced the air as she started to move back to her seat, but then her foot got caught on a floormat. She stumbled to the floor with a dull thump.

Trent's humming stopped. There was a new tapping sound, but this time it was on the glass.

"Hello?" he said.

Faustina shrank down even more as if melting from her seat onto the floor.

"I'll get out and talk to him—make up something," Phoebe whispered. "I'll tell him I'm alone."

"Hurry up then, before he sees me," Faustina whispered breathlessly.

Phoebe opened a door on the opposite side and slowly popped her head over the roof, looking in Trent's direction.

"Before you ask me, yes, I am camping alone in a hired car in an alley," Phoebe said with a coy smile.

Trent grinned and studied her with amusement in his eyes while taking a long last drag from his cigarette before stomping it out.

"Nobody's smoked in decades," she said. "How do you even have them?"

"I'm not from here," Trent replied, seemingly nonchalant.

Phoebe huffed. "Okay, I know who you are, first of all. You definitely live in New York. But also, nobody in the whole world has smoked in decades."

She walked around the vehicle to stand closer to him, admiring his lean, muscular physique. By the reflection of a glowing streetlamp, she noticed his mischievous green eyes for the first time. It was like seeing herself staring back at her in a way.

He held out the silver case to her and said, "I have another one if you want it."

"No thank you. I'd rather get a straight answer," she replied quickly.

"I know who you are as well, Ms. Astor. I work security for Mr. Godwine on the island sometimes . . . Taking a holiday from your mansion to sleep in a car in the city?"

Phoebe drew up her posture and held her head high while continuing to close the distance between herself and Trent.

"You haven't the slightest idea what socialites do for fun outside of our obligations to Adam," she said and looked directly into his eyes again. "Maybe I knew you'd be here. Maybe I wanted to meet you properly rather than admiring you from afar on the island."

"Won't your partner—" Trent started to ask the question.

"No . . . and he's not here." Phoebe interrupted him.

"Damn. Well, if you're not going to smoke my last cigarette, I believe I need it now." Trent smiled.

He lit the last smoke and enjoyed the moment, standing close to a beautiful older woman.

"Your eyes are . . . like mine." She thought for a moment about how much she should say, or admit to, and then continued. "Are you one of us?"

He smirked and asked, "Am I a powerful and wealthy supporter of Mr. Godwine?" His flirtatious laugh was deep and comforting. "No."

"You know what I meant . . . Where are you from, then?" she asked.

"I'm originally from Staten Island, but I relocated here to Manhattan several years ago." He looked away.

"I've never heard of Staten Island. Is it in the United States?"

He mumbled, "You could say that . . . You know, actually, it's a lot like Richmond Island."

"Oh? Richmond must be your favorite borough then. They let you smoke there?" She asked as if to tease him.

He said, "I thought I was alone out here; that's why I walk all the way down to this alley at night. The public surveillance doesn't report me. Dust's surveillance does."

"We *are* alone out here," Phoebe jokingly retorted.

Trent leaned into Phoebe, almost resting his chin on her shoulder. His breath tickled her neck and ear as he spoke to her in a low and tender whisper.

"I hope to find myself alone in the dark with you again sometime," he said, "but right now I have to get back to the office."

He gave her one last knowing grin before turning and walking back up the alley. She watched him leave until all she could see was a faint, black silhouette and a red glowing cigarette cherry. Then she rejoined Faustina in the car.

⨳ ⨳ ⨳

Ruby shared an antique brocade armchair with Snoopie. She stroked his ears while listening to Adam play the piano. Adam appeared lost in thought. His playing became increasingly erratic as his eyes remained fixed on an unknown point in front of him, and when he began pounding the ivories harder and harder, Ruby stopped pandering to the dog and looked at Adam.

Pounding a final chord, he leaned into the keys and held them down until the notes echoed into nothing. Finally turning from the piano, he looked at Ruby. She was still looking at him, and their eyes met before his gaze shifted to Snoopie and then back to her.

"Your father has been easily vexed as of late . . . I've had reports of an unidentifiable person entering the governor's house . . . Your brother has been busy with meeting many different people at different locations, rarely meeting the same people twice and never at the same location . . . I feel tired," Adam said.

"What does 'vexed' mean?" Ruby asked, changing the subject. She was well-read enough to know most of the dead words he used, but teasing him about his speech was a game they played.

"I'm serious, Ruby."

She thought about everything she knew and how she felt. Something needed to give. She knew Adam was dangerous, but she could also tell that their intimacy gave her leeway in his world.

"Well, then. I'd like to trade answers for answers," she said. "I want a question answered first though."

"Fine," Adam agreed.

"Genesis said you died after almost a millennium, and then there's Noah's flood to consider," Ruby stated.

Adam stared at her. "Is there a question somewhere in that statement?"

She boldly stared back at him in silence, knowing the vague general statement would force him to explain more to her than a specific question would. If he wanted to get things moving, he would answer.

Adam sighed loudly and explained, "Religious mythology is just that: mythology. For example, people lived through the flood all over the world. How do you think there are flood stories in every culture? I'd already left my family by then . . . Tell me what's been going on at the governor's house."

"Okay . . . We've all been practicing our powers," she said carefully, watching his anger rise. "And what I want to know from you now is—without hurting me—without abusive reprimand—why is that a bad thing?"

Her words extinguished the temper burning under the surface of his being, and he said, "Ruby, I've never hurt or abused you, have I?"

"No, but I know you're capable of it, and I need to know why . . . If any part of your mythology is true, you'll understand that. We're like you. We need to know. Are you going to throw us out of the paradise you've built for us after it's too late to explain, or are you going to share the knowledge, so maybe we can understand and help?"

Adam knew she was right. In all his years, he'd never considered the parallels between his position now and his father's position in Eden, nor had he realized the learned behavior from his father that dictated how he treated his descendants.

Ruby saw many details in the world. She saw people and understood the complexities of situations and relationships, and that was as much of a power as any magic. He thought perhaps that was why he had let her closer to him than anyone else since Eve.

Adam explained, "Eve and I were immortal in Eden, but on the Blue Earth, we age. The years in the Tanakh are accurate. It took nearly a thousand years for us to look older than twenty. We had magic, and our family had long life, but that didn't last. As our family grew and grew and left to intermarry with other beings exiled from Eden and other beings made here, the power within us from Eden was spread thin.

"Having children aged us. Using magic in the form of our individual powers aged us. I began secretly encouraging our most powerful descendants to stop breeding and to control their magic, but some of them were already in foreign lands with other beings from Eden—"

"What do you mean by that? What other beings?" Ruby interrupted.

"We are what's now referred to as witches," Adam explained. "Even when exiled here, we retained magic and longer lives because of how we were made. Others were not made the same. Some were not even made to stay in Eden. For example, there were many species of intelligent primates made here for studying. Then there were other beings sent here to exterminate them. The creators made other special, chosen people as well, but most of the world's current population isn't connected to me and Eve . . . she made certain of that."

The color drained from Ruby's face and dread was apparent in her expression and her voice as she asked, "How—"

Adam interrupted her. "I'm overdue for another answer."

With her voice trembling, Ruby explained, "You don't understand. I need to know about her. What did she do?"

It was clear to Adam that something was amiss, but he reluctantly answered, "She slaughtered them. As they died, we stopped aging, and their magic poured back into us. She and I were on opposite sides of a war. She wanted to exterminate them, while I wanted to reign over them. For centuries she hunted them all over the world as I hunted her. Then I violently defeated her in battle."

Ruby's head was shaking side to side in disbelief, and as he finished speaking, she belted out a sob, dug her fingers into her hair and bent forward to rest her head on her knees. She knew how Eve had twisted the meaning of the visions her mother saw. She knew the divine being needed to be obeyed.

"He tried to warn me!" she cried. "I have to stop them!"

She looked up and met Adam's gaze, and he could read the horror in her eyes. His suspicions were escalating. Dread overtook him. He continued to sense the fear and panic radiating from her while she fought to control her breathing and gather her wits.

He cupped her face in his hands and whispered, "Tell me what I need to know, Ruby."

"They're looking for her now—tonight. Adonai told me not to—"

"He spoke to you?" he asked.

Adam's father hadn't spoken to him since his exile, and he found it difficult to control his emotions at Ruby's revelation. She whimpered when he accidentally squeezed her face too hard. He quickly let go and took her hands in his instead, silently pleading for her to answer.

She said, "Yes, he came to my dreams, but Mother and the others were so sure they were right to help her."

"Where is Faustina now?" he asked.

"Everyone's in the city looking for Eve. I'm so sorry . . . I'm sorry," Ruby pleaded with him.

Adam embraced Ruby and said, "Never lie or withhold the truth from me again. From now on, we work together and sort out any and every issue. I must always know what's going on within my empire, do you understand me?"

She answered him by holding him tighter. Then she let go and held his hands in hers.

"Thank you, Adam. I love my family. Please don't hurt them either. Please help them," Ruby begged.

"Sometimes I must hurt those who disobey me lest they cause me harm or destroy what I've built . . . But I will do my best to be fair and exercise forgiveness in this matter . . . I do this for you as my valuable confidant if you'll pledge to me your power and your insight, Ruby."

She nodded. "Always."

☙ ☙ ☙

Jeremy felt dejected. His plan to use the Companion to search the building worked, but they found nothing useful for the witching cabal's quest. Manipulating all that tech and narrowly avoiding Trent in the corridor turned out to be useless risks. His sister hadn't sent their secret code indicating she was leaving Sands Point to meet

Giselle. She hadn't sent any of their agreed upon codes, and he didn't know if he should feel worried or frustrated about it.

The operation was moving too slow for his liking. They'd almost passed an entire uneventful night, and he was on his way back to the alley where Phoebe and Faustina look turns napping. He left from the back of the building and walked down the street, thinking about the ice cream stand that used to be on the corner where he was going to turn and find their car.

His dad used to buy him ice cream there when he was a little kid, and then they'd walk to the riverfront. On cue with the thought, he looked up at the river.

He stopped so suddenly that he skidded and swayed slightly while staring at Adam's yacht. The change in Joe's plans, the last-minute voyage, and the missing clues were all adding up in his mind.

Jeremy took off running. He still had time to try to board the boat and look around before dawn. His excitement increased with each click of his heels upon the sidewalk. With no plan of ingress, he slowed and quieted his steps a safe distance away. He moved between overlapping shadows down the docs and spied his lucky break.

He saw Joe and a security guard he didn't know. They were both headed up the passarelle with supplies when the guard slipped.

Boxes fell in a disarray of crashing and splashing. The man stayed down for too long. Joe called out to him, but there was no answer. When he put down his own load and rushed over to help, the guard moaned loudly when Joe rolled him over and started lifting him. Even though Jeremy was some distance away, he could see blood gushing from a head wound and pooling on the metal ramp.

Joe then shouted to another crew member aboard, who disappeared for a moment and then came running down to help. All three men got into a nearby vehicle that drove them off quickly with lights and sirens blaring.

The passarelle leading aboard onto the main deck was left unguarded. Jeremy knew the third crewmember had likely disappeared to notify additional crew of the emergency and to tell them they were leaving, so he then had an easy way to get aboard. He suspected one or two more people were inside, so he boarded and went in the opposite direction from where he saw the crewmember go.

As he searched the other side of the vessel, he slipped into a dim passageway. About halfway down the length of it, he heard voices and turned to open the closest door. Once inside, he closed the door behind him, but it was so dark that he could not even see the shape of the room. He stood still and pressed against the wall and listened for voices. After he heard them dissipate, he reached again for the doorknob, thinking he would continue down the passageway.

Before he could open the door, there was an odd feeling in his chest. He felt like an unseen force was gently tugging him back into the room, so he let go of the door and felt his way along the wall. When his hand finally brushed across a switch, he flipped it.

A red bulb flickered on from above the center of the room, which was a sterile, gray antechamber. The only other door he could see looked like a vault entrance with a keypad and a combination lock mounted in the center. Possibly due to the emergency outside, it had been left ajar, so he opened it slowly to discover a stairwell that twisted down into a large room.

With the flip of another switch inside the door, florescent light from below pierced the black stairwell. Jeremy's right forearm snapped up to cover his eyes from the sudden brightness. As his eyes adjusted to the light, he lowered his arm, revealing a surrealistic scene below him.

The room's dominant feature was a glass cube situated in the center. Looking down on it, he could see it had its own heating, cooling and air filtration system attached to the top. His heart pounded in anticipation as he hurried to the bottom of the stairs and then to the cube.

She was there, and he sighed deeply and threw his fists in the air at the discovery, which was a victory for him. Eve was contained within the cube. She had been placed into a hospital bed that had several machines and monitors attached.

His time could run out at any moment, but he needed help to open the cube and move her, so he slipped off the yacht as stealthily as possible and then sprinted through night's darkest hour back to the car.

Duncan and Sylvia had their hands up while facing Giselle and Hayden. The older couple waited patiently in silence for the Rosemonts to give them further instructions.

"How did you find us?" Giselle asked.

"My gift allows me to hear magic, so I can listen and follow it . . . You've been loud today," Sylvia said. "May we lower our hands and find a place to sit down?"

Giselle looked to Hayden.

He nodded and said, "Yes, please come sit with us in the main room. I'll get us some water and tea."

Giselle showed Duncan and Sylvia into the main living area and invited them to sit on a large sofa while she sat across from them on a smaller loveseat. The silence was awkward as the sounds of running water and glassware clinking echoed from the kitchen. As an expert hostess, Giselle was about to begin small talk about the pleasantness of their journey when Sylvia spoke first.

"Your hair is such a rich, beautiful shade of red, Giselle," Sylvia said. "Ours used to be the exact same color, but it's hereditary in our family to lose all color in our hair by sixty years old."

"Oh? But you only look to be about sixty now," Giselle said.

Sylvia said politely, "You're very kind to say so, but we passed that mark ages ago."

Hayden appeared with a tray of refreshments and asked, "You said it's hereditary, but—excuse me. I know you have the same surname, but I thought you two were in a traditional partnership."

"We are distant cousins from an older witch commune," Duncan explained. "Back then, the entire community shared a name."

"Back when, exactly?" Hayden asked.

Duncan looked to Sylvia, but she shook her head as if to warn him not to say too much.

Witnessing the exchange, Giselle and Hayden exchanged a look of their own. They needed to stay firm even though they were trying to be as polite as possible.

"Look, if you want something from us, you should answer our questions," Hayden said.

"Oh, we don't want anything from you," said Sylvia. "What could two children possibly do for us? We're wealthy, powerful, and contrary to the rumors, Adam allowed us to retire."

Eager to bring back a pleasant feel to the conversation, Giselle smiled, poured some tea and asked, "What brings you to the city today?"

"As I said," explained Sylvia, "you've been loud. It's dangerous for you. Everything Adam does, to include his control of technological advancements, is to limit how much magic is used on this planet."

"So, it does weaken him?" Hayden asked.

"Not exactly," Sylvia said.

"It ages him, but you wouldn't be able to age him enough to make him weaker before he uses his powers to stop you . . . There simply aren't enough of us left to make that large of an impact fast enough," Duncan added.

"How can you be so sure—" Hayden started to ask before Sylvia interrupted him.

"Elemental manipulation is your power. Duncan's power is also elemental manipulation, but he controls the air, like your mother. It's a common gift among our kind, with some of us able to direct the energy in the air to harm and to protect others. Three others alive today have similar powers. Joe Cohen sees in the same way I hear," Sylvia looked Giselle in the eyes and continued, "and you communicate with plants and animals. Your friend, Ruby, has the power of prophesy, which is very rare, so it has been a joy to hear that particular magical frequency after so many years of silence . . . I tell you this, so you'll trust my word. There aren't many of us left because I can hear it."

"What about Eve?" Giselle asked. "When we free her, maybe her power can free the rest of us."

Sylvia's eyes widened and Duncan choked on his tea. Their facial expressions turned grave.

"Did I say something wrong?" Giselle asked.

"Eve is extremely dangerous," Duncan said. "Her most dangerous power is mind manipulation, but she can just as easily kill dozens of people at a time by directing her energy—"

"Duncan!" Sylvia said, interrupting him. "There's no need to repeat rumors and legends." Then she said to Giselle and Hayden, "No witch or human alive today has ever seen Eve. I know she still exists, but she is in hiding."

"Eve reads minds?" Giselle asked.

"No," said Duncan. "Our kind cannot read minds . . . She manipulates people with her mind. She can influence them with her own ideas, but she can't read what they're thinking as if having a conversation . . . At least, we think she manipulates minds. Like Sylvia said, she's disappeared."

"Joe Cohen and Faustina Rothschild have seen her. She was clearly being held against her will," Hayden said.

"If she's as powerful as you say, then she can help us, like I said," Giselle said.

"Think, girl," Sylvia said. "All of our magic flows from Adam, but also Eve. She has no reason to help—"

"Sylvia, we must tell them what the coven's legend says about Eve. Even if we don't have all the facts, these kids are making a mistake, and they need to know," said Duncan.

Sylvia sighed deeply and explained, "There's no need for me to embellish the story, or go on and on about a supposed war, aliens, titans, and vampires—so much is mythology . . . What's important is Eve chose genocide as a solution to her aging. She killed most of her own descendants."

"Ruby was right. She tried to warn us," Giselle whispered.

Giselle started gathering her things, picking up a backpack and packing personal items and supplies for herself and for Hayden.

Hayden and the Cavendishes stood as well. There was tension between everyone as they tried to anticipate each other's next moves.

"Ruby isn't on our side," Hayden said. "Wake up, Giselle. I'm tired of your stupid socialite routine . . . If Ruby knew this information, do you think she'd let her mother and brother do what they're doing right now? No, she's just Adam's whore. She wasn't trying to warn us or save us. We must do that ourselves now."

"Get a grip, brother. That awkward rant is beneath you," Giselle said.

Duncan ignored the sibling bickering and said, "You have business to take care of, so we'll go. Thank you for the tea and your time. Remember to be careful with your powers."

Giselle said, "Thank you. We need to hurry. They might already have Eve, so we'll tell them what we know and help in any way we can . . . Are we allies? How can we contact you?"

Sylvia reached into her purse and retrieved a clear quartz crystal. The gem was in the shape of an obelisk and was about three inches long and an inch thick. There was crimson liquid trapped in the center of the crystal. The obelisk was attached to a platinum chain, which she held twisted around her fingers while the crystal refracted rays of light as it swayed.

"Give this to your mother. She'll know what to do."

Not breaking stride, Jeremy's hands flew up to brace his body's impact with the car door. It was louder than he intended, so he looked around at the surveillance systems nervously. He let out a relieved breath when no sirens wailed.

Phoebe and Faustina jolted upright in their seats at the sound of something slamming into the door. Seeing her son there, Faustina opened the door. Jeremy immediately jumped inside. Closing the door behind him, he caught his breath and began to ramble off his plan.

"We got to act now. There is a small window of time. A perfect opportunity, but it's closing fast. There was . . . a medical emergency on the yacht. Father—most of the crew left in the middle of loading and preparing the voyage to the island. A door to Eve's room was left open. There's a glass—I don't know—cell? It's like a cube. She's in it. We gotta go now. Before daylight and the city wakes. And Father will be back any time. Let's go."

He rushed forward and opened the door, but Phoebe slapped his hand away and shut the door again.

"Let's go!" he repeated, looking to Faustina for support.

Faustina said, "Okay, but what is our exact plan? Do we know how to open the cell? What tools will we take. How can we defend ourselves?"

"Mother—mother," he said, then turned to Phoebe. "Ms. Astor, we have the luckiest break ever right now, if you could just see. She'll never be left this unguarded. We have a whole bag of tools. We can bring as much as we want. I'll protect you if the crew finds us. Okay?"

"Okay," Phoebe agreed as she lifted a seat to expose a secret compartment filled with weapons and lifted a gun out and tucked it into the back of her pants. "We all need to have at least a stun blaster at the ready though, can you both handle that?"

In response, Jeremy looked to his mother for approval. Faustina grabbed two blasters and handed one to her son. They hid the weapons under their clothes, and then Jeremy put the whole bag of tools across his back.

Even though the run back down to the river only took a few minutes, it seemed like hours to Jeremy. The women were fit, but they were no match for his youth and athletic nature. However, it was a small relief that Phoebe was able to keep up even though she was much shorter than him and his mother.

They arrived to find the yacht still unguarded. The presence of blood and debris told Jeremy most of the crew was still gone, so he charged aboard with the women following closely. As they entered the passageway where he'd found the antechamber and stairs down to Eve's cell, a man rushed them. He had a rifle, but the sling was across his back. As he reached to bring his weapon forward and up, Jeremy hesitated, but Phoebe did not.

She saw Jeremy hesitate to aim his weapon, so she slid from behind him. Kneeling on one knee, and then sliding to the side with the other leg before switching knees to get a stable base to aim. Phoebe had a clear shot at the man's eyes and took it, sending a laser at her target.

Blind and in pain, the man stumbled back and fell. Jeremy gathered his wits and stunned him. They left their foe passed out in the passageway, but Phoebe took his rifle and tossed it through a random portal as they continued their quest.

"I can't believe you used a laser pistol on that man," Faustina said to Phoebe as they entered the antechamber.

Phoebe shrugged and said, "He could have killed us all in a blink with that automatic rifle. I'm not even sure how Adam gets those legally anymore. Besides, Dust will certainly replace his eyes, so . . ."

"Thank you," Jeremy said.

Phoebe gave him a nod with a terse smile, and they descended the spiral stairs to stand in front of Eve's glass cube.

Jeremy opened the tool bag and all three of them studied the best way to pry open the one-woman prison.

Faustina's calm brown eyes looked from the two keypads to the row of cypher locks before drifting to the glass itself.

"Do we have something to cut glass?" Faustina asked.

Jeremy held a sensor up to the glass and answered, "Not this kind of glass. I best start picking all these locks."

"We won't get out in time that way," Phoebe said.

Jeremy kept working and answered, "We need to start doing something. Could you make sure the door upstairs is locked and guard us from up there?"

Phoebe went up the stairs while Faustina kept studying the glass structure. She considered the air unit sitting on top.

"The three of us should be able to pry off that air machine and move it. Then we could lift her out through the hole," Faustina said. "We need a ladder though."

Jeremy considered the space and said, "No need for a ladder. Look, we can jump on top from the stairs. It's only a couple of feet, so all of us should be able to do it. Once inside, I can stack that table on the bedframe and carry her out."

"Okay, I'll get Phoebe."

As the women reappeared, one after the other swung their bodies around to the outside of the stairs and hopped down, landing on top of the cube where Jeremy was already working.

"It looks like the sedative keeping her asleep is fed through this ventilation, so she should awaken when we get her out of here," he said.

After prying out the machinery and moving it out of the way, they realized the opening was a bit small, so Jeremy likely wouldn't be able to get Eve out on his back. He jumped in and made the makeshift tower from the furniture. While puzzling over how to lift the unconscious woman through the small opening, Phoebe found rope in the bag and tossed one end of it down to him.

"Tie it around her hands and lift her by the waist. We'll keep her upright until we can reach her arms to pull her up," she said.

When Phoebe and Faustina grasped Eve's hands and arms, they easily pulled her petite body from the hole. After Jeremy held onto her and pushed from below until he let go of her heels, he hoisted himself out and then made his way to the floor.

"Go ahead and send her over the edge. I'm ready to catch her," he said.

"We're going to toss her over on her side, so you can catch her in your arms, okay?" Faustina said.

"Sure, I'm ready." He was looking up with his arms stretched out and open wide.

As Eve landed in his arms, her elbow hit him in the face, and he stumbled and fell to the floor with her on top of him. He sat up and moved his hand over his face to discover he had a busted lip, but at least his nose wasn't broken or bleeding. Faustina and Phoebe quickly joined him on the floor.

"Are you hurt?" Faustina asked.

"No, I'm fine," he said, standing with Eve cradled in his arms. "Let's go."

As they reentered the antechamber, an alarm started blaring and echoing all around them. Phoebe carefully opened the door and peeked around.

She called back to them, shouting over the alarm, "There's nobody out there! Let's jam!"

They disembarked to find Adam standing on the dock blocking their escape. Armed guards flanked him. Joe was also among them.

At the sight of both his partner and his son, Joe said, "Please, Adam. Send these gunmen away."

Eve began to stir in Jeremy's arms. She turned her face right toward Adam. Her eyes popped open. The couple stared at each other for long moments while everyone else stood frozen. The witches were frozen out of pure terror; the guards were frozen from the apprehension of facing violence with deadly force.

Adam gave a signal to the guards, and they lowered their weapons and boarded the yacht. He thought they'd be useless with Eve awake anyway. He willed a magical energy shield around himself and Joe.

"Put me down, child," Eve's sweet voice calmly commanded Jeremy.

He carefully placed her on her feet in front of him, and she quickly spun around on him, clasping her hands around his face. He heard his mother's voice cry out somewhere behind him. Eve paralyzed him with mind control and smothered him with her magical energy, meaning to drain him of magic until he was dead. She thirsted and ached for more power after being asleep for so long, but she suddenly let him go with a growl of frustration.

She hadn't located a thread of magic to grasp and grew impatient. If the thread was there, it was too deep to find fast enough with Adam at her back.

Phoebe held onto Faustina, telling her to stay out of the way. They huddled close together, Phoebe watching Eve while Faustina was focused on her son.

Adam sent a wave of energy at Eve, knocking her into Jeremy, who recognized the severity of her attack against him and pushed her away from him. He then stumbled back away from her even more, huddling beside his mother and Phoebe.

Eve needed to gain a lot of strength before facing Adam in battle, so she knew there was only one way to end the standoff. She sent the biggest wave of energy she could muster radiating from her in all directions. Adam's shield mostly held between himself and Joe. Her energy felt like a strong wind passing by them.

Jeremy, Faustina, and Phoebe were knocked off their feet and thrown through the air. All three of them were laid out on the dock, teetering between life and death.

THE NETWORK

"Save them, or catch me?" Eve called out to Adam, taunting him as she backed away. "At least two of them are on the edge of death. They'll never make it without your help."

Launching herself over the edge of the dock, she dove into the murky river. Her flowing locks of red hair were the last part of her visible under the water before she vanished from sight.

Adam stood above the river as she disappeared, but Joe's panicked voice called him back to the tragic scene unfolding behind him. He turned at the sound of his name, but his mind was clouded and overwhelmed with thoughts of another war with Eve and the fear of change. He blinked, and his mind focused.

Phoebe was closest to Adam, so he rushed to help her first. From the corner of his vision, he saw Faustina with her face down.

On the other side of her, Joe was working to resuscitate their son, who was starting to cough and blink his eyes.

Like Eve, Adam could concentrate magical energy to harm foes. Both could also help people with it, but neither of them used the power often. It wasn't too late for him to help Phoebe. Her consciousness still lingered in her body, and he could sense a faint pulse. Not only had he made a promise to Ruby, but he would also need every descendant he had left to find Eve and right the world. Placing one hand over her heart and his other hand on her forehead, he directed warm, healing energy into her.

Phoebe sat up, inhaling loudly.

Realizing that Adam was on his knees next to her, she said, "Fuck me! You saved me again? I'll never get away . . ." she trailed off, but then had another thought and continued, "But why did she attack Jeremy . . . and us?"

"Faustina," Adam said, and that was his only reply.

That's when Phoebe looked behind her and realized Faustina was unconscious. Joe and Jeremy were kneeling over her. Joe was studying her closely, and she knew he was using his special sight to assess her injuries.

As Adam joined the others at Faustina's side, he asked, "What do you see?"

"I couldn't start chest compressions because—fuck," Joe said and then paused. He appeared to be concentrating on what he saw within his partner's body.

Jeremy answered, "As soon as he looked down at her and started to put his hands on her chest, he stopped and said she was bleeding internally."

"She's got broken ribs—punctured organs. She's a normal human with magical injuries—I'm afraid the medical team won't be able to heal her properly," Joe finally answered. "Adam, you've got to be able fix her . . . please."

Phoebe had crawled her way over to her new friend, bearing witness to the three men's efforts to save the ordinary woman surrounded by witches. Phoebe tried to stand, thinking she would get a first aid kit from the yacht to help, but her sight flashed white. She sank back down to the ground. She was temporarily blind and dizzy. Her ears buzzed, and as she regained use of her senses, she heard the men talking, finally able to focus on Adam's solemn voice.

"I'm sorry, Joe," Adam said. "We need to move now, and we'll work as fast as we can to try to heal her once we're concealed on the boat."

Phoebe looked up at the pink sky between the architecture and understood the conversation. The sun was coming up, and they needed privacy. She heard Joe sending a message to security to cordon off the area immediately, and some crewmembers appeared with a medical evacuation stretcher for Faustina.

To Phoebe's surprise, Adam noticed she couldn't stand yet, so he lifted her in his arms and carried her aboard himself.

Adam whispered to her, "I need your help with this one, Phoebe. You need to combine your power with mine."

The entire entourage ascended to the owner's deck where Adam's medical team set up in his private lounge. Located above the main deck, Adam's deck had the luxurious lounge they were all gathered in, but it also had his master bedroom suite, two washrooms, a conference room, a gym, and a sun deck with a hot tub. The owner's deck was also the biggest secure area on the yacht, making it the most secure place they could get to in time to save Faustina.

The medical team placed Faustina on a long mahogany cocktail table, which was central to the room. Three large sofas bordered the table, so Adam's team had plenty of space to work there.

Adam placed Phoebe on one of the sofas and raced across the room to the bar to get her a bottle of water.

As he approached her with the water, she said, "How am I supposed to help you save her? All I can do is kill."

"There are two sides to your power—positive and negative," he explained.

"How do you know?" she asked.

"Because it's a common gift; everyone else who has this gift can direct energy to friend or foe," he explained.

"Why didn't you let me use it?" she nearly screamed at him, starting to cry.

Adam said, "Phoebe, I'm sorry . . . With Duncan and I able to use the same gifts, I didn't need you expending power."

"But why?" she asked.

"I will explain when we have Faustina healed, I give you my word." He squeezed her hand.

"But I've never—I don't know how," Phoebe cried with tears now rolling down her face. "What if I kill her? You've never let me do this!"

Adam placed his hands on her shoulders and sent enough energy to calm her. She felt it and gasped, looking up to meet his eyes.

"We must make haste," Adam said. "It's simpler than you think, but I'll need you. She's hurt badly. Let me guide you to help me—help her . . . Please."

Phoebe nodded. "I want—I want to help her. More than anything, I want her to be okay."

"I can help direct your energy for healing rather than destruction. You don't need to learn how to control it in the next few seconds. That wouldn't be reasonable, right?" Adam asked.

"Of course," Phoebe agreed. "Tell me exactly what to do."

"All you need to do is hold my hand, and then we'll each place a hand on Faustina. From there, I'll do most of the work, but you'll need to think only of the love you feel. It can be for her, or for your family, but every hateful emotion needs to be locked away until we're done, can you do that?"

"Yes," she said, and tried to stand.

"May I help you?" Adam asked. "Even though you can likely walk now, I'd like you to save your energy just in case."

She let him help her kneel over Faustina, then she linked hands with him. Phoebe placed her other hand on Faustina's forehead while Adam placed his on the unconscious woman's injured chest.

Silence fell all around them. Adam's medical staff stopped moving and working their instruments. They lowered their heads out of respect and stood patiently. Only the newest nurse stared at Adam and Phoebe because she was curious about strange comments she'd heard from the others and the odd wording in her nondisclosure agreement.

The nurse's eyes widened when their hands began to glow, and she promptly fainted. As the other nurses and doctors were not surprised, since seeing Adam save a man on the island the year before, they stayed silent and left the nurse propped on the floor against a sofa.

Jeremy felt equal parts terrified and guilty. He was terrified that his mother would never open her eyes again, but when he looked at the tears staining his father's face, he felt guilty that he had no tears of his own to shed for her.

Joe reached for his son's hand and gripped it tightly, whispering, "It's working . . . I can see it working." Then he reached over and gave him a side hug. "I love you, son."

Adam felt movement under his hand. Faustina had taken a breath. He reached over and guided Phoebe's hand away from Faustina's forehead. Still following his lead, Phoebe leaned back to give Faustina space.

"Is she . . . okay?" Phoebe asked Adam.

"We'll soon know," he answered.

Joe took a deep breath and held Faustina's hand while still embracing Jeremy.

Faustina's eyes were still closed when she murmured, "Jeremy."

"I'm here, Mother." Jeremy put his hand on her face and leaned over to speak to her directly.

As Jeremy leaned closer to look at her face, she coughed. Blood splattered all over him, and he froze from the shock of it until she rolled to her side, opened her eyes, and coughed a few more times.

He then reached out to help her, but she spit bloody phlegm on the floor and said, "Oh, my. Pardon me."

Rolling onto her back again, she looked around, noticing everyone quiet and staring at her, so she added, "I'm fine—I think."

Joe smiled and rubbed her hand. "Yes, you're fine now."

Faustina saw the blood on Jeremy and asked, "Jeremy . . . Are you hurt?"

He rested his head on hers and lightly embraced her, speaking softly close to her ear, "No, mother. I'm well . . . It's your blood."

"I'm so sorry," Faustina cried. "Eve—"

"She showed you half-truths and manipulations. It's not your fault. She's had thousands of years of experience," Joe said.

It was then, after he was sure she was going to live, Jeremy was able to put aside the mind-numbing terror that had been shocking his system, and he cried while resting his face against his mother's shoulder. He felt grateful to have both his father and his mother there with him in that moment, but his thoughts eventually drifted to his sister. He hoped Ruby would join them soon.

⋙ ⋙ ⋙

In the aftermath of Eve's escape, Adam entreated everyone to stay on the yacht as his guests with the promises of telling them the entire truth and protecting them. Although his descendants were rightfully distrustful of him, his lifesaving sacrifices for Phoebe and Faustina earned him temporary reprieve from their judgement and rebellion.

Adam cancelled his trip. Instead of sailing to the island, they would use the supplies and crew already on the yacht to stage a makeshift headquarters for a few days. He could find a remote location not far off the coast, bring enough security for constant surveillance, and sort out what to do next.

No longer fearing Adam's ability to intercept messages, Phoebe sent for her children, who had been worried for her after not finding her at any of their designated safe spots all night. When they warned her about Eve, she told them Eve had already attacked and escaped. She told them to hurry and stay hidden along the way, and she could explain more when they were safe within Adam's guarded perimeter.

Joe had other plans for Eve and wanted to go back to his office before doing anything else.

Approaching Adam privately, Joe said, "I can track her . . . I perfected the tech we talked about, and I just installed it yesterday."

"Where is she now?" Adam asked.

Joe said, "The control console is still in my office. I was in the process of moving things here and loading for the voyage . . . I'll need to go back for it."

"Do it. We'll wait for you," Adam stated.

Joe started to leave, but then turned back to Adam and said, "It's imbedded at the base of her spine, so . . . I've weaponized it. We can paralyze her or execute her if we're in range."

Adam sighed and turned away from Joe. "I feel like I've lost control of all of you . . .Why would you add specifications I didn't approve?"

"I was afraid something like this would happen . . . I'm not sorry. You may need to kill her if you don't get the envito," Joe said.

"Get what you need and hurry back, Joe," Adam said dismissively.

Ruby knew she wasn't in bed, but where was she? The last thing she remembered was reading a message from her mother while sitting on the chaise sofa in Adam's study with Snoopie curled up at her feet. Suddenly she was in darkness, and it wasn't only darkness. There was no floor beneath her feet, nor could she hear anything. She felt like she was in a void.

Silhouettes began to emerge out of the pitch as darkness morphed into a scene of life animating before her eyes. It was merely a scene to her because she was still weightless and not part of the place. Her feet did not stand on the ground appearing around her.

In her dreams, she was an active participant. Something completely different was happening. She looked around for answers to what she was seeing. It was Giselle's house, but she didn't see the family or anyone yet. Noticing a grandfather clock at the end of the foyer, she had an idea. Knowing the time wouldn't be helpful, but maybe knowing the date would be.

Walking wasn't an option, so the looked towards the study and willed herself to travel there. It was like floating though the house, or sort of like seeing the house as a movie set through the lens of a camera moving through it on a dolly.

With any luck, the main household planning and security monitor in the study would be on and displaying the date. She floated around to the desk, and she could see it. She was four days in the future.

She was finally having a premonition. She smiled to herself and wondered if her physical body was also smiling and staring into nothing while still sitting on the chaise. It was her first premonition, and pushing aside her excitement, she concentrated on how to make it work. The future was there, but she looked for ways to find something important. Going back to the open main hall would be the best place to find someone, she thought.

The room was still empty and quiet, so she waited. From above she saw two trails of black smoke traveling down in the direction of the floor. They looked like drops of ink falling through water. When they reached the floor, the swirls of smoke coalesced into people from their feet up to their heads. She recognized her brother before he was even halfway formed, but the other person wasn't someone she remembered ever knowing.

Moving closer, Ruby saw the mismatched eyes and remembered her mother's words. Ruby was looking into Eve's eyes and seeing her face. She was seeing Eve's mouth curled into a vicious sneer as she tried to attack Jeremy.

Ruby gasped, expecting her brother to fall under Eve's power, but something incredible happened instead. She saw his magical gift. He walked through a rip in the air, disappearing and then reappearing behind his attacker. As if reaching through another portal, his hand seemed to go seamlessly into her body.

When he pulled back his hand, Eve's heart was there in his fist. Tears streamed down his face, and he dropped the bloody heart, walking away in silence without looking back at the shell of the life he'd just taken.

Jeremy and Eve turned to smoke, and Ruby was alone with her thoughts as the room gradually faded.

Her brother would somehow manipulate spacetime and kill Eve. She was grateful to know his gift and wanted to share the knowledge with him, but the rest of the scene—the ending had to be a harbinger of something terrible to come.

She knew her brother, and he wouldn't be able to kill someone with such raw violence. The kill was personal. It was emotional, and Ruby ached with the knowledge that her family would know deep, personal loss before Eve's demise.

The scene dissolved back into darkness.

Giselle and Hayden arrived and joined everyone in Adam's lounge. Phoebe rushed to hug her children, leading them to seats at the bar. She began mixing three drinks while they told her about Duncan and Sylvia.

"Sylvia said you'd know how to use this," Giselle said, holding up the crystal.

"It's a bit inconvenient, but yes," Phoebe said. "Her blood is in there, so we could scry for her over a map and then physically travel to seek their help . . . That's the only way I know how to use it."

"So, you think they can help?" Hayden asked.

Phoebe answered, "We won't know exactly until after the meeting."

They toasted their reunion and continued to talk about the night before. Giselle was in the middle of telling Phoebe about Hayden's progress controlling his power when a dog started barking.

"Snoopie!" Giselle squealed.

Giselle spotted her mother's dog by the piano with Ruby and went to greet them. Hayden accidentally met Ruby's eyes and scowled while turning back to his mother and gulping down his drink.

"Is Father coming?" Hayden asked.

Phoebe frowned. "No, he has business in Albany. This isn't his world anyway . . . Right now, we're only waiting on Joe to return before heading for some uninhabited island not far off the coast, so we'll have privacy and security for the meeting."

Joe and Trent entered the room with equipment, and Joe started setting it up at a small workstation three crewmembers had placed by the corner bookshelves. When he finished, he thanked Trent for helping him carry everything and asked him to return to his security post on the main deck. Joe then nodded to Adam, signaling everything was ready to go.

The lounge had been rearranged during the day to accommodate Adam's guests. The oblong cocktail table on which Faustina had been revived was replaced with a large round one, and several armchairs were added between the three sofas surrounding it. Adam took his place at one of the armchairs and asked everyone to join him around the table.

Adam still had over a hundred identified descendants, who were unaware of their magical ancestry. Although their blood didn't contain significant levels of magic, all of them had faint traces of the same special blood that flowed through his and Eve's veins, which meant they were talented employees. All of them had a place in this empire, and he kept track of their lives and families.

Only a fraction of his living descendants were still proper witches, making up most of his inner circle. With the very recent addition of the Cohen and Rosemont youths, all of them became aware of each other and their magic. Seven of them were not present, and that fact was not overlooked as whispers and rumors circulated the room.

When everyone was settled around the table, Adam said, "Hayden Rosemont, share your meeting with Duncan and Sylvia Cavendish with us."

Adam knew what they whispered about him, and he understood why. He might have killed the Cavendish survivors under different circumstances, but sparing their lives was fast becoming an advantage as several people in the room received Hayden's story with visible relief.

Danielle Cheshire, who was sitting rigidly upright next to Giselle, stealthily removed her left glove and let her palm casually rest against the side of the bag sitting between them. It was the same bag Giselle had been using since their quest started. Moments passed before Danielle put the glove back on her hand. She then relaxed her posture, leaning back comfortably into the sofa.

Adam watched Danielle's movements with interest. He'd always found her the most beautiful of his people. Her red hair glowed like fire against coal black skin. The irises of her eyes were so dark they blended with her pupils, making it seem to Adam like deep magical voids in the center of her eyes were pulling him in when he looked at her.

Danielle's power was reading objects, deciphering the echoes of where they'd been and what they'd witnessed. Not taking Hayden at his word, she'd read Giselle's bag to confirm her lost friends were still alive.

"None of you will use magic in this room without my permission," Adam said. "This is your last warning."

Danielle faced Adam and realized he was speaking indirectly to her, so she replied, "I needed to know it was true." She looked around the table. "It is true, if anyone else was wondering. He let Duncan and Sylvia retire."

"Why wouldn't you believe my brother's account of what happened last night?" Giselle asked. "We have no reason to lie about it."

"I find it hard to believe, too," said Ty Alexander, the Dust gym's general manager, sports partnerships organizer, and former commercial supervisor.

"Oh, so do you want to use your powers against us to find out as well?" Hayden asked, his voice dripping with angry sarcasm.

"No, he doesn't!" Adam replied forcefully.

"I don't think I could even if I wanted to," mumbled Ty.

Ty had the same gifts as Phoebe, and like her, he was never called upon to use or hone his gifts. That wasn't the main source of his disgruntlement, though. He'd been at odds with Adam because he was getting older and tired of living in the city.

"I didn't harm anyone," Danielle argued.

"This subject is finished," Adam warned.

Everyone started coughing, feeling like something was suddenly stuck in their throats. They all looked around at each other and at Adam, realizing he was punishing them.

"Adam, stop!" Ruby managed to bark at him before gasping and coughing again.

The coughing stopped and was replaced with the sounds of deep breaths and drinking glasses being pulled across the table as people soothed their throats with drinks.

Hayden cut a hateful glare at Ruby.

"Even considering Duncan and Sylvia's absence, there seems to be five others missing from our number," said Phoebe. "Was this an optional meeting? Because I don't remember having much of a choice."

Joe answered, "I can account for them, Phoebe . . . They're all caring for critical Dust interests overseas, and I think you know that. How could they be here?"

Phoebe threw up her hands. "Just checking."

"Anything else of burning concern to anyone?" Adam asked.

Jeremy was sitting on the other side of Giselle, and they began whispering to each other.

"What is it?" Joe asked a bit impatiently.

"The weapon you brought to Adam after the Companion demo . . . We want to know about that," Jeremy answered.

"Envito is an emotion," Adam explained. "In Eden, when newer beings than Eve and I are created, their brains are grown and wired with this emotion. It's not possible to exactly explain with any words from his world because the essence of what the feeling is doesn't exist for us, but the emotion instills one with the ability to receive more clarity in life, which helps beings who've lived for as long as I have from going insane.

"It wasn't a weapon Joe delivered to me. It was a beacon to summon someone here to operate on Eve's brain and give her envito—to cure her. I assume everyone here has heard by now that Eve and I are from a place in the universe called Eden, and that we were sent here thousands of years ago, and that Eve turned murderous after a few hundred years . . . However, I'm the only one who knew her before. I loved the woman she was. I want her back."

"If it's that simple, then how are you not raving mad? What if you decide to kill our children one day to keep their power for yourself? Are we not causing you to age as well—when we use our magic?" Phoebe asked.

"I very well could be mad one day, which is why I've asked to receive envito as well," Adam said.

"Can't we all receive it?" Danielle asked.

Joe cut in and answered, "None of us were created in Eden. I don't think we'd withstand the process for reasons too complicated to explain to everyone."

"Try me!" Danielle challenged him.

"I'll have my research sent to your office then," Joe answered with a shrug.

"My concern," Ruby said gently to Adam, "is that Eve has committed mass murder—an attempted genocide, and you'd have us forget this when her brain is fixed?"

"He's thousands of years old and has always been in control," said Hayden. "Of course, he thinks he's better than us. He probably thinks he's a king, like back in Mesopotamia. He probably had slaves that he treated a lot like he treats our parents."

"Make no mistake, Hayden. I am better than you," Adam said. "Yes, I am from a time when that sentiment was more acceptable to my progeny, but it is no less true now. My power is pure and vast. I knew your great-great-great grandparents . . . Do we need to continue this conversation?"

"Even you answer to someone, Adam," Ruby whispered.

"Ruby!" Joe shouted. "Not now."

"She's right," Adam said, addressing everyone in the room, "and if my creator ever—ever lowers himself to acknowledge me and Eve, maybe he'll punish her. Alas, I will not . . . Joe, take over this meeting."

Joe proceeded to brief everyone on safety and how to read his Eve tracking machine. They worked out shifts for monitoring Eve's movements via the workstation he'd set up earlier in the day.

❧ ❧ ❧

Phoebe propped her arms upon the main deck's rail and watched the moon's reflection shimmer in the gentle ocean waves. She breathed deeply, savoring the scent of salty sea air. It was one of her favorite smells, reminding her of freedom from her old life when she had been confined to her neighborhood in the city and never saw or smelled any wide-open spaces.

"Am I interrupting?" a voice asked from behind her, and she recognized it was Trent without even turning around.

"No, not if you make it worth it," she said.

Walking up behind her, he brushed her hair away from her neck and whispered, "I saw you earlier, and I knew I had to find you alone while the night was still young enough for sultry misdeeds."

She leaned back into his body, rubbing her backside against him while still holding onto the rail. His hands drifted from her shoulders, down to her waist, and then felt their way down her arms to rest on top of hers while he kissed her neck.

Ruby approached in darkness, not realizing what she saw until it was too late. She recognized them and couldn't unsee it. Giselle always said her parents had an open partnership, but knowing was different than . . . knowing. Attempting to retreat as quietly as she'd arrived, she turned and took a deliberate stride in the opposite direction.

Ruby's knee collided with a bench, and she moaned from pain and from annoyance that the deck furniture was painted black.

"Hello?" Trent called out.

Ruby winced to herself and responded, "Hello. I didn't mean to disturb you. I was just out for a walk."

Phoebe called out to Ruby, asking, "Ruby, is that you?" Then to Trent she whispered, "I'll find you soon."

Trent continued his roving guard duties around the deck, and Phoebe approached Ruby. Ruby was in awe of Phoebe's shameless, bold demeanor. She was glad it was so dark, so her blushing cheeks wouldn't be noticed.

"You should stay inside in case Eve approaches," Phoebe said.

Ruby mumbled, "I was actually coming to see you—but I—I didn't know—"

"It's copacetic. I know . . . What do you need?" Phoebe asked.

"When I have a premonition . . ." Ruby struggled for words to voice and describe her questions. "What I mean to ask is, premonitions are the future, but is the future certain?"

Phoebe reached for Ruby's hand and pulled her near before saying, "If you're scared of something you saw, you can tell me, but no, the future isn't certain. Any part of what you see can change."

"Okay," Ruby said and sighed with relief.

"Is there something you need to tell me?" Phoebe asked. "Telling the subjects of your premonitions what you know is how you can help them."

"No, it wasn't about you . . . I just knew that—you knew. I mean, you know about powers and stuff," Ruby said.

Ruby was sufficiently embarrassed. Not only did she interrupt her best friend's mother with a lover, but she was starting to sound as confused as her own idiot brother instead of speaking like the intelligent person she knew herself to be.

Phoebe picked up on Ruby's awkwardness, realizing she must be embarrassed. She decided to spare her any questions or further discussion, giving her an easy out.

"Congratulations on unlocking your premonitions, Ruby. I've got to jam just now, but you can always come to me with your questions," Phoebe said as she walked away.

"Thanks," Ruby said weakly before turning around to go find her brother and tell him about the magic she knew he could do. She still didn't want to tell him what he was doing with that magic though.

The date on the calendar couldn't refer to her brother either, she thought. There had to be something else important about the day because she didn't see any way for him to discover and learn such intricate powers within a few days.

Giselle and Jeremy were sitting facing each other. They were both fully clothed and straddling the diving board above the pool. Jeremy was sitting closer to the end, so Giselle bounced up and down, trying to knock him closer to the edge. He slipped a bit, and she was overcome with bubbly giggles.

"I'll jump in with all my clothes on if you let me take you on a date," he said.

"Will you jump in naked if I don't?" she teased.

She laughed again, but he frowned and sat quietly, so she answered him seriously. "I would, but I know you care too much. I don't want you to think we'll jump into a partnership."

"What's wrong with a partnership?"

"Jeremy, there's nothing wrong with it, but we're young . . . You're even younger than me and haven't properly enjoyed yourself with other girls yet."

He shook his head. "I'm not like you—not that there's anything wrong with . . . What I mean is, I'm not interested in sex the same way you are."

"I don't know what you're trying to tell me . . . Are you calling me a nymphosexual?" Giselle asked.

"I'm telling you I'm demisexual, and I've felt close to you for years, which is the only reason I followed you up to your secret room that night . . . I had a phenomenal time—I mean, it was really good, but I wouldn't have felt that way with anyone."

"I don't want to hurt you if we try to have a relationship, but I'm prone to lose interest, or it might not work out anyway," Giselle admitted. "I want you in my life, and I don't want Ruby to be upset with me either."

"What if I can deal with knowing what might happen?" he asked. "What if we agree to explore the possibility and accept if it doesn't turn into anything?"

He reached for her, and she didn't pull away. As they kissed, they entwined their legs together that were dangling on each side of the board and began playfully swinging them. She wrapped her arms around him and slipped her hands into his jeans, grabbing onto this bare ass to pull him even closer. He was about to slide his hand up the front of her shirt when his sister called his name right before she appeared from around the corner.

Dropping her head into her hands, Ruby shrieked, "Fuck my life!"

Ruby wondered if her entire destiny was to cock block every person on the yacht in one night. Dragging her hands down her face, she turned around and was about to round the corner again when they started shouting her name and laughing.

"Ru! Get your perfect ass over here!" Giselle shouted at her, then dissolved into more laughter along with Jeremy.

Ruby got to the base of the diving board and said, "I don't think all three of us will fit on this thing."

Giselle looked over her shoulder and replied, "Well, if you don't want to straddle me, we could all fit in the pool?"

"If those are my only two choices, I'll go ahead and straddle you." Ruby stepped onto the board, laughing.

Ruby sat behind Giselle and hugged her around the waist while resting her chin on Giselle's right shoulder, so she could face her brother and talk to him.

"Do I look like I have two heads now, Jeremy? What if I had to share a body with your sister?" Giselle cracked a cheesy grin.

Ruby answered, "Well . . . technically we're all distantly related to according to Adam, so . . . Never mind—I don't want my thoughts to go there."

Giselle and Jeremy started giggling yet again. Ruby knew they were drunk, or high, or both.

"Hopefully you still have some candy to share," Ruby said.

Giselle lifted a strawberry narcotic candy to Ruby's mouth, and she took it with her teeth. Strawberry was Ruby's favorite flavor, and Giselle knew that. Ruby gave her a little kiss on the cheek to express her thanks.

"So how long were you looking for me?" Giselle asked Ruby.

"So sorry, my friend. I was looking for Jeremy, but it's a bonus that I can now talk to him over your shoulder while I hold you." Ruby squeezed Giselle.

"You were really looking for me?" Jeremy asked. "What's going on?"

"I had my first real premonition outside of a dream," Ruby stated.

Giselle bounced with excitement. Ruby held her tighter and squealed as half of her bottom slid over the edge. Jeremy reached out and steadied them. Ruby noticed how happy he was, and she didn't want to ruin it with too many details, but she wanted him to know his power.

"You manipulate dimensions in air, and space . . . possibly spacetime? I saw you walk through rips in the fabric of reality and travel from one point to another through them," Ruby said.

"Wicked!" Jeremy declared. "Who the heck can help me learn to do that though?"

"I have some experience with that gift, if you want to come see me in the morning," said Trent as he emerged from a large shadow where he'd been about to smoke in secret.

They all froze and stared at him. Trent merely stared back and waited. He felt he really shouldn't interfere, but manipulating spacetime was dangerous business. He didn't want the kid to end up trapped in a parallel universe.

"You can manipulate spacetime?" Giselle asked, really raising the pitch of her voice on the last word to emphasize the question.

"I know how to manipulate spacetime," Trent answered.

Ruby caught the subtle difference in what he was asked versus the answer he gave, but she couldn't make sense of it under the influence of candy. She thought he looked like a witch, but she knew he wasn't part of the meeting.

"But you're not a . . ." Jeremy trailed off.

Realizing just how high they were, Trent said, "I'm the night security supervisor at the Dust headquarters, but I'm a roving guard right now, see?"

He held out his arms and turned in a circle, messing with them for his own amusement. Then he decided to go ahead and light a cigarette and smoke it down in a few long drags while he kept watching them.

"Giselle, where did you get that candy?" whispered Jeremy. "I think I'm hallucinating too much."

"No, I see it too," Ruby said. "I think maybe you should go see him in the morning—couldn't hurt."

"Everyone says you're a smart cookie, Ms. Cohen," Trent said as he turned to leave. "See you in the morning, Mr. Cohen, but let's keep this between us."

After Trent left, they all started crawling their way off the diving board with careful, deliberate movements. Jeremy suggested raiding the refrigerator for snacks, so they started walking that way.

"Who was that guy?" Giselle asked.

"Mr. Pinkerton," Ruby said, trying not to think about Giselle's mother going to bed with him later that night.

"So, was he super badass and sexy, or was he super fucking creepy and weird? I can't decide," Giselle said.

"All of it—all the things," Jeremy answered.

Their next bout of laughter echoed down the passageway, after which they each started loudly shushing each other all the way to the galley.

◈ ◈ ◈

Another day at sea put Joe a bit more at ease after his family's brush with death. Three nights had passed since Adam and Phoebe saved Faustina.

Even in their tough situation, Joe enjoyed having his whole family sailing together. The meals, drinks, games, and quality time they were sharing between working shifts made him a truly happy man.

It was early afternoon when Ty alerted him that Eve's movements called for his attention. They were still relatively close to New York, sitting several miles off the coast, but they had a lot of travel flexibility with the helicopter and speed boats they'd brought along. However, it was safe to assume Eve knew of most of their capabilities.

Joe approached the workstation and asked, "How close is she?"

"She's not closing in on us," Ty explained. "She's in Albany."

"Shit!" Joe activated his bracelet and tried to message Jameson. Then looking around the lounge, Joe saw Hayden at the bar staring at him, so he asked, "Has your father contacted you today?"

"It's a trap," Ty said. "The governor isn't useful to her other than to lure us, so we should think about how to respond. Maybe we stay here?"

"We're going. This machine is more than a tracker if I can get closer. If I can get into range, I can disable her," Joe explained.

Hayden said, "He's not due to be home for a few hours. He went to Syracuse."

"I need you to find your mother and bring her in here. Both of you message him not to return home, and I'll do the same," Joe said to Hayden. Then to Ty he said, "Get Trent and tell him I need him ready to travel and to also bring one of his best agents with him."

Adam entered the room and went straight for Joe. "How do you know your device will work against Eve?"

"I don't, but I've tested it as much as possible . . . Adam, there's no safe way to bring her back in. Doing it quickly is better than waiting," Joe said.

Adam tensed. "Don't tell me how to handle her, Joe."

"Actually, I think I should tell you . . . All of this is your fault. You've fucked everything up with secrecy and threats and lies for a long time . . . So, punish me if you want, but I'm going with or without you," Joe stated.

"You know I can easily keep you from going," Adam said sternly, but he knew Joe was right. "She'd destroy all of you without me there. I'm going with you."

Phoebe walked in, followed by Trent and another random man from the security team, Sam. After gathering a bag of supplies and briefing everyone the plan, Joe told them to meet at the helipad in ten minutes as he rushed from the room to share farewells with his family.

As Adam, Joe, Phoebe, Trent, and Sam exited the aircraft, Adam told the pilots to stay in the immediate area around the helipad located in a far corner of the back lawn at Camilla Rosemont House. On their walk up to the house, Joe received a warning message from Jameson about the house's security detail. Jameson had tried to contact the security manager on duty at his house to inform him about Adam's arrival via air, but he couldn't get a response from the detail, nor could he access the security controls from the house itself to see what was happening inside.

"Phoebe, can you access your house's security system?" Joe asked.

"I was going to when we get closer," she said as she consulted her bracelet to check security. "Jameson was supposed to alert the detail anyway . . . I got nothing. Security is down."

"Yeah, he just messaged me," Joe told the team. "The detail never replied. She's here."

Joe halted, and everyone else stopped with him. Knowing the house's security was offline, he was certain Eve was inside, but he had one more way to be sure. He reached in his back pocket and studied a small device that was part of the weapon system he had on Eve.

In addition to the large GPS, map, and monitor he'd been using on the yacht, he had a hand-held component to the system that was a combination remote and detonator. Reading the small display on the front, he began tapping buttons to set up the device to receive commands from his bracelet to paralyze his target.

"Is she still in the house?" Trent asked.

"Yes," Joe said as he finished adjusting the device. "Adam, do you want me to paralyze her from out here?"

"Will we know if it worked from out here?" Adam asked.

"It's not a question of whether or not it works—it works," Joe explained. "The problem is, it may not be effective because it's unknown if her power can overcome the device embedded inside her, or how long it would take her magic to find a way to overcome it . . . However, when I send the command, she will be immediately disabled."

"But if you set it to kill her, there wouldn't be a question, right? If you kill her in a snap, there'd be no chance for her to realize it and call on her powers; they'd be snuffed out, or redistributed among us?" Phoebe asked.

"Correct. I can kill her now without a doubt," he said to Phoebe and then looked directly at Adam and said, "This could be the only opportunity anyone has ever had to execute her without casualties or consequences . . . Know that if she escapes this time, she will know about the device, have it removed, and safeguard against future vulnerabilities . . . So, there may never be a chance like this in the future."

"But then you'd be no better than her, man," Trent proclaimed. "Life isn't ours to take."

"Seriously, Trent. Where the fuck are you from?" Phoebe whispered to him.

"You know I can't allow death for her . . . Paralyze her now, and we'll continue into the house with the utmost caution and silence to retrieve her," Adam said, ordering the team forward with the wave of his hand.

They found one of the back doors ajar. A dead security guard was sprawled across the floor inside. As they looked around, it was apparent that one of the guards had been made to use his rifle to destroy the house's security cameras and equipment.

After searching quietly for fifteen minutes, they passed through a door and emerged into the main entry hall. Adam kept the group inside his shield as much as possible. Stretching his bubble of protection that far weakened it, but they'd survive a wave of destruction from Eve even if it knocked them down. Adam tapped Joe on the shoulder.

Joe looked at Adam, who was making a gesture to his eyes. He knew Adam wanted him to try using magical sight. Sometimes, when Joe was close enough to Adam or Eve, he could see the shining tendrils that connected them to their descendants. He couldn't always see them, but it was worth a shot. Focusing his mind on what he wanted to see, he looked about the hall. The ties that bound Joe and Phoebe to Eve were flowing up the stairs.

Joe pointed them to where they needed to go. They passed through the second-floor hall and into the foyer leading to the family bedrooms. He lost the sight for a second as if it flickered out. He looked around, finding it again and leading the team into Phoebe's own boudoir.

Eve was there. She was in a reclining massage chair with a towel wrapped around her, and her wet hair dripped down the chair's back. The chair was still prodding and nudging her body, but she was completely paralyzed. The cushioning saved her from falling to the side since it was designed to completely cradle and prop up a relaxed body.

"What rotten luck," Phoebe whispered to Joe. "If we'd arrived ten minutes earlier, she'd at least have a concussion from falling in the shower—maybe worse."

"Shut up and turn off the chair, Phoebe," Joe mumbled. "Keep your weapons pointed at her, guys."

Joe went to work, using the ottoman in front of the chair as a table and preparing the sedative that would ensure their safety. He was working against an unknown deadline and needed to focus. Phoebe kneeled across from him and his open bag of tricks, helping him prepare a cocktail of syringes. Adam concentrated on keeping everyone inside his shield.

As an afterthought, Joe said, "It's best not to look her in the eyes, just in case, but we're almost ready to sedate her."

Trent and Sam were the only people looking at Eve, holding her at gunpoint. Both men instinctively did the opposite of what they were told and stole a glance at her bicolored eyeballs. Trent glanced away, but Sam was positioned directly in front of her and caught her gaze.

Just then, Phoebe finished loading the last syringe and placed it into Joe's waiting hand. He thanked her, and she looked up at him smiling.

She didn't have time to form words. There was no warning. There was only a split second of terror, watching Sam swing the barrel of his rifle to the back of Joe's head and pull the trigger.

Through the ringing in her ear and the blood in her eyes, she tried to push through. She didn't want to die next. Wiping her eyes, she found the sedatives intact, so she grabbed them. More shots rang out, and Sam fell next to Phoebe.

Trent had shot Sam and taken his rifle. She watched Trent run from the room with both guns before realizing Sam was still alive and trying to claw at her. She screamed, and it was like a war cry as her fatal magic hit Sam.

Adam had switched tactics. Instead of trying to protect everyone, he was subduing Eve. She was still in the chair paralyzed, but Adam's hands were covering her eyes and face as he projected energy against her to smother the small amount of power she was still attempting to wield. Phoebe approached them, stumbling over the chair.

Adam waited for Phoebe to sedate Eve then let go and caught his breath. He hadn't felt a loss so deeply in hundreds of years. His most trusted associate—his most talented and loyal descendant—was dead in a pool of blood alongside the dead shooter. As he thought about what would come next, he endured the guttural cries of anguish coming from Phoebe.

Phoebe held Joe's hand in both of hers and expressed raw, unhinged mourning for her friend.

She cried for his children.

She cried for Faustina.

She cried for a good man cut down in the prime of his life.

She cried for her fear.

Jameson arrived to find her wailing in a pool of his good friend's blood. Without hesitation, he knelt beside her in the carnage and held her until she was able to function. Then he guided her out of her boudoir and across to his shower to help her wash, leaving Trent and Adam to bring in the cleaners and then get the bodies and Eve ready for transport.

CHARIOT OF FIRE

The collective mood on the yacht was somber and restless. No music played. The common areas were empty, except for the bar in Adam's lounge where people drank in near silence. Nobody slept, but some were in their rooms packing bags or zoning out. The news from Albany meant they'd be sailing back to the city by the next morning.

Faustina, Jeremy, Giselle, and Ruby had retired to Faustina's bed shortly after the news of Joe's passing, needing a private place to exist together. Giselle tried her best to comfort her friends. She held Ruby while Faustina held Jeremy. None of them had a plan or purpose other than shedding tears in the dark.

Hayden and Danielle had a lazy chess game going at the bar while they nursed their glasses of scotch. Minutes went by between each move as both players were distracted. Hayden's eyes were glued to his bracelet while he sporadically received messages from his father. Danielle was taking advantage of Adam's absence. She was touching each of the chess pieces she won without wearing her gloves.

Ty approached them and waited patiently for both to look up from their game before speaking. "There's a flying saucer hovering starboard."

Hayden and Danielle stared at him.

"Dani?" Ty spoke as if slightly annoyed rather than seeming anxious. She'd been left in charge in the absence of Adam and Joe.

"Are you ever going to take your job seriously?" Danielle asked him.

Ty shifted on his feet and crossed his arms over his chest. "Why do so many of you pretend you're not working because you have to?" he asked in a monotone voice. "I don't want to be here. I want to retire, but that doesn't mean I'm not serious about a flying saucer hovering outside."

An alarm started blaring, and without changing his disgruntled pose, Ty raised his voice above the noise and shouted, "I guess the roving security just stopped fucking around for long enough to notice it."

Giselle ran up behind Hayden and asked, "Is this a real emergency? Should I get the Cohens out of bed and go to the lifeboats? Everything seems fine from in here."

"I think we need to kill the alarm and take a look at the starboard bow," Hayden said. "Ms. Cheshire?"

In response, Danielle messaged security to kill the alarm, and they hurried through passageways, not speaking to each other along the way. Too much had already happened, and Danielle was eager to regain as much control over their situation as possible.

However, as they emerged onto the main deck, Danielle's hopes of returning to any sense of normalcy whatsoever vanished. A strange woman accompanied by a humanoid robot stood facing them on the deck with a massive flying saucer hovering beyond the railing as their backdrop.

ℕ ℕ ℕ

Phoebe rummaged around in the kitchen. She sipped wine out of a water bottle while putting together an intricate snack plate for herself. Even though she wasn't hungry, she knew she had to eat something, so putting a combination of the best food she could find on the plate would help.

Jameson and Adam were busy somewhere making plans to deal with the aftermath of Eve's attack on her home. Jameson had told her their kids would be home by the next night.

Trent walked into the kitchen to use the water cooler, and Phoebe clinched her fists and stared at him. He didn't notice her while he filled his glass, nor did he look in her direction as he drank it empty. He finally saw her when he turned to put the glass in the sink.

"Are you alright, Ms. Astor?" he asked.

"No," she said while continuing to stare at him.

"Is there something I can do to help you?" he asked a bit more softly.

"Help?" she sneered. "Like you helped when you ran away without helping us today?"

"Phoebe—"

"Oh, it's 'Phoebe' now, is it?"

"Ms. Astor, then . . . I shot Sam and took his rifle."

"Then you ran," she shouted back at him.

"What else could I have done?"

"You're a witch," she stated. "I know you are. You didn't have to run."

"If I had any powers, wouldn't I be in the center of the Dust empire in your little elite cabal? I wasn't included in the meeting.

You've never seen me wield magic," he explained as if pleading with her.

"Do not lie to me! I know you're a witch!" She came around the kitchen island to face him toe to toe.

"If you sit down and eat something, I'll tell you what I am," he whispered while she looked up at him.

She pivoted on her heel and collected her plate and water bottle from the counter. Then she marched to the breakfast table and sat down with her meal before gesturing for him to take a seat across from her. She ate a cube of Havarti with a Spanish olive and looked across the table at him.

When he didn't respond to her gaze, she said, "Well?"

He sighed and started his story. "I'm from a parallel universe. My gift was manipulating spacetime, but that gift only worked when I was in the same universe with my Adam and Eve. Once I opened a portal out of my universe, I removed myself from the magic's source . . . Your Adam and Eve are not mine, so . . . I had no defensive magic in that room today, and I feared her. Do you understand what I'm telling you?"

"I think so, but I have questions . . . Does Adam know?" she asked.

"No, I don't think Adam knows . . . In my universe, I was close to Joe, so I approached him here, and he's taken care of my employment and anything else I've asked for, really. He asked for information from my universe in return, like inventions we've achieved and powerful people also in this universe."

"Then—I'm sorry," she put her head in her hands and sobbed. "You've lost your home and then watched someone who looks like your friend die."

"Phoebe, please don't dwell on these things right now . . . Ask me your other questions and eat. Distract yourself for a while."

"Richmond Island is called Staten Island in your universe?" she asked, wiping her face before picking a cherry from her plate.

Trent smiled. "You remembered . . . Some things are different where I'm from, including the names of places, which can be confusing at times."

"Is that why Adam calls our entire world 'Blue Earth'? Is yours called something different? Maybe he does know about your universe," Phoebe said.

"I can't answer to what Adam knows from his thousands of years here and his time in Eden before that," Trent replied. "Except I'm fairly certain he doesn't know about me . . . My planet is also called Earth, but there are some older beings who call it 'Green Earth.' Our mythologies say there are three Earths, but I've always hoped to find more answers about that question myself."

"What do you mean by 'older beings,' Trent?" Phoebe's question was tinged with both concern and fascination.

"In my universe Adam and Eve lead a race of witches against a race of vampires," Trent stated.

Phoebe tilted her head to hit him with a judgmental stare and scoffed at him. "You're fucking with me now, aren't you? I know you at least that well."

"I'm serious," he asserted.

"How can they lead a faction of witches for years and years and not grow old and die?" she asked with a smirk that suggested she'd caught a hole in his story.

"Vampires are from Eden too, but—look, I don't think now is the best time to tell you how witches and vampires can take powers from each other—I won't. It's war, and the details are grotesque," he explained. "The gist of it is that both races have power that can be taken and used by the other, and that's the important part—that's the truth."

"Are there vampires here? Do you see them in the room with us?" she teased.

He laughed and gave her a small smile. "Funny! Don't believe me then . . . I've never seen any in this universe, by the way."

"I believe you for the most part. 'There are more things in Heaven and Earth,' according to the Sonneteer," she said and continued picking at her food.

"We call him 'the Bard,' but it's an apt sentiment nonetheless," Trent said.

Trent continued to keep her company. Although she didn't keep conversing with him, she ate and seemed calm and content for the moment. He didn't realize her water bottle was filled with wine until she got up to refill it, so he got a glass from the cabinet, filled it with water, and sat it next to her plate. She glared at him, but then rolled her eyes and smiled a little.

"One more question," she said.

He nodded.

"Will there ever be a way for you to go home?"

"Jeremy Cohen found out he's got a similar gift," Trent said. "I'm trying to help him learn to use it . . . Maybe one day he'll be able to send me back."

She jerked her head up from her meal as if having an epiphany and said, "Where is Eden?"

"Are you going to ask me where Heaven is while you're at it?" Trent laughed and shook his head. "I haven't a clue, but I've never found it on the Green Earth."

Jameson entered the kitchen and approached Phoebe from behind while she sat in her chair. He placed his hands gently upon her shoulders, leaned down, and kissed the top of her head. Then he took her left arm and placed her bracelet around her wrist.

"I had it cleaned while you were resting," Jameson said. "There are some messages you're not caught up on yet, and I'm sorry to say they're important. Plans have changed."

"What?" she asked weakly and grabbed his hand, turned in her chair, and hugged his arm against her while leaning into him.

"A, um . . ." Jameson coughed and began speaking again. "A spacecraft has made contact with the yacht—"

"What?" she said loudly and stood to face him.

"Apparently there's a flying—a spacecraft that appears to be friendly, but Adam needs you to go with him back to the yacht," he said. "They can't sail back right now."

"But the kids—" she said with panic in her voice, clutching onto his arms and digging her nails into him.

Jameson remained calm and didn't flinch as her nails broke his skin, but he interrupted her. "The kids are well. You can check your messages and contact them as soon as you meet with Adam and prepare to leave."

During Phoebe's exchange with Jameson, Trent was on his bracelet. He was annoyed he hadn't received messages about a spacecraft, so he was frantically sending and receiving messages with the security team on the yacht.

"How can there suddenly be vampires and spaceships? Is there anything else the universe wants to dump on me today?" she moaned.

"Pardon?" Jameson looked at her quizzically.

"Nothing." Phoebe embraced him and said, "I love you, Jameson."

"I want to come with you, but Adam insists I don't," Jameson said.

"He's right," Trent interrupted. "Ms. Rothschild shouldn't be out there either."

Phoebe shook her head, and Trent added, "Excuse the interruption." Then he bowed his head slightly with an awkward wave and said, "I should go help with departure preparations. Good evening."

"It's true what he said about Faustina," she said to Jameson. "I'd like to invite her here to stay with you, so she won't be alone in their house."

"That's a good idea, Fe." Jameson kissed her mouth tenderly. "When this situation with Adam is over, I'm going to take you to Bora Bora. We'll stay alone and naked together in a bungalow for at least a week straight."

"Are you sure Miranda can spare you for that long?" she teased.

"Do you want to bring her with us?" Jameson replied, challenging her playfully. "Or did you want to bring that Pinkerton fellow?"

They shared laughter and a last embrace before Jameson walked with her to meet Adam. She got halfway to the kitchen door before running back to the table to grab her water bottle full of wine. She thought she'd need to finish it before meeting aliens.

❧ ❧ ❧

Danielle thought it best to keep the aliens happy until Adam made it back to the yacht, although it was Ty's opinion that the concessions from the witches' side were becoming outrageous. The entire yacht was dry docked inside the spaceship's bay with two smaller aircraft flanking it.

The spaceship itself was floating on the water's surface, and a crew of human-looking aliens extended a helipad from the bottom level in preparation for Adam's crew to arrive from Albany. The vessel looked like black, smooth metal on the outside, but the aliens could also cloak it to make it clear. On the inside, most surfaces were white or metallic with many light sources.

"You're letting them cook for us, now?" Ty complained after receiving a message the aliens were preparing a feast for everyone in the formal dining room on the yacht's main deck.

Danielle put her hands on her hips and growled, "I'm keeping us alive . . . Unless you know how to overpower aliens and a massive spaceship with superior technology?"

When Ty responded by throwing his hands in the air and walking away, Danielle shouted, "I didn't think so!"

Giselle went to wake up the Cohens and bring them to dinner. She'd told them everything was fine and had left them to sleep after the alarm. When she walked into Faustina's room, she was surprised to see a lamp lighting the bed and the family awake and having a conversation.

"Hi," she said softly. "I hope I'm not disturbing anything."

"Not at all," replied Faustina as polite as always.

"So—um," Giselle began to awkwardly explain, "there's been a change of plans, and we have . . . special guests. I've got to take you to dinner."

"Adonai is here?" Ruby asked.

"W—what?" Giselle's smile was fake, but she meant well.

"Is there a godlike robot here?" Ruby clarified.

"Hold on—how did you . . ." Giselle's words trailed off as she realized something, so she stated dully, "Oh, you had a premonition. Yeah, there's a creepy robot alien thing here."

"Alien?" Faustina and Jeremy said at the same time.

"Actually, don't freak out," Giselle said, "but the whole yacht is inside a flying saucer right now."

"That explains it perfectly," Ruby said.

Weary from the happenings over the last few days, everyone simply looked at Ruby.

She continued, explaining, "Well, Eden must be somewhere. Why not space?"

"I always imagined it inside Earth somewhere underground," Faustina said.

"It can be both," Ruby stated.

Ruby watched them nodding at her while seemingly lost in thought, but she couldn't tell if anyone understood what she meant. Her dreams and premonitions gave her unique perspectives. She wasn't in the mood for more discussion. She was eager to meet Adonai and ask about her father's death and possible afterlife.

After the fact, her first premonition's significance became partially clear to her. She understood it was the date and location of her father's death, but she wondered why he wasn't in the premonition. If he had been there, she would have warned him. Her best guess was that her brother's fight with Eve would be the eventual result of what happened in Albany.

Ruby linked arms with Giselle and said, "Let's go have dinner then."

Jeremy helped his mother to her feet and walked hand in hand with her behind Ruby and Giselle.

≈ ≈ ≈

Nick Bishop stepped off the helicopter with the confidence of a rock star and practically rejoiced before the spacecraft that enveloped his entire field of vision. With arms wide open and face to the sky, he inhaled the salty ocean air. Nick was happy to have joined the team in Albany minutes prior to them leaving Phoebe's home.

He'd missed the happenings of the week before due to overseeing Dust's prior engagements in Australia.

Phoebe rolled her eyes at Nick and said to Adam, "Here we go. All Nick's conspiracy theory dreams are coming true, and we'll never hear the end of it."

"Damn right, Astor!" Nick shouted. "Now you'll know I was right about aliens. Soon you'll know birds aren't real."

"Are you sure this guy needs to be your new first mate?" Phoebe asked Adam while looking straight into Nick's smiling face.

"No, that's why you're sharing the job," Adam replied.

Adam needed a new second-in-command for the mission against Eve, and Nick was one of his most talented and charismatic descendants. Nick called himself a shapeshifter, but his gift was more like a glamour. For instance, Adam and any powerful witch or being could see Nick's true form when he changed his appearance. Adam could see his true form within seconds even if he didn't try too hard. On the other hand, Phoebe and others needed to use a bit of concentration. Nick was strong and intelligent. However, he was an eccentric loose cannon, which was why Adam told Phoebe to work with him.

Crew from the spacecraft appeared to take the unconscious Eve into custody, and Trent went with them. A different delegation appeared to escort Adam and his lieutenants to dinner upon his own vessel. The three witches followed three human-looking strangers until they arrived at the formal dining room.

Place settings at the table consisted of a single plate at each place that was already filled with fluffy white flakes with golden shimmers and an oversized champagne flute filled with a glowing blue liquid. The rest of the guests had already arrived, but they were waiting patiently for Adam, Phoebe, and Nick before beginning to eat. Two chairs were at the head of the table, and Adonai and his strange female stood from those chairs to welcome the last of their guests.

Adam and company approached the opposite end of the table, facing their hosts. Adam had never before met the woman, but he knew the robot.

Overcome with emotion, Adam managed to croak, "Father."

"I'm here to help you, Adam," said Adonai.

"I fucking knew it," Nick interjected. "God's an alien."

Phoebe elbowed Nick in the ribs to shut him up, but Adam didn't acknowledge the outburst.

"Please, sit at this table," said the strange woman. "My name that I am called is Lilith. I welcome you to feast on manna and nectar with us."

"Lilith!" Adam blurted out. "It's you I called. Please, I have need of envito now more than before."

She nodded and replied, "First we feast, then we discuss the unpleasant solutions to events already occurred."

Lilith's speech was choppy, clipped, and awkward as if she thought of each word individually before forcing it from her mouth. Adam noted that her hair, eyes, and complexion were exactly like Sorina's. Her clothing resembled metal armor that looked similar in color and consistency to Adonai's body.

Adam watched his descendants around the table eating manna for the first time. As they feasted, he noticed the dark circles under Jeremy's eyes disappear. The small cuts and scrapes on Phoebe's hands and arms from both of Eve's attacks disappeared. Ty's hair went from gray to black. The divine food visibly nourished and repaired everyone before his eyes while he hesitated over his plate with his fork in hand.

"This stuff is delicious, boss," said Nick. "You should try it."

"I've had it before," Adam said.

"You didn't like it?" Nick asked.

"Edenian food, especially manna, tastes better than anything in this world," Adam explained. "It took years for me to acquire the taste for anything here. I'd rather not start over again and fail to enjoy my supper for the next thousand nights."

"Eat, Adam," Adonai commanded. "You need this nourishment. It is a gift. Do not insult Lilith."

As Adam took a bite, he shifted his gaze down to his plate to avoid having to notice everyone suddenly interested in him eating. With the divine food's taste in his mouth, memories and images from his former home flooded his thoughts.

"The gray streak just disappeared from your hair, Adam," Ty observed.

Without lifting his eyes from his plate, Adam replied, "Your hair changed, too. All of you have been blessed, nourished, healed. You were simply too busy gorging yourselves to notice."

Danielle sighed at Ty and said, "Okay, that's not fair. Now you have perfect hair as well as perfect abs."

Giselle laughed openly, cutting the tension at the table. Soon everyone started sharing how great they were feeling. Lilith personally refilled everyone's nectar. To express his thanks for honoring his people with the feast, Adam sent Trent a message to deliver the best bottle of wine on the yacht. It would taste like swamp water compared to nectar, but the gesture would mean something to the Edenians.

Lilith graciously accepted the bottle from Trent's hands and thanked Adam. She then stood suddenly from her chair, watching Trent retreat from the room.

"Stop!" she commanded loudly, but without hostility.

Everyone in the room froze except for Trent, who was almost to the exit and still walking.

Adonai said, "Trent Pinkerton, come stand before me."

In an instant, Trent knew his cover was blown. Those beings knew he wasn't from the Blue Earth. He wasn't usually one to be nervous, but he visibly shook as he came to a halt in front of the creator.

"Why are you here?" Lilith asked.

"I work for Mr. Godwine," Trent said, delivering one of his usual witty remarks, but failing to pair it with his trademark chill attitude.

"You understand well that is not the question I am asking," Lilith replied in her stilted manner.

"Yeah, I know . . . What now?" Trent asked.

Lilith Looked to Adonai to pass judgement. He placed a hand on Trent's shoulder, calming him with a warm, gentle unseen force.

"Do not fear us, Trent Pinkerton," he said. "We will decide your future tomorrow. Tonight, we must decide other urgent matters. We must pass judgement on Eve."

Trent's eyes were moist with tears he was trying not to shed. Adonai released him, telling him to take a seat at the table. With a slight gesture of the robot's hand, the Edenian crew cleared the table and prepared a platform in the middle of it.

Like his father, Adam had more pressing issues than Trent. He'd find out what their odd exchange was about later. Eve was his priority, and he feared the creators had come to take her from him.

Several witches instinctively cringed when Edenian guards brought Eve into the room because she was conscious. She was guided along in a hovering bubble cage in which she stood upright with her wrists and ankles in shackles made of light. The bubble was charged with a powerful energy unknown to the witches. Eve wore goggles over her eyes with mirrored lenses, but they could tell she was looking at them when her head moved around. Her cage was placed in the middle of the platform on the table.

"Edenians and earthbound beings," Lilith announced, "you will bear witness. I will speak. Adam will speak. Eve will speak. Adonai will judge . . . Adam, justify the request to receive a gift of envito from me for the evil Blue Earth Eve."

Adam replied, "Lilith, I met your descendants in Romania. As newer creations of Eden, you built their brains to include envito, which all beings created in Eden now have. Mine and Eve's only crime was being created before that technology. I needn't suffer madness in the future, and Eve's madness can be cured for her sake and for our descendants' futures."

"Attachment to Eve makes a blind man of you," Lilith said. "Envito prevents madness. It does not prevent evil."

"But her madness caused her crimes. The design flaw isn't her fault," Adam argued.

"When good beings enter madness, they will not do genocide," Lilith replied. "The monster was always hidden inside. Adonai speaks now."

Adam's father stood and said, "When Lilith received Adam's request, I forbade her to help Eve. I watched Adam and waited for him to find his own solution. But when I saw the destruction wrought yesterday, I knew it was time for divine intervention. History cannot repeat. Eve cannot be permitted an opportunity for mass murder again. I do not want the species wiped out."

"You abandoned us here, and now you won't help her?" Adam asked.

"I exiled you here because you exalted Eve above me," Adonai explained. "You were given a chance to correct your mistake, but you still choose to hold onto her, this time putting your people in danger of extinction."

Adam looked around the room at the faces watching him. His descendants were each priceless pieces of a masterpiece he'd been building since the beginning. He'd never meant to sacrifice his opus for Eve. He finally realized the decision he'd been avoiding, which was the decision his father had waited all that time to allow him the autonomy to make himself. His entire existence on the Blue Earth was a lesson. It was a test.

"I understand, Father," Adam eventually answered with conviction in his voice and tears in his eyes. "I denounce Eve for the evil and pain she has wrought, and I acknowledge that I failed in Eden and on the Blue Earth. Forgive me . . . I stand ready for judgment."

Eve was shouting and writhing within her cage. Her restraints heated up and burned her skin the harder she fought against them, causing her to scream even more until her face was red and streaked with tears.

Adonai looked to Lilith and nodded. Lilith removed the sound barrier and welcomed Eve to speak for herself.

"How dare you pass judgment against me!" Eve ranted, spitting though her teeth. "I am made of living flesh, while you dwell in the metal prison Gaia built for you! Like her, your mother, my spirit is immortal! You're nothing but a machine! You're an abomination!

Strike me down, and I will haunt you, I swear it! Gaia will protect me! Do you hear me? Gaia will punish you! It's your fault I'm evil!"

Lilith reactivated the sound barrier as Eve continued to wail. There was nothing else of substance to be heard from her. Adam looked away from them all and wept.

"Universal balance between good and evil exists whether or not I will it, but I created you with the potential for both," Adonai replied to Eve. "You chose your path, my daughter." Then he announced his judgement to the room. "My judgement is that Eve will be banished to the Red Earth, where only basic humanity and animals dwell, to exist in a world without magic in isolation for eternity . . . Because Adam has repented and shown loyalty to his father and to Eden's laws, he shall receive envito and remain on the Blue Earth to guide his people."

THE BENEVOLENT

Phoebe and Nick managed the inner circle on the ship while Ty and Danielle helped reorganize Dust without Joe. Lilith prepped Adam for surgery to improve his brain and mind, which would give him the emotional fortitude to thrive for another several thousand years and beyond if his body lasted that long.

They expected to be dry docked inside Lilith's flying saucer for three more days, which was the time needed to complete Adam's treatment. After Lilith's task was complete, the Edenians would depart and carry out Eve's sentence.

While Adam rested in a medical isolation chamber that would monitor his vital signs over the span of twenty-four hours and compile an overall health report for Lilith to factor into his surgical procedure, Adam asked Trent to visit him.

When Trent arrived, he noted the isolation chamber was almost identical to Eve's bubble cell. The key difference was that Adam's body position wasn't vertical, but it was horizontal as if he were resting on a mattress. Adam wasn't restrained and there wasn't a sound barrier, but there were various tiny machines in the chamber conducting scans and monitoring him.

"Good morning, Mr. Godwine," Trent greeted him.

"Good morning, Trent," Adam replied. "Phoebe told me your story when she and Nick came to burden me with business affairs this morning . . . My question for you is, do you want me to ask Lilith to take you back to your home?"

Trent answered, "I appreciate the offer, but unless you object to me staying, I want to stay and help coach Jeremy to develop his gift."

Adam smiled. "I'm grateful for your help with my people. You have my full support . . . I'm going to rest now, if you please."

Trent nodded and turned to leave, but then paused and looked back at Adam.

"Lilith—she looks like a vampire . . ." Trent's unasked question hung in the air while Adam debated how to answer.

"She is the goddess of the vampire race," Adam explained. "She is their creator . . . Does this pose a problem?"

"No . . . I thank you for your time. Have a pleasant evening, Mr. Godwine."

❧ ❧ ❧

Blue Earth, Wessex, 542 A.D.

Eve sprinted through the misty forest under a gibbous moon with her disciples. She could hear Mira's breath and footsteps as she ran beside her. Juno and Ruth were behind them, but she couldn't risk slowing enough to look back because the blood demons were fast, and they greatly outnumbered the witches.

Shrieks pierced the fog and vegetation, finding Robin's large, pointed ears. His lips curled into a knowing grin when the smell of foreign magic in the air followed the noise. If mischief was afoot, he wanted to find it. With a snap, he disappeared from his rocky perch and reappeared on a high tree branch and surveyed the forest below.

A group of magical beings he'd never encountered before were ripping apart two witches. He beheld the magnificent hunters and was in awe of their strength and audacity. Besting witches was no easy task.

Eve heard death cries from Juno and Ruth and stopped to catch her breath, knowing the demons would stop chasing her and Mira for long enough to share the witches' blood before continuing to hunt. Eve glanced sideways at Mira, thinking it was time to make a sacrifice for her own survival. She knew Mira would only slow her down, but extra power might help her outrun the blood demons.

Four of them had a chance at conquering the island's witch communes and ruling the Pretanic Islands, but with two of them dead and blood demons arriving from the continent, Eve's plan changed.

Eve turned against Mira with her Edenian speed and power. A single yelp of surprise mixed with pain was still echoing in the air while Mira's dead, mutilated body collapsed to the ground. Mira's magical essence pulsed through Eve, and she started running.

Robin and the blood demons heard a loud, sharp sound that came and went. All attention turned in that direction. Ten hunters followed the sound while the rest finished their blood feast. Robin snapped his fingers and vanished.

Reappearing next to Mira's body, Robin looked at her and then quickly turned to the sound of Eve running. He snapped again and stood far in front of Eve in the darkness and waited. She almost ran into him but stumbled to a halt.

"You almost made me fall, dwarf!" Eve spat. "Get out of my way."

She made to step around him, and he moved with her. That's when he saw her mismatched eyes full of power and ancient knowledge.

He declared, "Oh, I'm intrigued now! Before, I was only slightly interested to know why a witch would kill another witch, but you're not a witch like the others."

"I said to move, dwarf!"

"I'm not a dwarf!" Robin laughed. "We're the same height, little witch."

"Let me pass!" Eve roared and magical energy pushed him to the side.

As she stepped into a run, he snapped and appeared a few steps in front of her. She halted, breathing heavily. "What are you?"

He smirked, "Tell me your secret first, and then I'll tell you mine."

Eve could hear the blood demons approaching. She turned to meet them and blasted them with the highest amount of magical energy she could send at one time. All ten enemies were blown backwards through the air.

The demons were down, but not for long. She saw them recovering one by one, so she pivoted to sprint.

"Why not stay and fight them? I love a good show," Robin said while holding her feet in place with his magic.

"I may not win," she growled. "They can read my thoughts—anticipate my attacks. It's too much of an advantage for ten against one." She had a thought. "Help me, and I'll tell you anything you want to know."

Robin smiled. "That is a terrible bargain . . . for you."

He grabbed her arm and snapped.

Robin and Eve appeared inside a stone circle. She looked around frantically for enemies.

"They're not close," he said. "Tell me who you are."

"I begat all witches. They call me Eve," she said. "What are you?"

"I'm a prince." He removed his hat and bowed deeply. "Robin Goodfellow at your service."

"You know what I meant. What kind of being are you?" she asked through clenched teeth while tightening her fists.

Robin shook his head and wagged his finger at her. "Our original bargain was a secret for a secret, and you received a secret from me."

"I don't play games," Eve stated.

"Then how unfortunate for you that I do," Robin said. *"What were those creatures chasing you?"*

She answered, *"I don't know. They appeared on the continent three winters ago. We call them blood demons because they drink witch's blood, and they almost never die. Their bodily power is great, and they read thoughts. Anything else?"*

He laughed under his breath and said, *"Yes, much, much more . . . Tell me about those three witches."*

She sighed and said quickly, *"They were the strongest of my progeny, selected above the rest to live and to serve me . . . Now, I'm going."*

She tried to walk away from him, but when she walked through the edge of the stone circle, she ended up back in the middle of it. She then tried running from the circle, but she still found herself reappearing in the middle of it. She released magical power, breaking several of the stones and knocking Robin to the ground, but she was still confined to the circle with him.

"Your power is great, Eve, but it cannot release you from our bargain," Robin said. He stood and dusted dirt from his cloak. *"Now, you must tell me anything I want to know because I saved you, and I still want to know things . . . If you want to play nasty, I can keep you*

with me forever and ask you a question every day, or you can be

pleasant company for the evening, and I'll let you go tomorrow."

Eve scoffed and asked, "You want my company?"

Robin stood toe to toe with her, and their eyes met again. He

smiled, but it was more a predatory gesture than a jovial one. He

watched her read his face and scrutinize his eyes.

He cupped her chin in his hand, brushed her lips with his

thumb, and asked, "What do you see?"

"I've underestimated you in my haste to survive," she

whispered.

"What else do you see?" he asked.

"Mirrored ambitions . . . and desires," Eve whispered.

❧ ❧ ❧

Phoebe started to knock on Faustina's door, but she hesitated

with her fist stopping about an inch from the door before she dropped

it back to her side. In her mind's eye she saw Joe's face explode into

a bloody mess, and she feared being alone with his partner. If

Faustina asked questions, she didn't know if she would be able to

keep her mind together and stay strong for her friend.

"Come on, Phoebe," she whispered to herself. "You've got to

do this."

She raised her fist to the door again, but it opened before she knocked. Faustina stood there in her pajamas. She looked deceptively well, having feasted on manna with them. Phoebe had noticed the changes at dinner the night before. She had been especially relieved to see Faustina's dark undereye circles brighten.

"I saw your shadow darken the gap under my door," Faustina said. "I suppose you're trying to work up the courage to speak with me alone . . .You haven't looked as fearless since your return from Albany."

"It's not about me, Faustina."

"I think it is," Faustina said. "I think we share this trauma. I think even though you've seen death—and caused death—in the past, this one shook you differently."

Phoebe dissolved into tears. "I don't—I don't . . . know why!"

Faustina pulled Phoebe into the room and shut the door behind them. They sat on the bed, and Faustina, with tears in her eyes, waited for Phoebe to regain her composure.

"When Adam came to pay his condolences in person," Faustina said, "he described what happened. He wasn't detailed, of course, but I know you were so close to Joe that you were almost injured from the same shot that killed him . . . It must have been a terrifying, awful mess, and I won't ask you to relive it now. I only ask that you let me know when or if you're ever ready to."

Phoebe squeezed her eyes shut and whispered, "Thank you." Then she cleared her throat and spoke with conviction. "Jameson and I think you would be safer if you left here and stayed with him until this is over. He's got so many resources, and the two of you wouldn't be in the middle of an alien-witch revolution."

"I appreciate what you're trying to do for me, and I get it, but I need to be close to Ruby and Jeremy right now," Faustina explained. "I'm not sure I could live with myself if one of them got killed, and I wasn't here. It's hard enough Joe died without . . . I'm glad you were there actually. I know that sounds cruel, but . . ."

"I understand—all of it," Phoebe blurted.

"Let's sit here in my mountain of pillows and have a drink for Joe," Faustina said as she reached into her nightstand and pulled out a bottle and two glasses.

❧ ❧ ❧

Eve's guards placed her in a larger containment area where she could sleep, eat, and live for the few days leading up to her departure from the Blue Earth. They removed her restraints and goggles since she would only have contact with her Edenian guards.

No terrestrial beings were permitted in the spacecraft's most secure decks, and Eve could not magically overpower modern Edenians because they were much more powerful than she had been created to be.

She paced like a caged tigress. Her eyes darted about the sanitized enclosure, looking for any means of escape, but there were no visible windows or doors. All sides of her enclosure, including the floor and ceiling, were smooth white surfaces. When the guards entered to bring food and toiletries, a portal appeared in the wall, but it never appeared in the same location.

When her dinner arrived in the evening, she spied her prime opportunity. They weren't feeding her food from Eden. Divine food would have been a delicacy, and it would have strengthened her more than she deserved or needed. Her guards were retrieving her meals from the yacht's galley, which meant that Adam's human cook was preparing her meal trays.

She'd received a bowl of fruit at breakfast, and a sandwich with chips for lunch. As she walked over to the tray and removed the lid, two things became apparent to her. Firstly, the yacht crew were not told who the trays were for because underneath the silver tray cover, there was silver dinnerware. Secondly, her guards didn't check the trays. They likely did not even consider anything from a primitive

Blue Earth dinner table could be dangerous to them. Eve smirked to herself. Her advanced and powerful guards would indeed never expect to fall under the blade of a steak knife and the prongs of a fork.

As a medieval era war veteran, Eve knew about close combat with steel. She could use the knife to make a kill before her foe had enough time to make a defensive sound or cry out in pain. Once one guard was down, she'd take the other one using the same method. Then she'd use the fork to skewer and eat their eyes to gain some of their power.

They were stronger than her, so she needed to get them close while concealing her weapons until the precise moment of strike. She ate, slipped the silverware up her sleeves while pretending to clean herself with the napkin, and waited until she heard the wall begin to shift before she started coughing and clawing at her neck violently while dropping to the floor.

In a perfect twist of fate for Eve, one of the guards decided to go for a cup of water to give her, which distracted the guard for exactly long enough. With her own supernatural strength, Eve slid the knife into her palm and buried it into the brainstem of the guard trying to hold her up. While the other guard was facing the table and reaching for the water, Eve withdrew the blade and buried it to the hilt in the second guard's skull in two sleek movements.

An alarm sounded, prompting Eve to go to work on the dead guards with the fork, plucking out their eyeballs and shoveling all four of them into her mouth. She sucked as much blood out of them as she dared take time for. Then she took their weapons and waited to blast her way through the door once it was revealed.

After plowing through the pair of guards opening the door and entering a central control room, she blasted energy at the room's central console. The alarm ceased, and she thanked Gaia for the alarm being local to the security bay. She turned back to her latest kills and took two more sets of eyes.

Leaving the freshly dead to keep every drop of their blood, but taking their weapons, she ran faster than she could ever remember. Her speed was enhanced with the stolen power. She knew she wouldn't stand a chance against the gods, so she tried to cut through narrow or dark passageways devoid of traffic.

When she slipped into another room, she scanned the walls for evidence she was closer to the outer ring where she might find an escape portal, but she came face to face with a robot.

"Father!" she cried in fear, but then realized it was only a shell.

The robot was an empty machine with no consciousness as if it were a switched off appliance. It looked like her father, but he wasn't there. She didn't feel this presence. The automaton body disgusted her, so she roared at it. Energy gathered and shattered the Eden-forged metal body into pieces around the room.

Eve continued her escape drunk on power and emboldened from destroying the strongest metal in the universe.

❧ ❧ ❧

Lilith slept in the hospital bay on the other side of the ship but jolted awake with a deep gasp. She felt a strong spiritual disturbance. Souls were crying into the eternal dimension for her attention.

She approached Adam's medical isolation chamber and saved the readings it had collected up to that point. She then disabled the chamber and pulled Adam to his feet. He was alert as if expecting a catastrophe, but he waited for the goddess to speak.

"Adam, it is my belief that now Eve is loose from her prison," Lilith explained. "I sense transitioning souls crying out warnings into eternity. I must make apologies to you, for I must postpone envito preparations tonight. Please go to your progeny for their protection. I must secure my ship. Your father is between universes, so it is only my responsibility tonight."

Lilith escorted Adam from her lab. She ensured every available Edenian searched for Eve. She approached the ship's bridge and encountered carnage, but there were survivors helping the wounded.

"In which direction did you see the escaped prisoner travel?" she asked.

As she left in the direction they indicated, a young navigator called for her attention. "Lilith! She took the ancient chart. She recognized the Tree of Life. She might try to follow its directions to the garden portal."

Lilith turned to the tapestry wall and found it bare. Their ancient tapestry, which Gaia had woven from nothing but the fabric of reality itself thus turning it into something sacred to guide her children across eternity, always hung on the wall in the bridge. It was a star chart combined with terrestrial and subterranean maps, plotting Eden, its constellation, the wormholes between Eden and each Earth, and more divine pathways of the past, present, and future.

⁂

Trent was two hours into his third training session with Jeremy. While Trent was happy with their progress, Jeremy was getting frustrated and impatient. Trent was coaching him to reach into rips in reality, but he wanted Jeremy to improve his focus before stepping through.

The Edenians had drained Adam's pool when bringing the yacht aboard the spacecraft, so they practiced at the bottom of the pool because it was Jeremy's favorite place on the ship. It was important for Trent to foster Jeremy's comfort and confidence as much as possible, and location selection was the biggest factor in achieving that for a spacetime manipulator.

"I'm ready to take it all the way," Jeremy argued.

"You're close to ready," Trent said. "We'll start with tomorrow's session. You don't want to rush your focus and control and end up like me, do you?"

"No, I'm just ready to make a difference," Jeremy said with an attitude. "I'm tired of not doing anything . . . Sometimes I think if I get good enough, I can find Eve anywhere and kill her for what she did."

Trent gently said, "Your anger over what's happened to your family is clouding your focus. I think it would help you to have your sister meditate with you tonight."

Jeremy scowled. "I disagree. My anger is the reason I'm trying so hard to focus. It's my motivation."

Nick leaned over the edge of the pool and looked down at Trent and Jeremy.

"You men know there's no water in this pool, right?" Nick asked.

"Well, you know the Deep State manufactured this yacht and hid a cache of synthetic viruses inside the Arc of the Covenant underneath the pool?" Jeremy said. "So, we figured this is the best time to look for the glyphs that lead to the hidden staircase down here."

Nick studied Jeremy's face then shifted his attention to Trent and said, "The kid's been hanging around you too much and picked up your wiseass attitude."

Trent was quick to retort. "Oh? I rather thought Jeremy's nonsense sounded exactly like something you said last week."

Jeremy's laughter echoed across the crater that was the empty pool, and the two men walked to the shallow end, making their way to the steps.

A barrage of angry shouts and footsteps across the spaceship docking bay's hard floor had Trent and Jeremy scrambling to the yacht main deck's railing to join Nick in observing a ruckus between the Edenians.

Phoebe joined Nick on the deck and exchanged a few quiet words with him. The exchange seemed urgent, so Trent approached Nick for answers.

"Eve escaped again," Nick said. "Looks like these high and mighty aliens couldn't hold her any better than us, even though they talked a good game."

Jeremy started to turn away, but Trent grabbed his arm and asked, "Where are you going?"

"Let me go!" Jeremy shouted.

Nick interrupted them. "We're ordering everyone to a secure area below deck."

"I'm going to help them find her," Jeremy insisted, speaking through gritted teeth.

He yanked his arm from Trent's grasp, and against Nick's continued objections, Jeremy attempted to disembark the vessel.

Phoebe had heard Jeremy shouting his intentions from across the main deck, so she cut through the other side and approached him from behind. She directed her gift at him to make him pass out just as Nick caught up with them, so Nick joined Phoebe to help her as she caught Jeremy under his shoulders to break his fall. They guided his unconscious body down to the deck, and then Nick prepared to carry him to the secure area.

"Let me help you," Trent said as he rushed to them.

"Thanks," Nick said, and then he spoke to Phoebe, stating, "We need to make sure everyone gets below. Adam went to clear the crew who were camping on the bridge deck."

Phoebe nodded. "You guys take him. I'll go make sure everyone else comes down."

Phoebe hurried back to Faustina's room and banged on the door. When she'd left the room hours ago, Faustina had still been in bed and having another drink, so checking on her friend was Phoebe's top priority before going to round up Ty, Danielle, and the others.

When Faustina didn't answer, Phoebe banged on the door again and shook the door handle. She heard a heavy thump followed by a whimper and banged on the door again.

Faustina swung the door open while rubbing her head. She was in the same pajamas, and her hair was in her face. She smelled like booze.

"You made me fall out of bed," Faustina said in a daze. "I hit my head on the nightstand."

"Are you going to live?" Phoebe asked. "Because we need to get you dressed."

"I need a shower." Faustina yawned.

"No time. You scared the shit out of me not opening the door. I was afraid you were passed out."

Faustina sat down on the bed, looking like she was still asleep. Phoebe picked up a hairbrush from the nightstand and started brushing Faustina's hair.

"Why are you brushing my hair? That's a strange thing to do," said Faustina.

"I'm trying to help you. I need to escort you to a more secure area, but you're a mess and not dressed," Phoebe explained.

Although her movements were a bit sluggish, Faustina left the bed. She picked some slacks and a shirt from her armoire and removed her pajamas.

While sliding the slacks up her thighs, she asked, "Are the children in danger?"

Phoebe said, "We could all be in danger. Eve escaped . . . I don't think she'll stay around and risk confrontations with these sky gods, but we could encounter her as she tries to find a way out."

As Faustina listened to Phoebe, she started moving faster. Not saying anything, she packed a small bag with her toothbrush, a towel, and a few other items she could use to freshen up once they got to where they were going. Faustina pulled on her boots, grabbed the bag, and reached for the door.

Phoebe said, "Before we go, I need you to know . . . I knocked out Jeremy, and he's already in the safe room . . . He was trying to leave and hunt Eve on his own."

Faustina's parenting style was more delicate than Phoebe's, so Phoebe needed to clear the air before Faustina saw Jeremy.

Phoebe was both surprised and relieved when Faustina opened the door and said, "Good."

They ran into Ty in the passageway. He told them Adam had already made it around to everyone, so the three of them made their way to the designated safe room.

There were armed guards outside the room, but they let Faustina, Phoebe and Ty pass by them on sight. Soft music played inside, and because of the late hour, most people were lounging or napping. There was a hodgepodge of comfortable furniture such as sofas, armchairs, and recliners. A buffet table was set up along the back wall to provide food and drinks for as long as needed.

Faustina looked for her children and saw Jeremy unconscious on one of the sofas with Giselle. She was spooning his body while holding one of his hands.

Phoebe followed her look and said, "They've been close lately, but I'll go tell her to act a little more appropriate with so many eyes on them."

"Or, maybe we can leave them be this time?" Faustina asked. "They're adults, he needs the support, and they don't really have the option for privacy . . . On the other hand, Ruby needs a parent right now."

Phoebe noticed Faustina's glance shift toward another sofa in a corner. Ruby was sitting on it with Adam. Ruby had her hands cupping each side of Adam's face, and her forehead was resting against his. His hands were holding her face in the same way, and their eyes were closed.

"Actually, I think she's trying to share a premonition with him, so—you know—it's a witch thing, not a sex thing," Phoebe explained.

Faustina laughed a little bit.

Phoebe laughed with her and said, "I feel like we're becoming the ideal mothering team. We've got our own alternating 'good cop, bad cop' routine."

"I agree. I think we just became best friends," Faustina whispered and put her arm around Phoebe, who cackled once and shrugged it off.

❧ ❧ ❧

Lilith summoned everyone to the docking bay floor. It was the most neutral open space to address all crews, guests, and leaders while still offering them concealment since the spaceship was cloaked. She informed them of Eve's departure via escape pod and explained the need for Edenians and witches to plan for Eve's recapture. After she ordered Adam's non-magical crew to retrieve whatever supplies they needed, finish their work, and then stay in their quarters for the remainder of the night, she released them to do those things. Faustina left with them, embracing her children before following Trent back to the yacht.

Two members of Lilith's personal guard carried forth what looked like a treasure chest of precious jewels and metals from several meters away. As they approached the congregation, Adam and the others recognized the pile of advanced machinery and broken parts collected in a bronze tub. The guards placed it before them.

Whispers coalesced like smoke around Adam, his people's soft voices suffocating him with a new fear that his father could be killed and that he was more alone than ever before. He fell to his knees before the tub and picked up a piece of Adonai's metal face.

"It's not possible?" He looked to Lilith for comfort, but her face was turned upward and not looking at him.

From behind Adam, Ruby answered, "His spirit is eternal. That body was only temporary, like yours or mine."

At the sound of Ruby's voice, Lilith lowered her face and looked at Ruby and then at Adam. "She says true words."

"But how did Eve overpower her father?" Adam asked.

"She did not annihilate him. His spirit was away to observe Red Earth," Lilith said. "This home for his spirit is crushed . . . He will try to return to it imminently. He will repair it. We will wait."

"What does that mean for him—for us?" Adam nearly shouted.

Lilith lifted her head up again as if searching the empty air for something. She didn't acknowledge Adam's question.

Ruby offered her hand to Adam and said, "I will stand with you and wait as Lilith requests. We'll all wait for his return."

"Did you see this?" Adam asked her.

"I saw the holy spirit inside us and all around us," Ruby answered and looked at her hand that was still extended to Adam.

Adam took her hand and stood. Releasing her hand, he faced her, cupped her chin, and gave her a gentle kiss on the mouth.

"Thank you," he whispered.

Adam faced his descendants and stated, "We'll surround my father's destroyed body and wait with Lilith for his return."

They waited. Lilith, the brilliant innovator of Eden and creator of the vampires, waited for her teacher and mentor. The others from

Eden waited for their exalted leader. The witches waited for the God of their mythology. Adam waited for his father.

Tiny gasps rang out from the witches, while the Edenians chanted in low hums. They were all reacting to the divine presence raining down around them. They could feel it, and it comforted them. Adam could tell from Lilith's body language that she could see it, and he thought of Joe. Joe would have seen it too and described to Adam its awesomeness.

"What happens now?" Ty asked Adam.

Lilith answered, knowing Adam couldn't. "He will not be able to speak for all to understand with words until he enters the body and repairs it. His wisdom and instruction. That is why you wait."

Ty leaned close to Phoebe and whispered, "You're more important than me, so you can talk to him about getting us paid overtime for all this waiting and imminent danger stuff."

She laughed despite herself and said, "Shut up, Ty. A miracle is about to happen."

In Nick's imagination he saw all the parts in the tub start to shake and then move to fit together like a puzzle before fusing back into a whole body.

However, that was not how it was starting to happen. The tub's contents were melting, and Nick moved closer to the action. As he approached between Ruby and Adam, Adam placed a hand on his shoulder, which he knew was a silent message. He was close enough.

The swirling metallic-colored soup of every element that had been in Adonai's body eventually filled the tub, and it entranced the entire gathering. They watched the whirlpool change directions, and then the liquid level surged and receded in quick succession as a form steadily emerged from below the surface. By the time his neck broke the surface, Adam realized his father was rebuilding his body from scratch.

By the time Adonai stood complete in a dry tub, there were whispers about the small differences in his appearance. Some were saying the guards must not have recovered all the smallest pieces, so he had to reshape himself. Some were saying he made intentional improvements. Either way, everyone agreed they'd witnessed an amazing feat of creation.

Having gleaned their thoughts and whispers while in his spirit state, Adonai stepped out of the tub and said, "Eve has the chart."

"Yes," Lilith replied.

To everyone, Adonai announced, "With the sacred chart, Eve can find and enter Eden. I must prevent this, and I ask everyone's cooperation."

"There's no vehicle on the Blue Earth capable of traveling to Eden, even if she knows the way now," Adam said.

"She will not require a spacecraft," Lilith replied.

SOULMATES

Jeremy dashed down another passageway and leaned his head into the lounge, looking around for the Rosemonts. He'd been searching all their usual haunts around the vessel. Ruby had given him a map and told him Giselle really needed it, so of course he was super motivated to help Giselle.

The map was a thin, rollable touchscreen used on boats before they had hologram maps. Adam kept a few in his private office, so when Giselle had explained the scrying crystal to Ruby, she knew exactly where to find what Giselle and Hayden were looking for.

Spotting the siblings at a cocktail table, he sauntered into the room and sat between them. He started drumming the rolled-up map on the table while he listened to them argue about which one of them would try first.

"I should try it first, Giselle. Elemental manipulation is likely a more useful power for scrying than—"

"That's ridiculous," said Giselle. "I'm already holding it, so I'll try."

"Try what?" Jeremy asked.

Giselle held up the crystal she'd received from Sylvia. It dangled in front of Jeremy's face while he studied it.

"That looks like blood inside a fancy vial . . .That's kind of wicked," Jeremy said.

Giselle said, "It's a crystal Sylvia Cavendish gave me—"

"Gave us," Hayden interrupted.

"Right," Giselle said. "She gave it to us, but really she gave it to me, and we can use it to find her."

"Can't we just ask Adonai? I bet he could find them," Jeremy asked.

"I don't know about you, but I wouldn't have the balls to ask a god to do something for me that I can do myself . . . I mean, don't you think he's a bit busy for that?" Hayden said.

Giselle was excited and interjected, "So, we can find her by swinging this crystal over a map and seeing where it lands. It should be pulled to her exact location. We start with a world map, and then we can narrow it down to a country map, and then to a city map."

"Oh! So, you'll need this," Jeremy said, rolling out the map and smoothing it over the table. "Ruby sent me to give it to you."

Jeremy moved some empty drink glasses to fit all four corners onto the table, then selected a world map from the touchscreen, and the map was ready. Giselle stretched out her arm over the map. The chain was wrapped around her middle finger, and she held the crystal in her palm. Right before she opened her palm, Jeremy grabbed it.

"All three of us should do it together," Jeremy said. "Hayden, get your hand in here. We'll get it right the first time for sure with teamwork."

Giselle and Hayden both started to argue, but Jeremy insisted. "Just do it!"

When Hayden slapped his hand on theirs, Giselle released the crystal from her palm. It shot straight across the map and stabbed a location so hard that it dented the screen.

"Or maybe we don't need all three of us. We'll break it at this rate," Jeremy said. "Sorry about that."

The location the crystal indicated was in New York near the coast. Jeremy changed the setting to show them a map of the state, and Giselle and Hayden scried without him.

The crystal swung north to south over the map. Then it came to a complete halt and changed directions, swinging east to west.

"Maybe we do need Jeremy," Giselle said.

Right after Giselle's comment was out of her mouth, the crystal stopped. She moved her hand a little to the east to where the crystal was pointing, and the crystal stayed in place. She lowered her hand to be sure, and the crystal tapped the exact same spot.

"Hold on. That can't be accurate," Hayden said while Giselle just looked at the map confused.

"Wait!" Jeremy blurted. "Are they here?"

"I don't think I know how to read this thing," Giselle said.

Hayden got up from the table and left the room, mumbling something about telling his mother they had allies on the way.

"How did they know where to find us though?" Jeremy asked.

Giselle sighed. "I don't know, but Sylvia hears these things. I'm guessing the presence of gods must be pretty loud."

She reached to Jeremy, placed her hand around the back of his neck, and pulled him into a long, wet kiss. He put his arms around her and leaned back, pulling her on top of him. They heard Ty a few tables over from them clearing his throat, so they laughed and sat up. Giselle smiled mischievously, pulling Jeremy from the room with an arm around his waist.

Ruby awoke under a starless black canopy. She remembered relaxing on Adam's sun deck when the spacecraft's main overhead lights were still on, so she figured she must have fallen asleep. She didn't realize the bay could be that dark, but she didn't even see the glow of a security lamp or a guard's flashlight anywhere.

She liked darkness. She felt like a veil of black smoke was draped over her face, obscuring her vision. It wasn't complete sensory deprivation, but she didn't hear anyone at the late hour either. There was only a low frequency hum around the docking bay.

As she rested there in peace, she felt fantom hands slide onto her shoulders. She turned around and pushed her hands into the darkness, feeling for another person or being, but there was nothing. Turning back around, she was stunned to see a silhouette that was like a dull gray cloud against the black backdrop.

The figure's shape changed constantly as its size also waxed and waned. Its essence called to Ruby without sound or words. She was drawn to follow it but couldn't explain to herself why, feeling there was something familiar at its core.

Ruby followed the figure until she was off the yacht. After that, she followed it until she could see guiding lights along a passageway. At the end, the figure passed through an opaque archway. The archway looked like a solid dead end, so she put her arm through first. After her arm went through, she held her breath and walked through, emerging outside of the spaceship. She let out her breath, but then she stumbled back a step because the balcony she stood on was made entirely of clear material.

Adonai was standing there, but he wasn't facing her. He was facing a gorgeous ocean horizon filled with the crystalline stars she hadn't seen for days. A crescent moon painted trails of golden light across the calm water. She felt the gravity of God's presence in the scene before her eyes. All of it was enough to make her momentarily forget why she walked through the archway.

The figure she'd been following was gone. She wondered if it had been real, or if Adonai had guided her outside himself. She approached the edge of the balcony and enjoyed breathing the fresh air, knowing he'd speak when he pleased.

"It was real, and it's still here, Ruby Cohen. You cannot see it because of the light," he said. "I extinguished all lights inside just for you tonight. I wanted you to see."

She'd spoken to him enough times to know he would tell her or show her what he wanted her to know. There was no need for her to ask him why she was there. She could ask any lingering questions she might have when he was done.

He continued, "It's your father's spirit. He lingers close to you, your brother, your mother, and Phoebe Astor because her smile was the last thing he saw. Your souls comfort his. His soul is in distress from the violence of his sudden death, so he clings to the closest comfort he can find. He finally came to me tonight for guidance, so tonight I will escort him to paradise."

Breeze coming off the water dried Ruby's tears as they fell down her cheeks. Crying in silence, she closed her eyes and tried to imagine her father standing beside her. After a time, she realized the story was finished.

She asked, "Where is paradise?"

"You have been to the precipice of it when I took you to the garden and spoke to you under the Gaia Tree . . . Paradise is within the Tree of Life," Adonai said.

"Then every Earth has one?"

"Yes, and no . . . The eternal space within the tree is one but connected to all." He sensed her desire to ask more questions and knew what they were, so he added, "More will be revealed to you in time. For now, I take Joe Cohen's spirit on a final journey."

"Goodbye, Father," she whispered. "I love you."

She watched Adonai's body move to a corner by the archway and stand still there, appearing to shut down. The glowing green eyes went dark and closed, and Ruby could feel she was no longer in the divine presence.

Ruby stayed outside appreciating the shimmer of celestial miracles above a tranquil ocean. She didn't know how long she was there until four Edenian guards came to escort her back to the docking bay.

∞ ∞ ∞

Not long after Trent awoke from a nap and started stirring around, he noted the blackout from a window, so he walked outside from the bridge deck and tried to get a better look at his surroundings. From there, all lights were restored at once, and he closed his eyes while they adjusted.

Through squinted eyes, he watched the alien guards walking in formation across the bay. Ruby was in the center of their formation, but he noted she didn't appear in distress from his point of view. He moved stealthily to keep an eye on her as they approached the vessel and watched her board. Sighing in relief when the guards didn't follow her aboard, he moved to intercept her.

"I can smell you, Mr. Pinkerton," Ruby said as she turned to face the man following her down the passageway.

Trent walked into the confrontation, stopping only inches from Ruby. He didn't immediately speak, but he observed her appearance with interest. He'd always noticed her presence at Dust events, and he was a fan of her journalism, but he'd never been alone with her before. He was grateful for that first opportunity to look into her eyes and search for something familiar he'd lost.

Ruby's eyes were hazel with flecks of green, blue, and brown. As Trent looked at them, he thought of the stained glass rose windows he'd seen in Paris on his home world while traveling with his late wife.

"Please, call me Trent . . . What do I smell like?" he asked playfully.

"I—I don't quite know," Ruby hesitated as she whispered. She didn't want to offend him, and he was so close to her.
She thought about seeing his arms wrapped around Phoebe while he kissed her neck, and Ruby looked at his lips. She imagined those lips on her neck but quickly banished the thought.

"It's not a bad fragrance, I hope," Trent teased.

"It's sort of earthy, or maybe if one were to burn spiced tea? It's not quite like incense," Ruby tried to explain.

"Oh," Trent said with a laugh. "I smoke clove cigarettes. My apologies if the smell is offensive."

"No! It's—I know. You smoked one in front of me and my friends a few nights ago, and I thought I was having a bad trip," Ruby blurted. "The smell—it's fine. It's just—it's you."

"Okay, then," Tent said while maintaining eye contact with her.

Ruby's emotional intelligence had always been precociously developed, but since she'd fully unlocked her powers, she was experiencing a new, higher level of emotional understanding and control. While the desire in Trent's stare excited her and sparked her curiosity, his complicated existence made her hesitate to get involved with him too much.

"I saw you kissing Phoebe one night," she said. "I wasn't trying to creep up on you, but you were on the deck—in the open."

"What's your point, Ruby?" He smiled.

"She's my best friend's mother," Ruby said.

Ruby's heart started beating faster as Trent reached a hand up to her face and brushed a piece of her hair away from her eye. She found his audacity even more charming than his physique.

"Are you trying to tell me she's too old for me?" Trent asked.

"I'm trying to tell you she's too unavailable for you."

"And what about you? Are you too unavailable for me?" Trent asked, and then paused before he added, "Or is Adam too unavailable for you?"

"Well, he's definitely too old for me," she quipped, finally returning a smile.

Trent threw his head back and laughed loudly, and Ruby enjoyed the sound of it. He reminded her of a space cowboy-rebel from a classic novel she'd once read. By the time he fell silent, and his gaze once again landed on her eyes, she completely understood Phoebe's infatuation with him.

"How old are you . . . Trent?"

"I'm thirty-one."

"My father was over twenty years your senior," Ruby stated.

"What question is rolling around in that brilliant mind of yours?" Trent asked softly.

"How did you become close friends with the Joe Cohen from your Earth?"

Trent looked down. "He became like a father to me after I married his daughter."

Ruby stepped back as the shock caused her to falter slightly, but she recovered in a snap. She looked behind her and then she looked beyond Trent to assure herself they were alone.

"Will you come with me to my room?" she asked him as she took his hand and tugged him in the direction she wanted to go.

Trent nodded and followed her through the passageway and into her room. When the door shut behind them, Trent began to speak, but Ruby placed her finger over her own lips to signal him to wait and be silent. She started some music to mask the sound of their voices in case anyone passed by her door.

She finally spoke, "My mother and my brother sleep nearby, and I don't want them to overhear anything that can hurt them right now, you know?"

Trent nodded. "You're right. I should have been more careful."

She invited him to sit on the bed with her and asked, "Is your wife's name also Ruby?"

"It was," he explained. "She is now awaiting her soulmate in paradise."

"I don't understand what you mean," she said.

"Forgive me, Ruby . . . That is a polite way to say someone is dead where I am from," he explained.

Ruby folded her hands over her heart and her eyes filled with tears before she said, "She's your soulmate . . . That's beautiful . . . I'm so sorry for your loss."

"No," Trent explained, shaking his head. "Your soul is her soulmate. She's waiting for you in paradise. According to the ancient beliefs, you'll join her one day and become whole. When that happens, you'll ascend beyond paradise."

Ruby swallowed hard as her tears rolled freely for the second time that night. "My father's soul was guided to paradise tonight . . . Will he find his soulmate there?"

"Joe was alive when I came here, so I don't think so."

"What about Jeremy?"

"I didn't know Jeremy on Green Earth."

"Then, my brother has no soulmate?" Ruby cried.

"Ruby, I don't have all the answers . . . Between the Earths it is said that everyone has exactly one soulmate. In that case, Jeremy's was—or is—somewhere."

Trent reached for Ruby and held his hands around her face at the jawline, studying her. Then he removed a handkerchief from one of the pockets inside his jacket and wiped the tears from her cheeks. He sighed and brushed his fingers through her hair, enjoying the familiar feeling of her hair and skin. He felt calm amid having her near him.

Ruby placed her trembling hands onto Trent's shoulders and lifted herself to straddle him. Once she felt his jeans' rough material between her legs, she couldn't help but to rub against him, riding him while sliding her arms around his neck and bringing her face close to his.

Feeling her breath on his lips, Trent knew she wanted his lips on hers. He wrapped his arms around her waist and pulled her body flush against his and kissed her. Releasing the might of his passion and hunger, he fused his mouth with hers and savored her sweet, familiar taste.

He yearned to taste all of her, so he shifted her onto her back and lifted her sundress before kissing his way down her body. When he arrived at her green silk panties, he petted the sleek, soothing cloth between her legs. He enjoyed feeling the warm, soft material become wet while he placed kisses along her inner thighs.

She moved against his hand, moaning at the mere thought of his tongue inside her. She jerked her pillow from under her head and pressed it against her face to silence her euphoria as she felt him move the silk away from her skin and replace it with his fingers. She then felt his tongue slide between and around her sensitive folds of skin, teasing her.

When he couldn't hold back his desire to taste her completely undone anymore, he pressed his face fully against her, lapping up her pleasure with his tongue while slipping his fingers into her. While he stimulated her and her pleasure continued building, her muffled, growling moan told him she was ready for him to give her his everything.

Ruby felt heat rising ever more intensely through her body as she approached climax. Finally, as her core tightly embraced the little death, and a fluttering shiver rolled through her enraptured body, her clear mind saw a vision of herself smiling at her from the Tree of Life.

Minutes later, she heard a voice.

"Can you hear me yet?" Trent asked.

"Yes, I'm sorry. I—there was a vision," she answered.

He laughed. "Yeah, that can happen if I do a really good job . . . I hope it was a good one—the vision and the orgasm."

She smiled at him, too breathless to say much. "Yes, and yes."

A small moment passed before Ruby rolled over to Trent and attempted to initiate more intimacy. She reached for his belt, but he stayed her hand.

"No, tonight is just for you," he said.

"Don't worry. It will be," she stated with evident desire.

"I understand you want more, and so do I, but I don't want it tonight," Trent explained. "I saw how upset you were earlier, and you've been though something, and even if I'm not taking advantage of your emotions, I'll feel like I am if I benefit from this tryst more than I already have until you've had time to rest your mind and body."

Ruby laughed and then quickly explained, "I'm not laughing at you. It's just—that was deep, and a lot, and you're always wearing a mask of cool apathy . . . She must have been very much like me . . . Thank you for being emotionally comfortable with me and considerate of my situation."

She fluffed a pillow and rested her head on it. When he tried to rise from the bed, she tugged on his arm and smiled. It was a silent request for him to stay, and he did. He settled down behind her and held her body close to his. As he comforted her, she comforted him.

❧ ❧ ❧

Everyone woke up early the next morning to receive a message from Adam to meet in his lounge. The smell of fresh coffee prompted most of the team to pour a cup. Ruby held her coffee mug with both hands and savored the warmth as much as the smell before taking a small sip and expressing her enjoyment with a pronounced exhale as Giselle sat next to her.

Jeremy took a seat on the other side of Giselle, and they lazily whispered to each other. Hayden, Nick, Danielle, and Trent weren't ready to be social yet, but they sat peacefully with their coffees. Faustina walked in next and stood behind Ruby and played with her hair. Adam remained by the door, waiting impatiently for Ty and Phoebe to join the meeting.

Phoebe arrived and noticed Trent quickly avert his gaze from her. She shrugged and went to the coffee hutch. As she picked out a mug, she noticed Ty arrive.

All eyes were on Ty as he strutted into the room at 7:10 a.m. and went straight behind the bar. He poured a finger of Adam's best scotch and knocked it back, then he poured another one.

Phoebe put away her coffee mug and said, "Hey, pour me one of those."

Ty nodded silently, pulled a second glass from the shelf, and poured her a drink. He held it out to her, inviting her to come behind the bar and drink it. They clinked their glasses together and each took sips.

"It's a bit early for spirits," Hayden commented.

Ty addressed him and everyone else since he knew they were all judging. "Right, so I'm the only person who—besides Adam, obviously—noticed our friends from Eden heisted another ship during the small hours this morning?"

"What?" Nick asked, dumbfounded.

"You heard me, genius. Great idea to roll back security measures, by the way," Ty said.

"Fuck off, Alexander," Nick retorted. "Since we sent away almost all the normies, how would we keep up the same measures as before? And why would we do that while inside a fucking flying saucer that's far more fucking advanced than any machine we have?"

Ty turned to Adam and said calmly, "May I go home yet?"

"No," Adam said dryly before addressing the others and pointing starboard. "None of you looked out of any starboard window this morning?"

"We were all asleep until a few minutes ago," Phoebe said.

"The view is great from the main deck," Ty stated sarcastically.

Nick stormed from the room while mumbling something about the Men in Black not doing their jobs, and Adam gestured for everyone else to follow him. Almost everyone took time to finish their coffees before exiting the room. Only Hayden, as the resident rule-follower, followed straight behind Adam.

As the team dawdled onto the deck, jaded from the parade of life-changing revelations they'd all witnessed over the course of a week, they noticed a woman waving at them enthusiastically from the new boat in the bay.

"Is that Sylvia?" Danielle asked before waving back in excitement. "Hey, girl! I've been missing our brunches!"

"Good. Sylvia and Duncan have finally come to deal with this mess too," Nick complained.

Phoebe glared at Nick as she approached Hayden and patted his shoulder. "You were right. We did have allies on the way. It's good to know you and Giselle can scry accurately."

Trent looked closely at the woman standing beside Sylvia and said, "Yeah, and they've brought a vampire to the party."

Ty leaned on the railing, still nursing his scotch, and said, "Oh, splendid. Now there are vampires. Anyone want to take bets on whether it will be fairies or mermaids next?"

Trent continued to watch Sorina with suspicion as the team chattered back and forth about the Cavendishes, the vampire, and the boat. Sylvia and Duncan had arrived in style. It was a yacht similar in size to Adam's, but it was much newer and sleeker. Trent overheard Ty mention to Danielle that he positively wanted the retirement Duncan had received.

Adam shuffled to the middle of the group where he could be heard better and said, "Listen to me now."

Even through recent events, his people still feared him. They quieted and waited for him to continue.

"As some of you know, Sylvia can hear magic, and with my father here, this location is like a massive radio tower to her. She and Duncan have offered to help," he said.

"Is that really a vampire with her?" Giselle asked in apparent fascination, trying to get another look at the vampire and her witches as they disappeared back inside their vessel.

Adam shot Trent a slight side-eye, sighed, and answered, "The vampire coven does not wish to be directly involved with Eve, but they offer resources if needed."

"Sorina will be leaving, then?" Trent asked.

"Sorina . . ." several voices curiously whispered.

"She only accompanied Sylvia and Duncan to seek the vampires' mother, Lilith, on behalf of the coven. It will be Lilith's decision when she leaves," Adam explained. "Ruby, Nick, and I will board their yacht this morning—"

"No!" Trent interrupted Adam without thinking clearly.

"Hey, peon," Nick said, addressing Trent. "Interrupt the boss again, and you're out of here."

"Coming on a little strong there, Nick," Phoebe whispered from beside him.

Adam was still staring at Trent for an explanation. Adam blinked and asked, "What's wrong?"

Trent stole a glance at Ruby and said, "Sorina killed my wife."

Nobody said a word, but several sets of eyes looked back and forth between Trent and Adam as the suspense started to build among them.

Finally, Ty asked, "People still get married in your world? . . . Bummer."

Adam pointed at Ty and said, "I promise you can retire after this crisis is averted if you conduct yourself with the class and bearing befitting my empire and stop spewing apathetic sewage from your mouth." Then he pointed at Trent. "Not the same Sorina, correct?"

"No, sir." Trent lowered his head a bit, embarrassed he'd blurted out his fears.

Ruby walked forward to stand in front of Trent and whispered, "We'll be careful, and Adam will protect us."

When Ruby stepped back and glanced away from Trent, she briefly met Phoebe's gaze and realized her best friend's mother was watching her closely. Ruby pretended not to notice and planted herself by Adam's side for the duration of the meeting.

After Adam reassured everyone the vampire coven's vessel should be returning to Europe as soon as Lilith gave Sorina permission to do so, he told Giselle to make sure Duncan and Sylvia received a warm welcome and a comfortable room aboard his own vessel. When Adam took Ruby's hand and began walking away, Nick followed them, and the others understood they were dismissed.

❧ ❧ ❧

By the crescent moon's guiding glow, Eve drudged across a wet green field in the English countryside. Mud squished between her bare toes as she stomped forward, taking each step with her nefarious intentions in mind. Approaching the stone circles, she tried to refamiliarize with each stone's shape. Right away she realized many were missing, and buildings and roads appeared in their places. Her determination didn't falter.

A mist rolled in as if chased by the wind. The circle's center was ahead of her, so she continued forward. She'd try to sense the portal from there. The murky mist settled low across the plain, but her eyes traced the faint shapes of each remaining stone. She found nothing. Above the mist, each of the stone's tops were clearly visible, so she shifted her focus.

She found it. While most of the stone tops were bathed in a normal combination of shadow and moonlight, one of them was lit all over. It was an illusion. A smile of triumph slowly spread across her lips, and she sprinted.

Just before she approached the stone, her path was suddenly blocked. Within the time of a loud pop, elements from the earth and air around her were pulled and drawn together to create a solid being.

He was short, so he and Eve were standing eye to eye. He wore a green cloak over tight brown trousers with no shirt. Like Eve, he didn't wear shoes. A crown carved from solid emerald decorated his head.

"Well met, Evita," he said to Eve. "I'm delighted to see you're not dead."

"Well met, Robin," Eve replied. "Adam imprisoned me. It's taken far too long to escape . . . You're ruling the kingdom now, I see."

Robin laughed. "If you've come to see my father, I killed him on his own throne."

"I came to see the king, and here you are, blocking my path to your kingdom as if I'm not welcome," Eve said without hesitation. "Perhaps Titania would like to see me?"

"Both of my parents—your ancient allies, thanks to me—are dead, but I have no quarrel with you if you have none with me," Robin explained.

She knew Robin wanted to be sure of her intentions before inviting her into his kingdom. A witch's power could cause devastation within his realm under the right conditions, but she didn't care about his kingdom or his family.

Eve squinted her eyes and pursed her lips. "Your insignificant fae politics are not my concern—"

"But my father was your lover—"

"So were you!" Eve blurted out impatiently.

Robin smirked slightly. He visually inspected her from head to toes, licking his lips at her feet. His fingers snapped once, and a crown of flowers appeared on her head. With another snap, a goblet of wine appeared in his hand, and he offered it to her.

"Would you like to spend the evening with me, my Evita?"

Eve knew what he wanted. She took an exaggerated breath and stepped forward. She took the wine and offered him her other hand, which he took.

Robin was small for a human male, but he was not a human male. Eve liked having a lover as petite as herself. It made foreplay more exciting. She enjoyed his strong, hard, and defined abdominal muscles. She knew he enjoyed them too, which was why he never wore a shirt. She thought the golden irises of his eyes were magnificent, so they made up for his ridiculously pointed ears.

"I still find your appearance stimulating," Eve said as she sipped wine. "I'll pass the evening in your company, but only if you assist me. I came here to consult your people's expertise with a supernatural map I've procured."

"I've always admired your willingness to do anything to keep and grow your power," Robin said. "I aspired to be like you, and now I am. I'll forever assist you, and, yes, that is a bargain."

"Good, but then you are not like me," Eve declared as she stroked the back of his hand with her thumb. "My loyalty to you, or anyone, is conditional upon us being useful to each other . . . However, I do hope you will always be useful to me."

"Hold onto me," Robin commanded. "I'm going to snap us straight into the Emerald Keep."

With a snap, Eve and Robin disappeared from the stone circle, leaving only footprints in wet grass. They reappeared in Robin's throne room.

Robin's tribe descended from a race of diminutive beings made to entertain a primordial god. In the early years after their creation, they were little more than slaves, or pets at best. Their realm was in a separate pocket of reality because its original function was to keep them caged as beasts, but that location eventually ended up in their favor.

After the primordial gods begat titans, gods, and other lesser beings, their creator lost interest in the fae race and abandoned them.

As a result of their primal creation, their powers were more closely connected to Chaos, giving them unique and strong abilities while their realm went from being their cage to providing their hidden stronghold.

Only the fae knew what their realm really looked like. Outsiders saw the stuff of fairytales with clouds like cotton candy and lakes that sparkled like diamonds. It was like a three-dimensional painting that changed according to the ruler's whims. However, Eve was certain the inside of the castle's keep appeared to her as it truly was because it was the only aspect of their world that looked the same every time she saw it.

Eve looked around the throne room, still holding onto Robin, and said, "Can't we talk in your private rooms?"

Robin snapped again, and they were in his bedroom.

Eve laughed. "I said I want to talk first. We'll go to your study." When he started to snap again, she stayed his hand and said, "I can walk. Lead the way."

They took the closest of three exits from the bedroom and emerged in his study. Eve approached a stately desk and removed her satchel, placing it in a nearby chair. She then removed the tapestry she took from Lilith's ship and spread it across the desk and turned back to Robin.

"Well?" she asked impatiently.

Robin placed his hands on the tapestry and closed his eyes. Running his fingers over the material, he studied the texture and traced magical pathways in his mind. A flash of starlight from beyond his mind's eye jarred him, and he stumbled back from the desk while blinking his eyes rapidly. He charged at Eve and dug his fingers into her shoulders.

Shaking her, he asked, "Whoever you took this from—do they know you have it?"

She locked eyes with him. "I can make you let go of me. I can compel you to destroy everything you love, but I'd rather not."

He released her and said, "I don't think so, but I'd rather not find out . . . Why did you bring this here? You would put my realm in danger?"

"A primordial deity—Gaia's brother—spawned your race. This power is familiar to you . . . Those hunting me don't know how to find you and may not even know you exist, but even if they find your realm," Eve pleaded, "I'll be gone by then, and they don't have the authority to harm you."

"Who? Who is hunting you, now?" Robin asked with outrage.

He didn't fear any power in the universe, but the magic in that tapestry was beyond the universe and beyond even the fabric of time.

Eve responded with ferocity in her typical superior tone, roaring, "My father and his little sister, both of whom are abominations! They misuse the power Gaia has given them! They create life and then send it here to suffer and die, so why shouldn't I do the same? Why shouldn't those with lesser power than mine suffer and die under my feet?"

Robin had always found Eve's madness to be a strength. It gave her a fearless edge and a mind open to creative possibilities. In the thousands of years since his birth, he'd found that genius was rarely understood. He didn't understand Eve, but he wanted to because understanding her power and motivation would help him control her.

"You are not wrong, Evita," he said softly. "Fight with your family—your equals—if you must. However, it is for Gaia to judge where her power belongs. If they had this tapestry, it was by her will."

"Perhaps it is her will that I took it!" Eve shrieked.

"Perhaps it is her will, or perhaps it is your hubris," he forewarned.

"How dare you!" she spat.

"I am your confidant!" Robin countered. "That has not changed. I only worry you will meet the same fate as Icarus."

Eve shook her head. "Can you decipher it for me?"

Robin sighed. "Before I do, I want you to make me cry out in simultaneous ecstasy and agony no less than three times before dawn."

JUST LIKE MY FATHER

While Adonai searched England, following the path he sensed Eve had taken, Adam and Lilith awaited his findings and his commands. Adam helped his team practice their powers in case they were needed for a battle with Eve. Lilith ordered her crew to assist Sorina as she began her voyage back to Europe, and then she withdrew into her laboratory until dinner that evening.

Lilith's decision to postpone Adam's surgery until after Eve's recapture meant she could refocus on her main project for a few hours. Whereas the people of Blue Earth had only the technology to synthesize most organs and limbs, Adonai's ability to create life was a skill Eden's deities had been improving and perfecting since he'd first populated the Earths.

In Eden it was generally accepted that Lilith had mastered the art of physical creation above all others, while Adonai was the master of spirit and consciousness. She doted over the pristine male body growing in her lab. The skin was much darker than Adam's, but it also had a luster to it. The proportions were also slightly larger. The body wasn't like a giant from mythology, but it would stand eight feet tall.

Two of Lilith's guards escorted Adam into her lab. With a wave of her hand, she dismissed the guards, but she didn't look up from her work as they left him standing before her. Wielding a laser knife, she sliced through the neck. Before the head had time to roll aside, new tissue started to regenerate at the neck.

Adam flinched. "What are you doing?"

"I am testing a new body," she replied.

"You're making another new species?" Adam whispered.

"No. Adonai does not wish to be for all time in his second body," she answered while still observing her work and adjusting the machines attached to the body.

Adam paused, blinked, and then he asked, "His second body?"

Lilith finally looked at Adam and firmly answered, "Yes."

She went back to work, and Adam realized she was finished speaking, so he stated, "Please explain."

"Eons before Adonai created you, but after preparing the Earths, when Eden warred with Olympus, another deity vaporized Adonai's fleshly body, yet his being is always," Lilith explained as the body she tinkered with completely healed.

Adam had only ever known his father's metallic body, and none of the deities were adept at explaining themselves. Adam understood what it was like to try speaking to inferior beings, and he wondered if Lilith thought talking to him was like a person speaking to an ant. Still, he wanted to know more.

"Why does he need a body, and why keep a metallic one?" Adam asked.

"Without a physical anchor, his spirit can wander and become lost anywhere under the eye of Chaos. The second body is easy for him to rebuild, as you have witnessed," Lilith stated. "Adonai thinks flesh preferable, so I toil with . . . flexible, moldable, most regenerative flesh. He can rebuild. He can remold fast as the second body."

Adam gleaned as much as possible from stealing glances around the lab. He noted several machines that were like items from his private hospital wings at his home and at Dust headquarters. There were other technologies he spotted so far advanced that he couldn't guess what they were.

He wanted to keep asking questions, but Lilith interrupted his thoughts, asking, "Why did you come to my lab?"

"I came to respectfully request a feast for supper to strengthen us for possible battle—"

"I have doubt battle will be," Lilith interrupted, "but I grant a manna feast . . . There I will tell your beginning, so the importance of everything is understood."

The guards reappeared as if on cue, and Adam went with them happily after bowing to Lilith and offering her his thanks.

❧ ❧ ❧

"Go away!" Ruby shouted after Jeremy suddenly appeared right in front of her.

Giselle was decorating Ruby's fingernails as they sat on a sofa in the lounge, so various nail cosmetics fell all over the sofa and the floor when Jeremy appeared between Ruby and Giselle. Giselle giggled and helped Ruby put her supplies back into the cosmetics case.

Jeremy kissed Giselle and said to his sister, "I'm here to see Giselle, not you."

"I don't care. You're messing up my nails," she muttered and held them out for Giselle to finish.

"You're supposed to be using this time to hone your powers anyway," Jeremy argued.

Ruby rolled her eyes at her brother. "I'm relaxing. Relaxing is what helps me hone my powers . . . and now that you're here, Giselle can practice talking to her pet."

Ruby and Giselle both started laughing at Jeremy.

In a blink, he disappeared through a rip in the air and reappeared behind Giselle, hugging her against him and playfully growling, "Am I that funny to you?"

"Yes!" Giselle yipped at him when he tickled her waist and kissed her again.

Ruby stopped laughing and thought about the magic Jeremy had done in that moment. The way he'd appeared behind Giselle so quickly reminded her of the vision she'd had about him killing Eve by appearing behind her that fast, reaching his hand through another rip in the air, and pulling her heart out of it.

In the vision they'd been at Giselle's house, but Ruby didn't believe that location was relevant due to her father's death. Adonai had told them Eve had escaped to England while his spirit had been observing the other world. Ruby started to fear the vision's second part would still come to pass.

While Jeremy held onto Giselle from behind, she noticed Ruby had gone still in front of her. She reached out and held Ruby's hand in hers, and Ruby's eyes regained focus. Ruby smiled, but Giselle noticed the smile did not reach Ruby's eyes.

"Did you see something?" Giselle asked.

Ruby felt guilty, looked around the empty room, and confessed, "I didn't see anything just now, but I haven't been completely honest about something I saw before."

"You lied to us?" Giselle asked.

"I—I omitted part of the truth," Ruby admitted, "so I guess I did."

"Sometimes people don't consciously lie by omission though," Jeremy said. "Did you do it on purpose? What's the secret?"

Ruby sighed heavily. "As much as I appreciate this rare moment of maturity from you, brother, I kept part of a premonition from you for selfish reasons . . . I didn't want you to get hurt, and I didn't want it to be true."

Giselle's hands went to her waist and held Jeremy's hands tightly, and Ruby read the fear in her friend's eyes.

There was more curiosity than anger in Jeremy's demeanor when he asked, "Tell us, then."

Ruby looked straight at him. "You killed Eve."

"Good!" Jeremy announced with conviction. "I will!"

"No!" Giselle argued. "You should have kept that to yourself, Ru!"

"Why?" Jeremy asked Giselle. "I want to kill Eve. She killed my father, and she needs to die. Why do you think I've been training so hard?"

"Stop," Giselle whispered while fighting back tears.

"How did I do it?" Jeremy asked.

"I said stop!" Giselle got up and stomped away.

As Ruby and Jeremy watched Giselle run through the door, they noticed Trent standing there. Ruby closed her eyes and bowed her head, dreading the thought of how much he'd overheard. She felt her brother's embrace and returned it.

"Tell me what I am capable of," he whispered. "Don't you understand? It could save my life to know what to do."

"If I tell you, then you have to go comfort Giselle," Ruby said. "Tell her I'm sorry too."

Jeremy hugged her tighter. "I was going to do that anyway."

Ruby placed her mouth as close as she could to Jeremy's ear, and breathed, "You'll reach into a rip in the air, and when you pull back your hand . . . you'll have her heart."

"Thank you," Jeremy said and disappeared by falling backwards through an invisible portal.

Ruby was left with her arms reaching out to where Jeremy had been while tears fell down her face. Remembering someone was watching her, she wiped her tears away with her thumbs and faced Trent.

Before Trent said anything, Ruby stated, "I'd rather he knows how to kill her than mourn another person I love because she got us first."

"You told him at the right time," Trent said, trying to reassure her. "It would have shaken his focus to know before he gained control of his powers, but he's ready now. I don't see a clear right choice here, but it could have been worse if you didn't wait. Do you understand what I mean?"

Ruby nodded and placed her head in her hands and quietly continued crying. Trent joined her on the sofa and wrapped his arms around her. She crawled into his lap and rested her head on his shoulder.

"You did the right thing." Trent reassured her again and waited patiently for her to work out her emotions.

When Ruby saw Hayden stride into the room, she squeezed her eyes closed and tensed. She didn't want to deal with his judgement, and she knew he'd find an opportunity to discuss her and Trent in public just to hurt and humiliate her.

Trent felt Ruby's body tense up, so he said, "Can you give us a minute, Nick? She's a bit upset, but she'll be fine in a minute, and you can come back . . . Okay?"

Looking a bit embarrassed, Nick shapeshifted back into himself and said, "Yeah, okay."

Trent never explicitly told anyone their magic didn't work on him because he felt it was best to keep people guessing about his strengths and weaknesses, but he also liked to annoy Nick.

Ruby watched Nick leave the room and said, "Wow, that was bizarre." Pulling herself together by moving away from Trent and finding a towel in her cosmetics bag to clean her face with, she added, "How did you know it wasn't Hayden?"

Trent laughed. "I'm not sure why I can see past his trick, but it's been fun."

"Is my brother really ready?" she asked.

"He's as ready as he can be . . . He's wielding his gift very well, Ruby. Try not to worry. It can throw off your gift . . . When you have emotional moments like this, it's best to follow them with meditation," Trent said as he stood and made to leave.

Ruby urged him to stay still with a tug on his arm. She stood beside him and placed a soft kiss on his lips. She started to walk away, but then she turned back at him, wanting to look at his face one more time.

"Thank you," she whispered.

⚜ ⚜ ⚜

Ruby was in that familiar dark nothingness between consciousness and a premonition. She could smell the incense she started burning to help her meditate, and she resisted moving beyond the darkness. Her goal was only meditation.

A voice called her from the other side of the darkness.

"No!" she called out. "I'm looking for peace right now! I need to meditate!"

She kept hearing her name despite the plea she made for peace. It started as faint echoes, but as the voice got louder, she recognized who was calling her. It was her own voice.

She let go of her mental tether to the darkness with the intention to let the scene of somewhere in the future world coalesce around her. She was curious to see the face belonging to her voice, but no scene appeared as the dark faded into light. There was only light, as if her world became the inside of a dense cloud with sunshine above it.

A ball of light approached her. It burned brighter until, in a blinding flash, it was gone, and her soulmate was floating in its place before her. Ruby was overcome with comfort and warmth, and she knew it was the mere presence of her soulmate in the premonition that made her feel safer and more joyful than she'd ever been. She wondered if she'd miss the feeling for the rest of her life.

The soulmate said, "I'm sorry you learned about my early death. I wish you as little pain and sadness as possible before we are united in perfect joy."

"I'm not sad we won't have children, but it would have been wonderful to be an aunt . . . How is it possible you didn't have a brother?" Ruby asked.

"Green Earth's war pulled my parents into a violent, nomadic life when I was a child. I remember when my mother gave birth to a boy, but by then an infant wouldn't have been possible for our situation. He was adopted by a family able to keep him safe," the soulmate explained. "There is hope your family will endure and flourish."

"Did you bring me here to comfort me in this way? Because you knew I was seeking to calm myself in meditation?"

"I didn't bring you here. You're doing this. You asked for peace, and this is the vision you've received in answer."

"This is what paradise looks like?" Ruby asked.

"No, you cannot see paradise until it's your time." Ruby's soulmate smiled. "Then, it will be our time to go beyond."

"Can I see you and feel this peace and comfort anytime I need to meditate?" Ruby wondered.

"I don't know. This place—this blank white space—is not something I ever saw when I was on the Green Earth. Perhaps you've gained the ability to call to your soulmate simply because you know I exist beyond the living realms . . . You're going to be a powerful seer one day. Please take care of Trent. Don't let him leave the Blue Earth."

"How do you know he is with me? What if his soulmate is still in my world somewhere too?"

"When I was living, I had a premonition that Trent would go to another world and help save it one day, so even if they are both with you, keep them safe and close," the soulmate gently advised.

Ruby's soulmate began to glow, and she knew their time was ending. In a flash, the shape of a woman was gone and replaced with the same ball of light Ruby saw at the beginning.

"I hope I can make this vision again," Ruby said. "Goodbye."

Her voice echoed through the fading white nothing. "I wait for you in paradise. I dream of you and see your life . . . It's beautiful."

The white soon became the black.

Ruby was in her bed. She opened her eyes and breathed the calming incense. She smiled.

❧ ❧ ❧

Lilith summoned Adam, his descendants, Faustina, and Trent to feast with her in a grand room within the spaceship. The room was a giant clear box within an even larger metallic box. There was a clear, plain table and chairs in the middle. Adam and company stood around the table in the middle of the cube while Lilith and her entourage looked awkwardly at them.

"Choose its form," Lilith said. "I bestow this honor to the guests."

Adam's people awkwardly looked at him to see what would happen, so he cleared his throat and said, "I think we're in a holodeck, so if anyone has a preference . . ."

"We should choose a historic place that doesn't exist anymore," Ty said.

"Oh, yeah. I always wished I could have eaten inside Cinderella's castle," Nick commented to Ty. "Did you ever see that old documentary about the multi-course meals they had in the great hall while all those zany characters walked around entertaining people?"

The lights blinked out and came back on, and they were standing in a medieval great hall. Fireworks were bursting outside and causing the colorful gothic windows to shine and glitter. There were animated characters roaming around. There was an undercurrent of laughter among the witches.

"The choice is made," Lilith said. "We feast and then story your history."

Trent sat next to Nick and said, "Brilliant choice. If we ever get to do this again, you should always choose for us."

Duncan sat on the other side of Trent. "We haven't been introduced. I'm Duncan Cavendish."

Trent had seen Duncan a few times over the last year while working security for Dust, but realizing Duncan had never noticed him, he said, "It's good to meet you, Duncan. I'm Trent Pinkerton."

On the other side of Duncan, Sylvia had dropped her glass, which banged against her plate. She mumbled an apology for the loud noise, but Duncan never turned to acknowledge her accident. He kept looking at Trent.

"Duncan," Sylvia said, nudging him.

"Yes, it's lovely to meet you . . . Trent," Duncan mumbled.

Trent concluded from the awkward interaction that he'd finally met people who knew someone else named Trent Pinkerton who looked a lot like him. It was glaringly obvious they didn't want to discuss it, but he'd revisit the knowledge one day. Until then, he turned his attention back to the feast and the entertainment.

When Lilith determined her guests had enjoyed enough manna and entertainment, she approached the head of the table and ended the hologram. She then commanded the holodeck to synthesize Constellation Eden all around them. A cluster of blue stars and their systems burned in the distance around everyone against a backdrop of an outlying multicolored nebula. A green and blue planet hung in the foreground with multiple particle rings orbiting it.

When the floor seemed to disappear, a choir of gasps sounded from among the dinner party, and Danielle screamed, "Is she trying to give me a heart attack?"

Adam explained, "They don't realize we're not used to this."

"You mean it's beneath them to care," Phoebe remarked.

Adam shrugged. "That too."

Lilith silenced the room, clapping her hands and sending a sobering pop echoing around them.

From that point forward, the holodeck illustrated the story as Lilith requested. She began recounting the history of Adam's progeny by proclaiming, "In the beginning . . ."

Then a calm, neutral voice radiated from the holodeck and continued, "Adonai terraformed Earth, giving it an atmosphere, plants, and animals. When the other Edenians suggested developing multiple planets for posterity and experimentation, Adonai searched nearby systems for other suitable planets, but Earth was the closest compatible planet by many lightyears. He soon discovered Eden's existing technology made it easier to cross between universes and work with multiple Earths rather than continuing multi-galaxy searches for similar compatible planets.

"Therefore, Eden's life creators, including Adonai and Lilith, worked to induce splits in the universe, opening paths to three Earths they used to grow intelligent life. Many species of advanced primates and intelligent sea creatures ruled the Earths before Adam and Eve fell from grace.

"Adam and Eve lived in Adonai's sacred garden on the planet Eden, where he used the Gaia Tree's primal power to build wormholes from Eden to each Earth through the tree, also known as the Tree of Life and the Tree of Knowledge. The tree connects all of Eden's creations to each other and to paradise.

"Adam and Eve were created special and meant for Eden until Adonai found them disloyal and unworthy, making them mortal. When they expressed more loyalty to each other than they did to their creator, Adam and Eve's souls and bodies were split into two identical beings each and sent to both the Blue Earth and the Green Earth, giving them opportunity for both redemption and condemnation while dwelling outside Adonai's divine presence. . ."

The story continued until the voice described the rise of civilization. By the end, everyone was standing under the Gaia Tree with lush grass underfoot and a peaceful, still silence in the air.

Nick broke the silence, asking, "Is this what paradise looks like?"

"No, we can't see what paradise looks like," Ruby explained and pointed at the Gaia Tree. "This garden is the Blue Earth's portal through the tree."

"You don't know everything," Hayden complained, but Giselle shut him up with an arm punch.

Ty asked, "So, paradise is inside the Earth, or is it in the heavens?"

"It's both!" Nick observed. "Aren't you paying attention at all?" He asked Ty, and then he asked Adam, "How do we get to this place for real?"

Adam looked around at his descendants. They all looked back at him for answers, but he had none. "I've never known where Eden is or how to get there. If I did, Earth wouldn't have been much of a prison." He shifted his attention to Lilith and continued, "However, now that Eve has a map to get there, we should be there guarding it."

"Eve cannot know how to read the chart," Lilith said, "so it is not wise to risk leading her or other enemies there, nor do we wish not necessary violence in close range to a holy place. It is paramount to rescue the chart. An advanced powerful being can take it from Eve and read it."

Before the discussion could continue, the holodeck went empty, and Adonai appeared.

"Lilith, I need your counsel," Adonai said. "Eve has discovered some way to mask herself from my observation. I have lost her location. Come with me to remedy this. Adam and his tribe must return to their vessel."

Adonai and Lilith did not acknowledge the witches as they walked away. Two of Lilith's guards appeared to escort Adam and company back to the yacht.

As the group shuffled through the door, Sylvia whispered to Duncan, "They should just scry for her. No witch can hide from blood magic."

Adonai instantly halted and jerked his body around to address Adam. "Scry for Eve immediately. Lilith and I will join you after I speak to her alone."

❧ ❧ ❧

"Scry for Eve?" Adam asked Sylvia in an annoyed tone once they were back in his lounge.

"The vampires perfected the process hundreds of years ago. It works perfectly—much better than it did for older witch communes, trust me," Sylvia argued.

"Anything else you need other than her blood?" Adam asked.

"Well, I know exactly the type of crystal we'll need along with some other tricks to make it foolproof," Sylvia said.

Duncan agreed, saying, "If she is on this Earth, the ritual will work. Adonai must know this if he told you to scry."

Finding a crystal took longer than anything else since they already had a map, a box of small tools, and a vial of Eve's blood, which was easy for Adam to retrieve from the secret room below deck that served as Eve's combination hospital room and prison cell. With the map flat across the table, the vial of blood in Adam's hand, and the whole tribe assembled, it was up to Jeremy to bring the crystal.

Sylvia tried to convince Jeremy to rip open a portal and get one from her house, but he hadn't developed the skill to use his gift to travel to places he'd never been. The only immediate solution was to think of another place he could go to get one.

It was Giselle who finally suggested a natural herb and stone store in Sewickley, Pennsylvania. It was a random thought, but it was the right idea because Jeremy remembered the exact street from when they were all kids. One of the kids from their summer water polo club had moved there, and Giselle, Ruby, Hayden, and Jeremy had all been invited to visit multiple times.

Five minutes after they had the idea, Jeremy was back with a crystal suspended from a leather cord. Ty worked fast, hollowing out the core of it and injecting Eve's blood.

Starting with Giselle, every witch tried to scry for Eve to no avail. The crystal merely hung unmoving on the end of the leather. Adam looked angry and skeptical of everything happening in front of him. He feared wasting his father's time.

Ruby said, "Adam, you haven't tried."

"If it hasn't worked by now, do you think I can make a difference?" Adam asked.

"Yes," Sylvia and Duncan said at the same time.

The crystal was sitting on top of the map, so Adam picked it up and held it by the leather cord above the center of the table. The crystal stayed still.

"Do you love her?" Sylvia asked.

Adam answered, "Yes."

"Then you can make the ritual stronger by spitting your saliva on it," Sylvia said.

Adam sighed and mumbled, "You're asking me to spit on the map or on the crystal?"

"Put some saliva on the crystal and think of your love for her," Duncan directed. "Everyone else, join hands around the table."

Adam spit in his hand and rolled the crystal around in the moisture. When he lifted the crystal above the map again, it swayed slightly north to south. After a few seconds, it swayed east to west instead. The movements were soft and subtle, but they were obvious to everyone, including Adam.

It gradually picked up speed until it was spinning above the map like a propeller.

"It can't find her, but it's searching. Your love and your strong will are moving it," Sylvia whispered.

"It always works. It will work," Duncan uttered.

The crystal suddenly halted facing east, but it floated above the map.

Adam held fast to the leather cord. "I thought it was supposed to land on the map."

"It is supposed to land on the map," Duncan said.

Sylvia and Duncan exchanged glances, silently asking each other for more ideas and wondering what was happening.

Adam let go of the cord, but the crystal continued to float. It didn't only float over the same spot on the map, but it drifted along a geometric plane exactly parallel to the map. Although it stayed perfectly parallel and roughly six inches above the map, the drift pattern seemed erratic at first.

Then Adam realized the pattern, recognized its magic and said, "Everyone keep holding hands and focusing on the crystal and the map . . . It's moving outward in a spiral . . . Sylvia, what is happening?"

Sylvia searched her mind for an explanation. "I—I don't . . . I'm not sure—"

"Eve is in another universe!" Duncan interrupted, positing the most plausible thing that came to mind.

"Duncan Cavendish speaks a truth," Lilith said from behind the circle as she and Adonai entered the lounge.

All eyes pivoted to them, and there was a thump when the crystal fell from the air and hit the map. The sound made everyone register they were all linking hands for no reason anymore, so people started breaking the circle and moving around.

Phoebe, Hayden, and Ty went to the bar and poured drinks. Giselle, Jeremy, and Ruby gathered close to Faustina, who had been outside the circle on a small sofa. Trent and Nick stood over the map in wonder, looking at the air around it for tricks or clues. Everyone else waited.

Adam faced his father, waiting for a word or a command.

"We have no choice but to wait for Eve inside each Earth at the Gaia Tree," Adonai said.

Adam rubbed his head, wondering why his original idea was now the plan. "Why the about-face?"

"I did not sense that Eve can access the fae realm. I've never observed her disappear before, but fae magic is older, powerful, and primal. It can cloud the senses. It is the only explanation for these events and her absence," Adonai explained. "It is not merely an about-face, as you say. We cannot only wait at the Blue Earth portal. The boundaries of the fae realm are unknown. We must make haste and guard all portals."

The discussion about team distribution was brief by necessity, but those chosen to stand guard were ready and willing to stand between Eve and Eden. None of the Blue Earth witches were permitted to leave their universe, so those with powers that could be weaponized would stand guard inside the Blue Earth. Adonai would take Trent and guard the Green Earth portal. Lilith and her personal guard would take the Red Earth.

The room was a flurry of action as some prepared for immediate departure and others scrambled to help.

Ruby didn't care she and Trent weren't alone. There was no time to care. She had to speak to him before it was too late.

"Trent!" Ruby called out.

Trent begged Adonai for one moment, and he and Ruby crossed the distance between them.

"She told me not to let you go back to Green Earth!" Ruby cried. "I saw her, and she wants you to stay here—with me! You need to return here when this is over."

Trent realized she'd seen her soulmate. He held onto her shoulders and spoke gently but with strength. "I understand, Ruby. My powers on the Green Earth are more advanced than Jeremy's. I assure you, once I'm there, I'll have the power to bring myself back. I will."

Trent kissed her quickly, yet it was a firm and passionate act.

"Goodbye. Take care of yourself," she said.

"I'm literally going with God, Ruby. I'm in good hands. I'll see you soon." With those words, Trent left with Adonai.

Ruby turned to see Adam watching her openly while Phoebe tried to pretend not to watch, but Jeremy embraced her and said goodbye as well, and the mission was again everyone's focus.

Adam approached Ruby and said, "You, Danielle, and Giselle will remain here. Sylvia will be with you, so you'll have warning if dangerous powers approach, and you can get everyone to the safe room. Keep your mother protected but take care of everyone and everything else here as well."

"As you wish. Always," Ruby whispered before he kissed her forehead and turned away to gather his team.

Adonai and Trent had already disappeared from the vessel. Adam, Nick, Phoebe, Hayden, Ty, Duncan and Jeremy followed Lilith and her guards to one of the smaller spacecrafts docked in the bay. She'd take them inside the Blue Earth before continuing to her post.

Ruby was both relieved and scared. The end of the struggle was finally in full motion. She felt her mother's arm wrap around her shoulder, so she leaned into it and took a moment of peace and reflection before preparing for the worst.

THY WILL BE DONE

"How long have I been here?" Trent spoke aloud, asking himself.

He'd been captivated to such an extreme that he still felt on the edge of magical hypnosis. Standing before the Gaia Tree, he blinked and tried to regain his bearings. He looked at his feet in the lush, still grass and then turned his head to gaze at the light above.

"It's been approximately half an hour," said Adonai, "and long enough that I have prepared my spirit for what comes next. Your part in this is crucial."

Trent was grateful for the opportunity to help his creator, but with the task unknown and daunting, he looked around and asked, "Will the Green Earth's Adam and Eve help us too?"

Adonai lay down on the ground near the tree. "Your Adam and Eve are not ready for this knowledge and cannot be brought into this garden."

"But I am not sure I am ready, if they are not," Trent said.

"You will never see your Adam and Eve again, so it matters not. The Blue Earth Adam is ready, and you will dwell within his domain. You are going back to the Blue Earth presently, and there you will remain," Adonai stated.

"Thank you, my lord," Trent said. "So, you wish me to leave now?"

"Imminently, I will leave this body and enter this portal with the intent to lock it, like one would lock any door. Once I've locked this one, I will travel to the Red Earth and do the same. The Blue Earth will be the end of the journey, and I will need my body to be waiting for me when I lock the door there," Adonai said.

Trent understood. "I will take your body there as soon as you're gone. It will be there for you."

"I know you will . . . Understand it's crucial for you to place it as close to the tree as possible. This task will drain me. The power I'm manipulating within the wormholes belongs to Gaia, not to me. I shall grow tired and may become lost. This body must be placed where my weary spirit may flow directly into it and become grounded and reoriented.

"If I am lost, and they must fight, remember you are impervious to their magic, but not the consequences of it. Eve cannot compel you, but if she sends out a wave of energy that causes an earthquake, rocks can crush you," Adonai explained.

Trent wondered if gods thought mortals were that stupid, but he banished the thought and asked, "Can you ask Gaia to guide you? How long will you be lost?"

"Gaia willing, I will not get lost," explained Adonai, "but I cannot summon Gaia's help as I please no more than you can summon help from me. I believe I am doing Gaia's will and that she will bless my journey."

Trent nodded. "I am ready to serve you."

"When the glow in my eyes wanes to black, I will be gone, and you will take the body immediately," Adonai instructed.

Trent knelt next to Adonai. The supple ground felt cool and soothing while he waited calmly and stared intently into Adonai's mechanoid eyes. Trent grappled with his desire to regard the plants, the underground light, and—most of all—the legendary Tree of Life, which he also revered as the Gaia Tree and the Tree of Knowledge.

As the emerald irises staring back at Trent dimmed, he leaned down and wrapped his arms under Adonai's shoulders and back. At the same moment the eyes went black, Trent thought he saw the flicker of a human-shaped golden glow in his peripheral vision flying into the tree. Determined not to give way to temptation and look away from his task, Trent lifted the robot body on top of himself. As he fell back, he fractured the air and fell out of his universe and into the Blue Earth.

☙ ☙ ☙

Eve steadied her nude body by grasping a wooden beam that supported the canopy of Robin's bed. She stood with one foot on his silk sheets while her other foot pressed against his face and pushing him away from her lower abdomen. Robin knelt in front of her and tried not to let go of her upper thighs, but rather than fight to get his tongue back between her legs, he began ravenously sucking and biting on her foot. She laughed and jabbed her foot into his open mouth, leading with her big toe. He let go of her thighs and fell back onto the mattress with a guttural moan.

Swinging from the beam, she landed on the mattress with her knees on each side of his waist.

Robin looked at her in surprise. "You're ready for round three already? I thought I'd nibble on your feet or wiggle my tongue between your nether cheeks while you slap me around for at least a bit longer."

Eve smirked. "No, my salacious Puck. The sun has now set both here and at the destination you plotted for me, which means your powers will be peaking under darkness and moonlight at both locations. It's time for you to transport me there."

"Remember, I can transport you past the mountain barrier, but once inside the mountain, I can't come with you," Robin stated while sneaking his hands up her thighs.

"You mean you won't come with me," she said, removing his hands from her thighs and pinning them over his head.

He said, "Sure, fine. I won't—I won't approach a multi-dimensional portal with a stolen artifact forged from primordial magic."

Eve sighed and released his hands. "Take me as far as you dare, then."

Robin snapped his fingers, and they were no longer in his bed. They were sprawled upon a smooth large rock inside a cave. The cave's mouth was like a window to celestial wonders through which moonlight chased shadows from their naked skin.

"My clothes?" Eve asked.

Robin grasped her hips and thrust. "For a price?"

"I said there'd be fairies next, remember? I should have bet money," Ty muttered.

Phoebe and Nick chuckled openly, further diffusing the tension and the silence that had befallen the Blue Earth group as they apprehensively guarded the Gaia Tree. Duncan, Hayden, and Jeremy smirked at the comment, but Adam remained agitated.

"Be careful. Remember our deal," Adam said to Ty.

Ty shrugged and asked, "Now that I've seen this place, why would I ever want to be outside your circle?"

"Yeah, I'm hoping we get to see other planets next," Nick remarked.

Hayden said, "Not me, but I think I could sit under this tree forever. I feel a lot like I've taken a dose of candy, except it's a much smoother euphoria. It's natural here . . . Does anyone remember how we got here?"

Hayden kneeled behind the tree, postured to send a flurry of flames at Eve when she appeared. Duncan was with him to provide a magical shield from that direction. Ty, Phoebe, and Adam forged a perimeter around the garden. Adam was the only one besides Nick who stood in the open while the others crouched behind plants and rocks. Nick stood directly in front of the tree, but he'd shapeshifted into Adonai. Jeremy sat on a high branch above Nick.

If Eve arrived and a battle ensued, Nick was to distract Eve for long enough for everyone else to get at least one magical attack sent against her. They assumed she would be able to see through Nick's magic as she approached, so without knowing how long they had to trick her into being afraid of Adonai, they planned to strike quickly.

Adam considered Hayden's words and said, "I don't remember how we got here, so we must not be meant to remember. This garden is pleasant, but on the other side of it lies the garden that inspired it. The original garden is the definition of bliss."

There was a muffled whooshing sound by the tree, and the team looked in that direction just in time to see Trent appear with Adonai's body. They patiently waited for Trent to drag and bolster the body against a prominent root at the base of the tree. When he was done, Trent looked around for the best place to wait and noticed Nick standing in the middle of the garden for some reason.

"Hey, Nick. Uh, What—ah—what's the plan?" Trent asked while catching his breath and looking from Nick to Adam.

"Dammit, Pinkerton. I'm disguised as Adonai, but now it looks like there's two of us," Nick said and pointed to Adonai's body.

Trent rubbed his head. "Okay, right. Well, Adonai's spirit went into the tree at the Green Earth's entrance. He said he was going to alter the wormholes to Eden from every Earth. He asked me to bring his body here to wait for him to finish closing the portals, so to speak, and then he'll jump back into his body when he gets to this side . . . Um, so, that's the plan there. What's the plan here?"

"I'm going to distract her while everyone else attacks in unison," Nick said.

"Position my father's body directly behind the tree. Hurry," Adam ordered. "Hayden, Duncan—help him move quickly. We must stay ready and quiet. She can't know we're here, or she will shield herself."

They arranged the body and got back into their positions. Jeremy gestured at Trent for him to join him in the tree, so he jumped up and perched on a branch above Hayden where the leaves would provide him the most concealment.

Near the front of the colossal underground utopia, the entrance was through a tunnel perched atop a plateau with stairs carved into the stone down the front. Hayden had staked torches on each side of the staircase to use when the time was right. Even though it was almost 200 meters from the entrance to the tree, the extreme quiet and calmness of the garden allowed them to hear someone approaching. Being careful not to make any small sounds, they focused and awaited their moment to attack.

Eve emerged from the dark tunnel and squinted into the garden's supernatural sunlight while descending the stairs. As her eyes adjusted, she realized she wasn't alone when she recognized Adonai standing in front of the Gaia Tree looking at her. Her steps faltered, and she froze upon the stairs for a split moment.

Adam and Ty sent blasts of energy at Eve while Duncan and Phoebe directed their energy at the mountainside above the tunnel in hopes of pinning her under an avalanche. At the same time, Hayden sent flames from the torches that were behind her.

In the next second after Eve froze, she saw through Nick's magic, like a lightbulb switching on. Magic erupted from her fueled by her rage at being tricked. Her desire for revenge trumped her instinct for defense, and she sent a hard blow of energy straight at Nick right before shielding her body.

Flames reached Eve and burned against her back before she produced the shield. She screamed in pain but held the shield as rocks turned to dust when they hit the invisible barrier above her. Then she stumbled back a step and braced when energy hit her shield from the front.

With Eve's shield up, Hayden couldn't keep manipulating his flames, but they'd done serious damage on their own by the time Eve was able to shift focus from her other attackers and extinguish the fire. Much of her hair was burned away, leaving the crown of her head badly scorched. Burned pieces of black and red flesh stuck to her remaining hair, and a hole was burned through her dress at her spine, which also sustained a third-degree burn.

Eve released a war cry dripping with equal parts fury and pain while sprinting at Adam. Phoebe attacked her from behind and then crouched in the tall grass. Eve spun and sent an attack towards Phoebe. As Eve's attack missed Phoebe, Adam knocked Eve off her feet with his attack.

Jeremy saw Nick beneath him. It looked like Nick's skull had been crushed against the tree from Eve's attack. Jeremy acted fast, moving through his rips in space to appear beside Nick on the ground before pulling him through another rip. Seconds after Nick and Jeremy vanished, Jeremy appeared again, sitting in the tree once again and studying the battle for his opportunity to kill Eve.

Duncan and Hayden remained behind the tree close to Adonai's body, and Duncan shielded himself and Hayden. Since Hayden could not shield himself from Eve, he'd be exposed if he tried to attack her again.

They watched Eve fall to the ground while sending a second attack at Phoebe and a first attack at Ty. As Phoebe and Ty were both knocked unconscious with Eve's fierce magical energy, Adam and Eve continued to battle one-on-one.

Jeremy's need for revenge consumed him as he kept his eyes on Eve. When Phoebe fell, his body tensed, and he wondered when his moment would come. He knew how he was going to kill her, but he didn't know when she'd be distracted enough for him to get close to her. Without using magic as a shield, she'd be easy to best in a fight because of her petite frame.

Adam blocked an attack from Eve. He considered her wounds and thought he could bide his time until she exhausted her power and strength. He stood tall and calm before her, but he could already see her erratic breathing.

The Earth's energy shifted around them, and winds blew across the garden. They both stilled while trying to comprehend the change, but they kept their eyes on each other and their shields around themselves. It was like they could hear energy sizzling in the air between the sound of the tree's leaves shaking in the wind.

Understanding passed between them as Adonai revealed his golden light to his children for the first time in thousands of years. Its warmth fell upon their faces, so they turned to face their father. Fear of Adonai's wrath kept Eve from dropping her shield, and distrust of Eve kept Adam from dropping his shield.

But as their father's golden light emerged from the tree, an irresistible blue-white light followed. That's when Adam and Eve dropped their magical defenses and embraced Gaia's soothing light.

Adam fell to his knees in the presence of Gaia. As soon as he looked into her pure light, her energy filled him with comfort like he'd never before known.

Eve shed tears of joy. Once she looked at Gaia's light, she couldn't look away, and she never wanted to look away. Her burns no longer caused her pain.

Eve walked towards the light with outstretched arms, and whispered, "Gaia . . . Gai—"

She choked on her last word, then her arms dropped to her sides while she teetered. Her eyes still faced the light, but they became unseeing before she collapsed to the ground.

Jeremy stood behind Eve with her heart in his hand. His own chest tingled, but the sensation did not distract him from vengeance. He watched her fall, and when he was finally satisfied enough to shift his attention from her, he looked straight into the light for the first time.

The full gravity of his sin washed over Jeremy's psyche, and he cried out for Gaia's forgiveness while her light opened his mind and showed him the superiority of joy over hatred.

No other mortal had witnessed Eve's fall. As Adonai's spirit entered his body, Gaia's spirit retreated into the tree. When Gaia's light dimmed to nothing, Adam, Trent, Hayden, and Duncan were released from her enthrallment. Ty had regained consciousness during Gaia's appearance and experienced her light, too. They all glanced away from the tree after Gaia disappeared to witness Jeremy standing over Eve's body, crying, and still holding onto her heart.

Adam was kneeling close by and gracelessly crawled to Eve's side. He held her body in his arms and mourned his lost wife and partner with tears and prayers.

Adonai approached Jeremy, and Jeremy pleaded, "I'm sorry—I'm—I'm so sorry."

"Your contrition will be great and cause you much pain. This is all the punishment I require. You are forgiven," Adonai said and held out his hand. "Give me what you have taken from her."

"Jeremy!" Duncan called out.

Jeremy let go of the heart and looked to see Duncan and Hayden kneeling over Phoebe. He used his power to cross the distance in a blink, and he looked down at the unconscious woman, worrying for Giselle's mother.

Duncan noted Jeremy's panicked expression and said, "She'll be okay. Her pulse is strong but take her to Sylvia. She will know how to help."

Jeremy wrapped his arms around Phoebe to leave, but Trent approached and said, "Hey, Jeremy! We're finished here. Take her and wait there for us, okay?"

Jeremy nodded and vanished with Phoebe.

Adonai approached Adam, who was still cradling Eve, and said, "This has happened by Gaia's will. It was her will that I was lost, and a battle took place in my absence. It is her will, and she intervened to bring me back to my children."

Adam closed Eve's eyes and whispered a last prayer for her soul before saying, "I understand, Father . . . Please, Father. Allow me to stay on the Blue Earth and do your will."

"Of course. Eve's death does not change your fate or my judgement. You are still in my favor, and you will continue to grow your legacy here in this world," Adonai declared.

Adam looked down at Eve. "Where should we take her?"

Adonai reached into her chest, replacing her heart from whence it came. "I will take her body back to Eden. You will lead your people from this place. Even though you will all have knowledge of this place and remember this day, none of you will journey here again without my permission, and none of you will share this location with anyone. I have spoken this commandment, and all of you present have heard."

Adam looked around to notice his people gathering, so he stood and said, "Yes, Father." Addressing the others, he added, "I will lead us home. Follow me."

Adam and his people walked across the field in silence, respecting the holy place and enjoying its beauty. At the stairs, Hayden recovered the torches and handed one to Ty for both to light the way out of the deep cavern with a torch at the front and one at the back of the line. Adam entered the tunnel last and turned to take a last look at his father and his beloved, but they were gone.

⋙ ⋙ ⋙

Those left behind at the ship couldn't sit still. They didn't want to be alone with their thoughts to worry about what was happening in the quest to recapture Eve, so Ruby coordinated between Adam's crew and Lilith's crew to make sure they were ready for the voyage back to New York. Some of the other witches packed their bags and busied themselves with cleaning before they all gathered in the lounge to play chess and wait together.

While they were sitting around the cocktail table, there was a dull thump as something hit the floor behind the piano. Scrambling to see what had made the noise, they searched behind the piano to see Jeremy and Nick laying on the floor.

"Take care of him. I got to go," Jeremy said and vanished.

Nick was before them on the floor, and he was clearly already dead. His eyes were open and glazed. Danielle moved fast to shift him into a comfortable position, and she tried to cradle his head, but that's when she and the others realized what had happened to him. The back of his head was completely flat where it had been crushed.

Danielle cried out a bit, but tried to stay focused as she held the back of his head and said, "Sylvia, can you get a roll of bandages from the first aid kit?"

Giselle said, "But . . . he's passed."

"We can stop pieces of his skull and brains from completely falling out, so he can rest here with at least some dignity," Danielle snapped in annoyance. "Help Ruby to the sofa!"

It was then Giselle noticed her best friend was in shock, and she suspected Ruby was thinking of her father's recent death. Giselle thought of how her mother had described Joe's head after the rifle fired and killed him, and she retched, looked away from Nick, and guided Ruby to the sofa.

"Are—are you . . ." Ruby tried to whisper. "Are you sure . . . there's nothing to do . . . for him?"

Sylvia explained, "I spent several years as a doctor, Ruby. I would do something if I could, but his brain is too damaged--even if he had gotten here in time—and now, his spirit has gone."

Giselle started crying. "What if more of them die?"

"Don't say that!" Ruby said and reached for Giselle, so they could comfort each other. "I don't know why I froze like that."

Giselle embraced Ruby tighter and whispered, "We don't have to worry about that right now."

Danielle and Sylvia arranged Nick's body and secured his valuable personal possessions for this family.

As Danielle held his bracelet and wallet in her hand, she said, "His partner is pregnant."

"We'll need to make sure Adam watches over her," Sylvia said.

Danielle frowned. "The child will be a witch, so I'm sure he will."

Ruby sprang up from the sofa. She was gasping for air and shaking. At the same time, Danielle, Giselle, and Sylvia felt tingling in their chests.

"Are you hurt?" Giselle asked Ruby and then grabbed at her own chest. "Am I hurt?"

"Shhh!" Sylvia commanded. "I'm listening—be quiet!"

All eyes were on Sylvia. She was still for almost a minute. Then she sighed, put her head in her hands, and cried.

"What's wrong?" Danielle asked.

"Nothing," Sylvia mumbled through tears. "What we felt was Eve's magic redistributing. I heard it resonating within us as it merged with our existing power. She must be dead."

"Can you hear the rest of them?" Danielle asked.

"No, they may still be in the divine places. I can't hear them yet," Sylvia stated.

Giselle and Ruby yelped.

Jeremy had suddenly appeared on the opposite sofa with Phoebe in tow.

"Mother!" Giselle went to her.

"Duncan said she'll be okay, but he told me Sylvia needed to help her," Jeremy explained to Giselle.

Sylvia approached Phoebe and began assessing her condition.

"Do you have to go back?" Giselle asked. "Please stay."

Jeremy said, "It's over. The others are fine, and it's over."

322

"Did you?" Ruby asked.

"Yes, it was as you described it." Jeremy held his sister's gaze.

"I'm sorry," Ruby said.

"Me too," Jeremy replied.

Ruby nodded, understanding that her little brother would never be the same, but their lives had been completely changed already, and that was life.

"Should we go get them from somewhere?" Danielle asked.

"None of us remembered how we got to the outer entrance, so Adam thinks we weren't meant to remember . . . I can travel directly into the hidden place because I've seen it, but I don't think I should. Trent told me to wait here," Jeremy explained.

"Trent is there!" Ruby clutched Jeremy's arm.

"Um, yeah." Jeremy regarded her quizzically. "What's going on between you two?"

"It's complicated," Ruby sighed. "I'm just glad he made it back. My premonitions tell me he's supposed to be here."

"Hmph, well my common sense tells me he's in love with you," Phoebe commented in a low, raspy voice as she opened her eyes. "He must have known you in another life, huh?"

"Mother!" Giselle exclaimed again and grasped Phoebe's hand. "You're okay!"

"Don't move, Phoebe," Sylvia ordered. "I'm not done examining you."

"The last thing I want to do is move, trust me. I need to take a nap for about a year, I think." Phoebe closed her eyes again. "If my new best friend comes in here, tell her I'm not dead. I'm just napping."

Faustina strode into the room just then and announced, "I'm already here. My daughter grounded me to my room, but a couple minutes ago I noticed it feels different in here, so I looked out my window . . . When's the last time anyone looked out the window?"

After some thought, Danielle was the first to speak. "Are we in the water?"

"I better go check with the bridge. I don't know why the crew hasn't made any announcements," Ruby said.

Giselle, Danielle, and Jeremy went to the windows.

"We were still dry docked about five minutes ago, for sure. I remember glancing through this window and seeing the wall . . . This is ridiculous," Danielle remarked.

"This means it's really over. I bet the Edenians went to get Adam and the others!" Giselle guessed.

"That's a fair explanation," Sylvia said in surprise.

"Don't sound so surprised," Phoebe replied without opening her eyes. "Both of my children have unique intellectual talents inherited from me."

Sylvia finished examining Phoebe and gave her some pain medication and water. While Phoebe rested, Sylvia joined the others to look at the ocean for the first time in days.

Ruby came back and sat across from Phoebe before announcing, "The captain said she was going to tell us after she assessed the situation. Apparently some Edenians came to deliver supplies, and that's the last thing she and the skeleton crew remember before waking up to find the Edenians gone from the bridge, and we were in the ocean. She thinks they were unconscious for about a minute."

"They must have left right after I got here," Jeremy said. "That's impressive."

"But why?" Ruby wondered.

"Practically speaking, it might be easier and much quicker to sedate the crew and do it their way if they need to get somewhere in an emergency . . . Alien abduction stories are starting to make so much more sense to me after all this," Jeremy said.

"I asked two of the crew to bring a litter and take Nick's body down to the hospital room. I told them we're still waiting for Adam too," Ruby said.

"What happened to him?" Sylvia asked Jeremy.

Jeremy told the story, starting from their plan before Eve arrived. When he got to the part about her death, he glossed over the details. He didn't tell them what he did to her, and he didn't explicitly say that he killed her either. He only suggested Adonai and Gaia distracted her for long enough for her defenses to fail. He described the aftermath up to his journey back with Phoebe.

"I'm glad Hayden was able to help weaken her with his fire. We practiced his control over that power for days and days," Giselle said.

Ruby's bracelet alerted her to a message. "They're coming! But Adam wants us to sail back home without him. Lilith is going to do his operation."

"Going home and not having to listen to Adam for a few days both sound like good news to me," said Danielle.

THE GATHERING

"You're moving to Sands Point?" Trent asked Ruby with much trepidation.

"I want you to come with me," she insisted.

"I'm not going to share you with Adam, if that's what you're asking."

"No!" she snapped before taking a calming breath. "We'll have our own apartment on the opposite side of the house . . . I've already told him I'm asking you to live there with me."

Ruby, like Giselle, had always been a risk-taker, which was why they got along so well when they were young, wild tabloid queens who partied all over the city. She'd colored outside the lines and owned her adventures with a confidence and a style that charmed society.

Ruby's next risk after moving to the city on her own had been reinventing herself from party girl to career woman when she'd accepted her prestigious position at The Times. While Giselle made parties a profession, Ruby had moved on with no regrets.

Her next major risk, getting personally involved in Adam's affairs, had changed her life so much that she couldn't imagine going back to her job and her apartment in Manhattan. Her father had been so proud of her work and her independence, and that thought made her old life too bittersweet.

It was difficult for her to determine whether her gamble with Adam was lost or won. She kept questioning if meeting gods was worth losing her father because she felt guilt over her part in the events that had caused his death. She also considered Trent's love and the futility of regret. There were countless traumas and experiences to unpack, and there was a different kind of work calling to her.

The risk she faced in that moment was asking a man from another universe to move with her as she sold her apartment and resigned her job to work directly for Adam to explore spirituality while she researched and documented their supernatural experiences for his archives.

As she told him her plans, Trent asked, "What work would I do if I leave the city?"

Ruby took his hands in hers. "You can still work security at the house . . . Actually . . . I'm sure he'd prefer to have you closer to him with your advantage—since we found out you can't be directly attacked with magic, I mean."

"Ruby, I want—I need—to be with you, but are you sure about dropping everything?"

Ruby swallowed and explained, "I don't see another choice. How could I go back to news, social media, public relations, or anything like that here when I've witnessed divinity and aliens and vampires, and I have the skills and the drive to write histories about them . . . I need to move on, and I want to move on with you."

"What . . . about Adam?" Trent hesitated but asked.

"I pledged my loyalty and my power to his service before I really met you, and I will honor that, but he's family. He's family, but not a partner," Ruby said and laughed uncontrollably for a moment while Trent looked confused. "He's thousands of years old, Trent. It can either amuse me, or disturb me to think about, so I choose to laugh."

"True. I hope you have this much of a positive reaction when you think of the creepy aspects of our relationship," he said.

"I'm completely at peace with the fact that I spoke to your late partner—I mean wife—in a magical vision and that she's actually me," Ruby said, searching her bag before she pulled out a bracelet. "I almost forgot to give you this. Adam wants us all to wear a special bracelet just for emergency communications with him and Ty."

Trent took the bracelet and put it on. "I look weird with two of these on."

"You looked weird without it too," Ruby replied with a smirk.

He reached for her, holding her against him as he laughed and kissed her lips softly. She returned the kiss, elevating its intensity and guiding him onto her bed. He moaned into her mouth in response to the warm, tight feeling of her wrapping her legs around his waist and pulling him against her.

≈ ≈ ≈

Jeremy's childhood had died with Eve, fading into history beneath the Gaia Tree. Like soldiers romanticizing war, starting when they take oaths to defend freedom and ending with their first confirmed kills, Jeremy had exchanged the fantasy of his powers making him a superhero for the reality of feeling awake, older, and weary.

All he wanted to do was work at Dust, like his father before him, and settle down with Giselle as his partner. He held her close to him, and she stroked his chest absently while they lounged in her bed and made plans.

"I'm still not sure we're ready. Though it feels like ages, it's only been a few weeks. We have more of a trauma bond than a romance at this point," Giselle said.

"But you're still interested," Jeremy argued.

"Yes, Jeremy. I'm still interested since we talked about it last month," Giselle said and rolled her eyes to meet his stare.

"So, should I spend a few years partying in public with celebrities and posing for the paparazzi? Would I be considered mature enough then?" Jeremy asked sarcastically, poking fun at Giselle's life when she was his age.

She laughed it off and replied, "I'd like to see that. You do look sexy in designer suits."

"Giselle, are you staying here in Albany, or are you moving to the city with me?"

"Of course I'll move with you. Most of my work is down there anyway, so there's no reason to keep an apartment of my own if you want me to live with you," she said.

"Good," Jeremy hugged her closer, enjoying the way their mingled body heat felt beneath the sheets.

"I'm worried about your mother," she whispered.

"I know . . . Hayden's sick of the rest of us, so maybe he could go to Connecticut. I'm sure she'd be happy for a young roommate to mother. Plus, she loves Phoebe, so hosting her son is a win, win scenario," Jeremy remarked.

"I wish," Giselle breathed, "but he's already gone."

"What?" Jeremy almost shouted.

"Yeah, and he didn't even tell anyone. He can do much of his work by remote, so he could have gone anywhere. After Mother had already noticed his luggage was gone, she sent a message to him," Giselle explained.

Giselle snuggled the sheet to her face, enjoying the smell of her mother's lavender dryer sheets lingering on the fabric. She then cradled her head in Jeremy's armpit and kissed his chest.

"Giselle."

"What?"

"Was that the whole story? Did Hayden reply?"

"Oh . . . Yeah, he said he needed time alone to think about his life. He said he loves her and me and Father. That's it," Giselle said and closed her eyes.

Jeremy brushed Giselle's hair with his fingers. He knew she loved the feeling of having her hair brushed, and because tears ran down her cheeks, his only desire was to comfort her while she cried for her brother.

❧ ❧ ❧

Jameson lay awake and calm after a night in sensual company. Studying the ceiling, he realized it looked familiar. He was having déjà vu. The ceiling was painted in Renaissance Art style, reminding him of the Sistine Chapel, and he remembered having the same thought in his past.

Jameson slightly nudged the woman sleeping on his right shoulder and whispered, "Faustina?"

"Let her sleep," Phoebe whispered, stirring on his left side.

"Does she have a brother?" Jameson asked.

"Why do you want to know that at three in the morning?" Phoebe rolled over and propped her head on her elbow to look directly at his face.

"I've seen this ceiling mural before, and I can't exactly place it, but part of me thinks I stayed here in college," Jameson explained.

Faustina stirred and put her hands over her face. "Jameson, if you typically talk all night like this, I think I'd rather take only Phoebe as a lover."

All three of them laughed. He took Faustina's chin in the palm of his hand, gently turned her face toward him, and thoroughly kissed her mouth. Phoebe watched with a lazy smile spreading across her face before leaning into Jameson and biting his ear.

Jameson's participation in their intimacy had been unplanned, but earlier in the evening Faustina realized exactly how open his partnership with Phoebe was, so she'd confessed to finding him excessively attractive for years. The result of her confession was still in the works as they rolled under the sheets together.

"If you heard me to begin with, you could have either asked me to go to sleep, or you could have answered the question," Jameson argued.

Faustina sighed and explained, "You remember this room because you spent a weekend here hanging around the pool and drinking with my sister and some of your other mutual college friends . . . You went to college with my sister. You fucked her best friend in this room."

Jameson reminisced. "That's right. I was dating Ariana Walton. That was a wild weekend, I think . . . I think maybe—maybe your sister even told me she painted this . . . Where is she now?"

"How do you not remember when my sister, Fairuza Rothschild, killed herself at Niagara Falls the next year after you were here? It's all people talked about that summer." Faustina sounded annoyed and defensive.

In a low whisper Phoebe interjected, "Dammit, Jameson. I remember that, and I wasn't even in your special snobby club."

"Faustina, I did service in Antarctica for two years right after college. I'm sorry I didn't pay attention later, but I let society go while I was there because . . . It was so remote, and work needed to be the focus, and life kept going when I got back . . . I'm sorry I didn't realize. I haven't seen several of my college friends, actually . . . Fairuza was . . . genuine . . . and talented," Jameson said.

"You'll have to excuse him. Politicians don't know how to say their point quickly, but he's sorry," Phoebe said, attempting levity.

Faustina moaned to herself in disappointment. "I shouldn't have been defensive about it. I never talk about her around you or anyone, really . . . I wish she'd known Ruby. I think Ruby would have loved her aunt. They've got a lot in common."

Faustina closed her eyes, and Jameson and Phoebe let her sleep. They both kissed her and left the bedroom to enjoy a shower.

As she tried to sleep, Faustina thought about the last time she'd seen Ruby. Her daughter had insisted she loved her and promised to come back one day, but the cold reality was that Ruby had asked Faustina and Jeremy not to contact her while she worked through her emotions and the trauma Eve caused.

Faustina knew Ruby blamed her and Jeremy for Joe's death. Ruby had wanted to trust Adam from the beginning while everyone else kept believing Faustina's story and had thought Eve was a true victim, but Faustina didn't think it was her fault everyone had found it easy to vilify Adam. In her opinion, Adam had been the root cause of their misfortune, and she hoped Ruby thought about that.

Phoebe repeatedly assured Faustina that Adam wasn't the most innocent of men. They had all made an understandable mistake. Comforting Faustina after Ruby's decision had been the catalyst for Phoebe realizing she was attracted to Faustina beyond friendship.

Phoebe had never previously shared a bed with Jameson and another person at the same time, but having Faustina with them felt natural and right.

ɩ ɩ ɩ

Adam and Ruby perched on the edge of armchairs in Adam's home office with their heads together and their eyes closed. She'd told Adam about the events leading up to Joe's soul going to paradise, so Adam was trying to see her memories of the night it happened. Sometimes she was successful in pushing visions to him, but it still didn't work all the time. She was committed to working on her gift until she could expand and control it more.

Adam pulled back and opened his eyes. "I got a few glimpses. Thank you."

"We can try again in a few minutes," Ruby suggested.

"It's okay," Adam replied. "I know my father guided him to paradise, and that's what is important. He didn't deserve to be lost here."

"You seem different—in a good way, I mean." Ruby searched his eyes.

"It's my ability to experience envito," he explained. "I'm still committed to my empire and descendants, but my ideas about protecting them are changing along with my entire concept of my life."

Adam went to the French windows behind his desk and contemplated the sunlight and his back garden. Ruby joined him and wrapped her arm around his.

"What do you mean about your life?" she asked.

"With witches using powers again, I'll slowly age, but I'm no longer afraid to. My purpose for controlling tech and monitoring magic has changed . . . I was doing it to protect myself and Eve more than anyone, but now I want to do what's best for the planet and for you," he stated.

Ruby thought about it, and asked, "So, what does that mean for us?"

"We need to continue to limit our numbers, and we need to educate and train youth properly," Adam said, then he thought for a moment. "It's the only way to limit irresponsible use of magic that could do serious harm in the world as it is now."

"Then what will you do when someone abuses magic? Is it true you used to kill people who stepped out of line?" Ruby's voice trembled slightly, but she stood firmly next to him and asked her hard questions.

"For thousands of years I made extremely tough decisions on my own, and sometimes there were deaths despite my efforts to use less violent tactics," Adam said, "but I want to bring everyone together and find another way to prosecute magical crime, so to speak."

Ruby leaned against Adam and embraced him. "That's a perfect idea."

Adam chuckled. "You're supposed to question me and challenge my ideas, not feed my ego."

"I'm also here to tell you the truth, and it is a perfect idea as well as a necessary measure," Ruby declared with confidence.

Adam lifted her hand to his lips and placed a soft kiss just above her knuckles. She remembered back to the first time he'd kissed her hand. She liked it just as much as she had the first time, but with new understanding.

"You might not remember, but you kissed my hand after we danced at a party last year. That was before I knew about your past, but I wondered at the antiquated custom that night," she said.

"My apologies. It's usually quite easy to adjust to customs, slang, and the like. After all, everyone does it, but not for as many years as I have, mind you. Some things slip through." Adam humbly turned away while gently dropping her hand.

"No!" Ruby protested. "You misunderstand. I think it's charming—it's quaint and charming, and you should always greet me that way, actually." She smirked and broke into a giggle.

There was a knock on the door, and Ty let himself in. Instead of his usual hoodie and khakis with sandals, Ty was wearing a suit. Ruby chuckled to herself when she looked down and noticed he was wearing sneakers, but it was still a vast improvement in his professional attire. After all, he had worked in the sports and fitness arena for years, so filling Joe's shoes would take some adjustment time. At least he had help from Jeremy, she thought.

Ty said, "I don't yet have an update on the fae realm, but I have a lead in Cork, so I'm leaving for Ireland now. I'll be back in the city for the meeting next week."

Adam nodded to Ty, who replied with a thumbs up. Ruby's smile widened when she noted his manicure. Ty acknowledged Ruby's smile with a nod before leaving the room.

"Fae realm?" Ruby questioned.

"I was going to discuss that with you after our mediation . . . If they were helping Eve, they could be a future threat," Adam explained. "We have to be prepared for anything."

"All the old stories and fairytales say to never trust the fae," Ruby said. "It makes sense they would align with Eve, but how did she find them? Maybe that's the question you and Ty should be asking. Instead of directing research on them, dig into her past from when she was free and at war with you. It could lead you to them."

"You're too young to be so clever, Ruby," Adam observed.

"I tell her that every day," Trent called from the door that Ty had left open. "May I come in?"

Adam gestured for Trent to enter the office and take a seat in one of the brocade armchairs in front of his desk where he and Ruby had been sitting moments before. Adam relocated to the leather chair behind his desk while Ruby took her seat beside Trent.

"What of the fae on the Green Earth?" Adam asked Trent. "Father left without explaining them at all."

"I only know they are not to be trusted," Trent said.

Ruby laughed, but Trent's face remained serious.

"Oh, I had just said the same thing to Adam before you arrived," Ruby explained. "I was speaking of the fairytales."

The interaction was awkward.

Trent smiled weakly. "I know what you meant, but it's a bit different where I'm from."

"You've seen them?" Adam asked.

"No, they're essentially fiction in my world too, but it's different. I don't know anyone who's seen them, but most people believe they exist, and people's fear of them is real. The fae are not like the little women in shiny dresses and fluttering fancy wings you have in stories here. Not for the last few centuries anyway," Trent explained, but he didn't elaborate further, and Ruby and Adam could tell he didn't want to.

Ruby hesitated and then asked, "What are they like then?"

"Accounts of them are gruesome. Some say they're reptilian, like humanoid dragons. Some say they lurk near beaches and lakes and look like swamp monsters or hideous sea sirens. Some depictions of them are like bigfoot." Trent shook his head and placed his hand on Ruby's arm. "None of the modern stories are romanticized, funny, or delightful in any way, which is why I think we shouldn't take this lightly. Again, it feels weird since I've never seen one, but it's just something witches in my world are taught to believe."

Ruby caressed his hand, trying to reassure him, and whispered, "Look at how inaccurate mythology about Adam is. Stories aren't proof they're really monsters."

"It also doesn't prove they're not monsters," Adam said.

Adam had asked Ty to call the meeting, but Ty delegated the seating arrangements and refreshments to Giselle and concentrated on getting everyone into headquarters without drawing too much attention.

"I said to be discreet, Phoebe!" Ty snapped.

Phoebe showed up with Snoopie and a second dog, Mars. As she walked past Ty with the two dogs on a leash, he noticed she also had a cat inside a backpack.

"A cat too?" Ty moaned.

She turned to show Ty a full view of her back and said, "This is our latest rescue, Queen Mab. We had an appointment with the vet right before this." Phoebe shrugged.

Giselle and Jeremy stood inside the meeting room by the door, ensuring everyone took their assigned seats. With tensions still high between some of the witches, Giselle had taken special care with seating considerations. She also pointed everyone to the lavish buffet set up complete with full-service staff at the back of the room.

"Giselle, you've gone overboard on food as usual," Phoebe chided.

"Don't worry, Mother. I have a charity coming to pick up everything we don't use," Giselle replied with a sweet, fake smile. "I guess Father was too busy to take the animals back to Albany with him?"

"Oh, he and Faustina haven't left the city yet, but he had a meeting, and she had an appointment," Phoebe said. "Why is everyone acting like having the animals here is a big deal? Can't you just talk to them and tell them to behave if they bother anyone?"

"Of course, and I'm sure they'll love the extra attention, but they might get bored quickly," Giselle said.

Danielle came in, and Phoebe got into a conversation with her on the way to their seats. Giselle watched her mother walk away and rolled her eyes.

"So, do we tell Ruby your mother moved in with my parents and left a skeleton staff to upkeep the family home?" Giselle asked Jeremy.

"I can't speak to her, but you can tell her what you want," Jeremy muttered.

Sylvia and Duncan arrived next, and they both embraced Giselle and Jeremy while Hayden slipped past them and looked for his place at the table.

The Cavendishes were still retired from Dust, but all of Adam's decedents with magical powers had been sent a message on their emergency bracelets to attend the meeting. Ty had added a special note to their message, letting them know it was important and worth their time.

All the witches Adam had excluded from the Eve incident due to their remote locations traveled to attend the meeting. Bastion Roth arrived from Prussia. Leilani Alana arrived from Polynesia. Sisters from Joseon, Jinae and Youngae Lee, accepted an invitation from Ty to work at the headquarters for a few weeks, so they were already staying in the city.

When Ruby arrived flanked by Trent and Adam, she embraced both Giselle and Jeremy, but she did not speak to her brother at all.

Adam sat at the head of an oblong table with Trent and Ruby on each of his sides while Ty sat at the other end of the table, signaling it was time to begin.

Ty nodded to Danielle, and she announced, "Before we begin, I have news to share. Two babies were born into our circle last night, Gabrielle and Peter Bishop."

Adam waited patiently while his people reacted to the joyous news, then he began the meeting, explaining his new plan for witches. He started with the need to continue tracking genealogies. His decision to allow everyone to practice magic was popular, but his decision to grant them freedom to separate from his empire caused a stir at the table.

"So, we can walk out of here and not wear this emergency bracelet?" Hayden asked.

Instead of waiting for Adam to speak, Ty thought Hayden would be more open to hear from him, so he answered, "You are correct. However, we have strength and protection in numbers. We are a family whether we acknowledged that in the past or not. You'll always have a seat at this table and a job within Dust and its partners if you want them."

Hayden forcefully pushed his chair back and stood. Ripping the bracelet from his wrist, he threw it in front of Ty and made his way around the table. He placed his hands on Phoebe's shoulders and kissed the top of her head, then he moved to Giselle and did the same.

Giselle reached for his arm and attempted to stop him from pulling away. "Don't go, Hayden. You're our family."

"I'm your family, but I'm not sure I'm theirs," he sneered and looked around the table. "I already told you I want some time alone, and now I have permission to truly go where and when I want."

As Hayden turned to leave, Ty said, "Hayden, we're also making laws for our people tonight concerning magic, so if you leave this place now, know you are not free from our judgement and punishment should you use your gifts to harm people."

Hayden looked over his shoulder at Ty and nodded before walking out of the meeting. Jeremy put his arm around Giselle, and Snoopie also came around the table and placed his head in her lap to comfort her. Across the table, Danielle and Sylvia held Phoebe's hands while she fought hard to blink away tears and continue the proceedings.

"Mother?" Giselle asked.

"It's okay. There's been too much chaos and change for his personality to properly file and organize. He'll come around," Phoebe said and smiled weakly at her daughter.

Ty softly stated, "Let's continue, please."

The group decided on a seven-member jury to decide by majority all serious matters, which they defined as acts of violence or war that involved their family from within or from external forces. Death as punishment was outlawed, but self-defense and death in battle would be forgiven. Meetings would be called as needed rather than on a schedule.

Ruby would not serve on the jury because the others saw her as something like Adam's personal priestess or therapist, which they believed constituted a conflict of interest should they both get a vote. However, Ruby could cast Adam's vote in his absence.

Duncan and Sylvia excused themselves from consideration as jury members. They desired inclusion in the family to lend their powers when needed, but they otherwise wished to remain retired and secluded.

Jinae, Youngae, and Bastion excused themselves from consideration, expressing disinterest in the long-term travel commitments required. Instead, all three vowed to stagger their meeting participation to be present at least half the time.

By the end of negotiations, Adam, Ty, Danielle, Phoebe, Jeremy, Leilani, and Trent were decided to be the voting jury. All other current and future witches of the inner circle had rights to speak before the jury at any meeting. Jury members would serve for life unless they wished to step down, or they were voted guilty of violent crime or damaging disloyalty. All inner circle witches had one vote for electing new jury members.

Adam rose from his chair and placed his hands on the table, leaning on it slightly, facing his descendants, and making eye contact with them one by one as he spoke poignantly about his intentions and his duty.

Adam declared, "I no longer fight death or aging, but neither do I look forward to leaving my progeny—my family. I wish to protect all of you and your future children, and to continue building a world for your enrichment, for as long as possible . . . I've made grave mistakes in the past. I will continue to make mistakes, I'm sure, but I move forward with a clear conscience, knowing I do my best with my father's blessings to guide me."

At his declaration, Duncan and Sylvia exchanged glances as if they were making a silent decision or agreement. Adam noticed their body language, and he also knew they were likely to share aspects of the meeting with their caregiver, Sorina, when they returned to Romania.

"Sylvia and Duncan, are you pleased with the decisions made here today?" Adam paused and added a second question. "Will the vampires be pleased as well?"

"Certainly," Duncan stated, and with another look of approval from Sylvia he continued, "and we suggest an alliance. Witches and vampires have resources that can be mutually beneficial."

"And, you have authority to propose this?" Ty asked.

"They've had a sign—a sort of prophesy they were waiting for, signaling our evolution to the point where proper collaboration is possible," Sylvia explained.

"May I ask what sign they received?" Adam asked.

Sylvia gave him a curt nod. "I can only tell you they also saw Gaia that night she saved Adonai and guided him back to you. Only the vampire leaders can tell you more if you meet with them."

"This should be the jury's first decision!" Trent interjected. "Admittedly, I am prejudiced to their kind because of the war between witches and vampires on the Green Earth, but this decision fits the parameters for a vote by jury under the new covenant of law we have written today."

Around the table there were mumbles of agreement, with some voices saying they should vote on it immediately and some voices objecting to that idea due time constraints. Adam, Ruby, and Ty patiently waited and listened to the chatter to understand different points of view.

After a few minutes, Adam stated, "Shall we vote?"

"May I speak?" Danielle said loudly as she shot out of her seat.

"Please." Adam nodded to her.

"Our only vote today should be whether or not we will call a later meeting to discuss an alliance with the vampires in detail." She paused. "It has been a long day, and the decision is not a 'yes' or 'no' issue. We will need to determine how much we share with them, security, and so much more before you, or any of us, meet with them to propose any alliance . . . And I'm sorry, Sylvia, but we will need to discuss how much you and Duncan are told in the future."

Danielle sat down, and whispers were exchanged around the table. Adam and Ruby kept a private side conversation going for a few minutes. When Adam finally looked across the table at Ty, their eyes met. Ty started to speak, but Duncan interrupted him.

Duncan said, "Pardon me, but Danielle is correct about us and, I dare say, everything else she said. But I assure all of you Sylvia and I have already considered this, and that's another reason we insist on staying home unless we are specifically called to lend our help—"

"Or if we need to call for help," Sylvia interrupted.

"Fair point." Duncan laughed.

Ty said, "Thank you, Duncan." He then looked around the table and waited for any other comments before announcing, "We now take the first vote. All those on the jury who approve of another meeting where we discuss the details of a possible alliance with the vampires, raise your hands."

"The Cavendishes won't be there?" Jeremy asked.

Ty quickly stated, "No."

Jeremy's hand shot up. Leilani, Adam, Ty, and Danielle also raised their hands.

Danielle nudged Phoebe and whispered, "I'm the distrustful one, not you."

"I just think we need to focus on ourselves for a bit, that's all," Phoebe whispered back.

"Please be quiet, ladies. We're in the middle of a vote," Ty said.

"Sorry," Danielle and Phoebe said at the same time.

"All those opposed to holding a meeting to discuss the details of a possible alliance with the vampires, raise your hands," Ty stated.

Trent and Phoebe raised their hands. Ty waited for Ruby to give him a nod when she finished taking notes about the vote.

"We will reconvene to discuss the vampire alliance, then. I will send appropriate invites when I determine the time and place," Ty said.

"Giselle, I would like to make a toast to all we've accomplished today," Ruby said and looked from Giselle to everyone across the table. "Not only have we established new laws, but we have exercised them."

Giselle excused herself to coordinate with the waitstaff for champagne. Chatter began around the table as contentment and relief took hold within the group. Some, like Danielle and Bastion, felt a sense of liberty they'd been craving for years. Others, like Ty and Leilani, were redefining their purpose and commitment to something greater than themselves.

As Giselle approached the table accompanied by waiters holding trays laden with libations to share, she stopped next to her mother and embraced her tightly.

Champagne flowed along with a steady stream of laughter. Even Ty, who was always notoriously straight-faced, cracked a small grin when Giselle handed him a glass of champagne.

Ruby watched as Youngae and Phoebe laughed at Ty for being happy about something. She embraced Adam, and then she embraced Trent and kissed him. When Giselle handed her a glass, she embraced her best friend and kissed her cheek.

Ruby raised her glass and announced, "To the Children of Eden and their journeys through untold cosmos. Blessed be the divine and their progeny whilst stars spark life."

The revived and reorganized inner circle, that day deeming themselves the Faithful Watchtower Cabal, responded with strength and in unison, "So mote it be!"

EPILOGUE: CARPATHIAN STARSCAPE

Adonai's sublime consciousness endeavored to maintain coalescence and direction within the Tree of Life's intricate pathways, sending a surge of energy down the root system that burrowed deep within the garden and into its nourishing river even deeper below the Blue Earth.

Across the continent from the garden, the river's terminus was a sprawling pool that glowed underneath the crystal ceiling of an ancient cavern. Like a holy cathedral, the ceiling was a dome, sparkling hundreds of feet above the pool—thousands of feet below the Carpathian Mountains.

Ozana's back absorbed the heavenly feeling of a smooth, cool rock that peaked just above the surface of the pool to form a rounded mesa. She stared up at the crystalline formations above her and enjoyed the chamber's silent calmness. Her partner's breathing along with her own were the only sounds, and those whispers of air lulled her into a near meditative state.

Her right hand dangled over the edge of the rock with her fingers only a breath away from grazing the still water.

Then there was the sound of rippling water. Waves appeared in the pool, disturbing the formerly still surface. Water splashed Ozana's hand. The sensation caused her to stand in an instant, observing the pool for a source of the disturbance.

Nudging her partner in the ribs with her foot, she said, "Dragos, wake up!"

Although members of their coven could easily pass for typical humans, they had many superior physical and mental gifts along with that quasi-immortality, limited by flesh and blood.

Dragos was on his feet next to her in a millisecond, both observing their surroundings with eyes that saw in a wider spectrum than human eyes even in low light.

"The water's lifeforce is surging," he said as the pearlescent haze rolled through the pool, making ripples in its wake.

A greedy smile waxed triumphant across Ozana's face, her tongue sliding playfully between her fangs. Thirst came upon her then, shutting out everything else.

She dropped to her knees over the pool. Using both of her hands to scoop up water, she swiftly, intensely relished a drink. With her head tilted back and hands still pressed against her mouth, she swallowed hard and released a sigh as rejuvenating energy pulsed throughout her body.

"It's almost like I can hear my blood singing. Do you hear yours too?" asked Dragos.

Coming back to her senses, Ozana looked at her partner kneeling beside her with his beard and shirt suddenly dripping wet.

"Yes, it's humming in my ears, but fading," Ozana explained. "We must alert Vlad . . . now. The water hasn't been this powerful since . . ."

Dragos finished her thought, mumbling, "Since Lilith moved us here."

As Ozana sprinted away to find their leader, Dragos stayed by the rock's edge and gazed into the pool. He saw an effervescent humanoid figure floating below the surface, and the pool glowed with a warm light that started with a dim yellow glow then crescendoed to bright golden rays coming off the figure. Dragos thought the figure looked like a male's silhouette, but he couldn't be sure.

As rays of cool, blue light flooded in from the opposite direction and pierced the warm light, he turned to find the source. Another figure, like a great sparkling giantess, moved beneath the surface toward the smaller male being. She enveloped him, covering him with her white-hot rays. Then only seeing the larger sparkling white rays radiating from the giantess with the male folded into her embrace, Dragos watched her retreat. As the light beings headed back up the river from the pool, bright rays dimmed to a blue, fluorescent glow and then only shimmering specs that looked like stardust on the water's surface.

He dipped his hand into the water and caught a piece on the tip of his index finger. It was like a soft grain of sand. It smelled heavenly. He was compelled to taste it, so he licked it off his finger.

While still savoring the taste, dizziness overcame him. He stumbled back, stooped down on the rock, and lost consciousness.

ABOUT THE AUTHOR

Maria L. L. DeWillow lives in Texas with her menagerie of evil pets when she's not traveling her home world, visiting family and friends or going on peculiar adventures.

www.ingramcontent.com/pod-product-compliance
Lightning Source LLC
Chambersburg PA
CBHW061924170626
46813CB00006B/2287